MURDER AT COTTONWOOD CREEK

Books by Clara McKenna

Stella & Lyndy Mysteries

MURDER AT MORRINGTON HALL
MURDER AT BLACKWATER BEND
MURDER AT KEYHAVEN CASTLE
MURDER AT THE MAJESTIC HOTEL
MURDER ON MISTLETOE LANE
MURDER AT GLENLOCH HILL
MURDER AT COTTONWOOD CREEK

Hattie Davish Mysteries

A LACK OF TEMPERANCE
ANYTHING BUT CIVIL
A SENSE OF ENTITLEMENT
A DECEPTIVE HOMECOMING
A MARCH TO REMEMBER

Published by Kensington Publishing Corp.

MURDER AT COTTONWOOD CREEK

CLARA McKENNA

KENSINGTON PUBLISHING CORP.
kensingtonbooks.com

This book is a work of fiction. Names, characters, businesses, organizations, places, events, and incidents either are the product of the author's imagination or are used fictitiously. Any resemblance to actual persons, living or dead, events, or locales is entirely coincidental.

To the extent that the image or images on the cover of this book depict a person or persons, such person or persons are merely models, and are not intended to portray any character or characters featured in the book.

KENSINGTON BOOKS are published by

Kensington Publishing Corp.
900 Third Avenue
New York, NY 10022

Copyright © 2025 by Anna Loan-Wilsey

All rights reserved. No part of this book may be reproduced in any form or by any means without the prior written consent of the Publisher, excepting brief quotes used in reviews.

Without limiting the author's and publisher's exclusive rights, any unauthorized use of this publication to train generative artificial intelligence (AI) technologies is expressly prohibited.

All Kensington titles, imprints and distributed lines are available at special quantity discounts for bulk purchases for sales promotion, premiums, fund-raising, educational or institutional use. Special book excerpts or customized printings can also be created to fit specific needs. For details, write or phone the office of the Kensington Special Sales Manager: Kensington Publishing Corp., 900 Third Avenue, New York, NY, 10022. Attn. Special Sales Department. Phone: 1-800-221-2647.

KENSINGTON and the K with book logo Reg. U.S. Pat. & TM Off.

Library of Congress Control Number: 2025939898

ISBN: 978-1-4967-4853-9

First Kensington Hardcover Edition: December 2025

ISBN: 978-1-4967-4854-6 (e-book)

10 9 8 7 6 5 4 3 2 1

Printed in the United States of America

The authorized representative in the EU for product safety and compliance is eucomply OU, Parnu mnt 139b-14, Apt 123
Tallinn, Berlin 11317, hello@eucompliancepartner.com

In loving memory of Victoria Thompson,
an inspiration who I was honored to call my friend.

CHAPTER 1

―❧―

Montana, July 1906

What a splendid day to dig for bones.
Lord Atherly wiped his brow with his sleeve and swatted at the swarm of mosquitoes in one fluid motion. He did it unconsciously, his focus intent on the eroded hillside on the far side of the creek he and young Master Smith were driving beside. In June, the lush, green pastures of the New Forest had given way to the dry badlands of Wyoming, which now were being replaced, tossed aside like a bucket with a hole in the bottom, for these promising, untapped foothills of the Rocky Mountains.

Of course, if they'd found what they sought in Wyoming, not even a herd of wild horses could've dragged him away.

Chuckling at his pun, Lord Atherly removed the wide-brimmed felt hat he'd bought in Cheyenne and swatted more vigorously at the buzzing swarm about him. His mirth faded as fruitless days searching for ancient horse fossils came to mind. They'd gone over the same ground as those giants in paleontology Cope and Marsh for weeks and had very little to show for it. Could this hilly, grassland terrain be the expedition's new beginning, their eagerly anticipated breakthrough? With renewed determination, he shoved his hat back on.

Bracing for another jolt of the wagon, his attention momentarily shifted from the hillside to the stained knees of his trousers, the perspiration and dirt smudge on the back of his hand clutching the side rail. When he joined Gridley's expedition this summer, he'd insisted on leaving behind his mollycoddled life at Morrington Hall for a few months. He had eaten food cooked on an open fire, smelled of smoke more often than not, did without a valet, and slept like the others in tents of thick canvas that did little to keep out pests or the occasional horizontal rain when storm winds blew sideways. His lady wife would hardly recognize him. He barely recognized himself.

"We're almost there," Master Smith, whom those closest to him called Junior, said as their wagon rumbled past a rare stand of shrub brush. For a stream named Cottonwood Creek, it had surprisingly little vegetation taller than the grasses growing along its banks, save for one massive, ancient tree, its roots half-exposed from years of erosion, clinging precariously to the hilltop they were approaching.

The young chap urged the horses to cross at a shallow point in the rushing creek.

Stella's half-brother was a small but surprisingly muscular boy of twelve who carried a harmonica in his breast pocket and himself with the surefootedness of the numerous pronghorn that covered the prairie. Ready with a smile, his countenance was handsome, open, and guileless. The moment Lord Atherly met the young chap, he recognized the familial resemblance to his daughter-in-law.

And Stella hadn't even the pleasure of meeting the young chap yet. Happily, that was about to change. As prearranged, Stella and his son and heir, Lyndy, were to visit Stella's mother once they'd completed tying up their affairs in Kentucky. Of course, the timing was suspect. They could've crossed the Atlantic at any time. Most likely Frances had instigated the trip, thinking him incapable of looking after himself. Her concerns were both touching and irritating. Like the woman herself. But whether he had Frances to thank or not, won't it be splendid?

And yet . . . could he be a bit homesick?

Lord Atherly received the obligatory letters weekly from Frances, keeping him abreast of all that pertained to the running of the estate and nothing more. But that differed little from when he was at home. No kind words of affection, no pining for his return, not even one inquiry into the success of his endeavors. The one constant was his wife's fretting over Stella and Lyndy's failure to produce an heir. And in every reply, which was few and far between, Lord Atherly disappointed her by refusing to concern himself about it.

As if fretting over it ever affected the outcome. Besides, the couple hadn't even been married a year. As usual, Frances was being ridiculous.

As were almost everyone else he had encountered since his arrival. Of course, those on the expedition shared the same passion, and the Smiths were highly accommodating, but these Americans were a breed of their own. They were friendly, informal, and well-meaning—on the whole. But they weren't ones to listen to him with feigned interest, as a lord of the manor might expect, let alone with rapt attention. And where else would a man spit tobacco into a spittoon while visiting a lady in her parlor? Or brag about the size of his purse or the multitude of his progeny? And who else dare call the eighth Earl of Atherly "snobbish" for his well-bred deportment or "foppish" for his well-tailored attire? No, no matter how much Lord Atherly had assumed Stella's year with them had prepared him to be surrounded by her fellow countrymen, no matter how much he embraced the wild nature of the former colony, he had few illusions left. Here, he was the odd one out. And yet he was in his element.

Thank you, Stella, my dear, he offered in silent appreciation. Without his daughter-in-law's inheritance, none of this would be possible.

As cold sprinkles, kicked up by the horses, splashed him, Lord Atherly was not immune to the beauty of the water—the sunlight sparkling on the ripples, the clarity that allowed him to see color and patterns on the fish that darted from their path—but it couldn't hold his attention. His focus settled on the eroded channel originating from the sprawling roots of the tree.

"Ma said you might want to take a look around here," Master Smith said, leaping from the wagon. He secured the horses to a heavy tether weight Lord Atherly marveled the youth could wield so easily, and scrambled up the hillside, a shower of pebbles and loose soil raining after him.

"Come on, Lord A." He urged the older aristocrat with an encouraging and slightly impatient wave of his hand.

Lord Atherly sized up the climb and, feeling equal to the challenge, charged ahead. He'd planned a deliberate, dignified ascent, but one footfall on loose scree a dozen or so yards up, and his hopes were dashed. He'd taken a few steps sideways toward the eroded furrow Master Smith headed toward and, without warning, lost his balance. He flailed his arms about like a ghastly, over-encumbered bird desperate to take flight but to no avail. He fell, his hip striking the hard ground before sliding back the way he'd come. When he finally came to rest, his body had created a furrow of its own.

With a controlled skid, Master Smith descended toward him but stopped abruptly. "Gosh, is that what I think it is?" He pointed, his sun-beaten face keen on something on the ground. "You must've unearthed it on your way down."

Lord Atherly, a moment ago pleased to have simply stopped moving, winced at the boy's blunt observation of how careless and destructive his descent had been. But eager to look at what he'd disturbed, he struggled to his feet, kneading away the pain in his hip, and gingerly joined the lad.

"Good Lord!"

Ignoring the loud crack above them, the pair, middle-aged British aristocrat and young American chap, bent at the waist, side by side like stage performers taking a bow, peered at a row of teeth and a bit of fossilized bone protruding from the soil.

Then Lord Atherly saw nothing more.

Viscount "Lyndy" Lyndhurst dropped the satchel he'd been carrying for Stella to the platform, barely registering the thud it made as it hit the planks, and tugged at the lapels of his tweed jacket. The town that stretched across and away from him was unlike anything he'd ever seen. Stepping out of the scant shelter afforded by the railway's wooden awning, he was immediately accosted by the acrid smoke of a blacksmith's forge. Blinking it away, he surveyed the hodgepodge of unpainted shacks, narrow red brick buildings, and the imposing three-story, pale sandstone hotel sharing the same dusty street, wide enough to accommodate four carriages parked side by side. He felt like a man who'd just stepped onto the moon.

Where the bloody hell are we?

He'd seen garden wall moss older than anything in this burgeoning town. A quaint countryside village with a High Street, this was not. With its grandiose name, Colter City—an homage, he assumed, to John Colter, the famous American frontiersman—the town obviously aspired to be more.

"Have you spotted your mother?"

"Not yet," was his wife's optimistic reply.

Bustling about them was a cross-section of humanity Lyndy had only read about. A weathered cowboy strutted past, his spurs jingling with each step. A saddle was flung carelessly over one shoulder while a six-shooter hung at his hip. As he passed, he exchanged a friendly nod, revealing the sharp contrast between his black skin and the shock of gray hair peeking out from under a well-creased Stetson. Just like the Buffalo Soldiers Lyndy had read about. Across the street, a middle-aged man in a well-tailored, silk changshan directed workers unloading a freight wagon with YI XU HUANG & CO. stenciled in white letters on the side. Clutching a clipboard, he licked a pencil and checked off each crate as it passed. On opposite sides of the platform, two travel-worn couples in homespun attire conversed animatedly—one pair, surrounded by stacks of travel trunks, argued in German, while the other, hugging and kissing, spoke rapidly in a tongue as foreign as the landscape.

Mumbling something indecipherable in the way of apology, a chap in chaps and reeking of tobacco bumped into Lyndy's shoulder, knocking him sideways and realigning his gaze to the seemingly endless panorama of sky and mountains beyond the town. Granted, he and Stella had had plenty of time, three days in fact, to ponder the passing landscape, an ever-widening vista, an ocean of swaying grass unbroken but for the occasional sod hut, meager one-story wooden home, or small collection of hodgepodge businesses and dwellings that constituted a village here. He'd seen pronghorn antelope, the occasional small herd of wild horses, and countless ground squirrels that stood sentinel, even in the searing hot sun, beside one of many burrows in what Stella called "prairie dog towns." Yet not once did he see the majestic American Buffalo he'd dreamed of, nor the dust storm kicked up by infamous cattle drives. From what Stella had said, and to his utter disappointment, both were consigned to the past. The open range had been fenced in with barbed wire, and the buffalo nearly hunted to extinction.

As their train chugged west, he and Stella had watched the mountain ranges grow, remarking on the magnificence of their jagged, snow-capped peaks, but now, having crossed them, Lyndy still sought words to describe the experience. Not even the Highlands of Scotland could compare. This town sat in the vast valley encircled by their peaks. And here he was, just one more soul in the crowd, dwarfed by a land barely touched by human hands. Lyndy had never felt so small or insignificant in his life.

And yet never so alive. After the cultivated disappointment that was Kentucky, Lyndy couldn't be more thrilled to step foot into the actual "Wild West." With his heart pounding and his senses heightened, energy surged through him. He retrieved the satchel and stepped off the platform—right into a pungent pile of horse dung.

Laughing, he was scuffing the bottom of his shoe in the dirt when Stella called him.

Despite her porcelain features being flushed with excitement, her wide-brimmed hat tilted too far to the side, his lovely wife didn't seem worse for wear. As always, she complemented her surroundings, adding glamor and beauty to even this exotic landscape.

"Lyndy!" Grasping for his hand, she roused him from his musings and vigorously waved the other. "Look!"

Weaving her way through the crowd, enthusiastically waving back, was Stella's mother, Mrs. Katherine Kendrick Smith, a comely middle-aged woman with a becoming smile to match her daughter's. Sun-tanned and dressed in a plain cotton shirtwaist, woolen brown skirt, and floppy felt hat, she bore little resemblance to the stylish matron he'd met at his and Stella's wedding. Beside her strode a small, serious boy, in suspenders and on the cusp of manhood.

"Mama!" Stella shouted, giddy with joy. "Mama! Over here!"

Lyndy happily allowed Stella to lead him through the crowd to meet his mother-in-law halfway.

"Come here, Sweet Pea!" Katherine Smith beckoned her daughter toward her. Stella flung herself into her mother's arms, the two women clinging to each other like ivy vines on Morrington Hall.

Eyeing the women with a tinge of embarrassment, the lad kicked at pebbles beneath his feet.

"May I introduce myself? I'm Lord Lyndhurst, though friends and family call me Lyndy. As you may suspect, that's my wife, the Viscountess Lyndhurst, hugging your mother." Lyndy extended his hand to the lad. "Who might you be?"

"I'm Eugene Smith, Junior. And I'm pleased to meet you, Lyndy." The lad shook Lyndy's hand with the seriousness of a man sealing a life-altering deal. "And I don't mind calling ya that since I suspect we're kin."

Each brushing away welled-up tears, the women hesitated a few more moments before pulling apart.

"Eugene Smith? Then that makes you . . ."

"That's right, Sweet Pea." Katherine Smith removed the boy's cap and ruffled his hair. "Your brother."

"Ma." The boy squirmed away, out of reach, and readjusted the cap on his head.

"My brother." Stella whispered the words with reverence as if they had a holy meaning. Perhaps they did.

Unlike Lyndy, who'd shared his childhood with his sister Alice and cousin Owen, Stella had spent much of her life alone. Her mother left when she was young, and her father was distant at best, manipulative and abusive at worst. Instead, Stella had kept company with governesses, nannies, and stable hands.

Now, suddenly, she has a brother.

"Pleased to meet you, sis. You and Lyndy can call me Junior. Everyone does." The lad held out his hand.

"And you can call me Stella, though not everyone does." They shared a quick laugh as Stella pumped his hand. "And you probably guessed," she added, "Lyndy is also Lord Atherly's son. Where is he?" Stella searched the crowd as if expecting him to materialize on her say-so. "His telegram said he'd meet us."

"Too enthralled in digging up fossils to remember which day we were to arrive, I suspect," Lyndy said with a lighthearted jab. At home, Papa was often too engrossed with his fossils to remember to eat.

"What is it, Mama?" Stella asked, a furrow developing between her brows. More sensitive to these things than Lyndy, she must have sensed what Lyndy was only now noticing—a shift in his mother and brother-in-law's demeanor signaling something wasn't right. Suddenly, neither would look Lyndy in the eye. "What's happened?"

"I'm so sorry, Sweet Pea. I'm just so darn excited to see you, but I just don't know how to say it."

"Say what, Mama?"

Junior scuffed the ground again. "I did go back for Lord A."

Lord A? A year spent in Stella's company, as well as members of her family, still hadn't prepared Lyndy for how informal Americans were, their lack of hesitation to show affection in public or to divulge personal information to a stranger, their casual use of Christian names—to name a few. He'd even witnessed a grown man, Stella's uncle, crawling about on all fours playing "horse" with his daughter "riding" his back in the drawing room. But he never thought he'd live to hear his father, the Earl of Atherly, be referred to as *Lord A.* And from a boy.

Lyndy could almost hear his mother's scathing retort.

"Where's Papa?"

Katherine laid a hand on Lyndy's arm, sorrow and pity shining from the eyes that, not moments ago, had cried in joy. Lyndy flinched. He stepped away the moment she removed her hand as if a little distance could shield him from what she was about to say.

"I'm so sorry, Lyndy, but your father . . ." Katherine Smith bit her lip, shaking her head as if the words wouldn't come.

"Bloody hell," Lyndy whispered, removing his hat and shuffling two more steps back. He was desperate to know but loath to hear what she couldn't seem to say.

It was Junior who, finding a pebble, kicked it without regard to the passersby and exclaimed, "He's gone, Lyndy. Lord A's gone missing."

CHAPTER 2

Franz "Harp" Richter leaned against the wagon, the worn sole of his boot stiff against the wagon spokes, and pulled from his vest pocket the instrument that gave him his nickname. That—and a small satchel containing two cotton twill shirts, an extra pair of matching wool drawers and undershirt, a comb, and the new Bible his mother gave him—were all he'd carried when he'd come alone to this country. He'd built a cabin, a family, a life. But now, the clothes were gone, and the Bible was sold. He was alone in the world again. The mouth harp was all he had left. Its well-polished silver plate flashed blindingly in the sun, but Harp had already closed his eyes to the bustle of the depot traffic. Hired hands loading goods onto freight wagons, porters pushing carts laden with steam trunks, weary passengers eager for their midday meal didn't slow when he loosely cupped his hands, rough as leather, around the back and sides and began to play. When the jaunty tunes did little to improve his mood, he indulged his melancholy and struck up "Hänschen klein," a nursery song about a boy who leaves home to see the world. A couple arguing in his native tongue about whether to spend money on a room in town or strike out now for their claim did stop their bickering long enough to appreciate the sad, harmonic melody that evoked the old country. But when he was through, the notes still echoing between the train depot and wagons parked alongside, they picked up where they left off.

Harp gave the new homesteaders six months, maybe less.

If they couldn't even make such a simple decision before they left the depot, how would they survive drought, blizzards, crop failures, and disease? Harp almost didn't. Life here was all he'd hoped for when he emigrated from Germany and headed west, looking for the promised land. But he'd been tried by backbreaking work and heartbreaking loss. Would he have come had he known what awaited him? Harp asked himself that every day.

Pocketing his instrument, Harp glanced over his shoulder at the wooden crates lining the bed of the wagon. They weren't too heavy for him to lift and haul to the freight office, but Terry was supposed to be here to help. Professor Gridley was an easy man to admire and work for, but Harp wouldn't ever know what he saw in that dummkopf. And why should he care? Harp was just a hired hand at the dig. But he was also a man. While supervising the packing of all these fossil specimens to be shipped to some museum in the East, Terry had scolded Harp like some boy in short pants. What difference did it make that a fossilized bone be packed in this direction or that? And yet there was still no sign of him. If Terry cared so much, where was he?

When the wind shifted, bringing the harsh, tarry smell of creosote from the railroad ties, Harp shoved off the wagon. He lowered the wide brim of his hat to block the sun and searched the crowd again. He spotted the rancher's boy and wife hugging and kissing a wealthy, young couple. Wasn't the Englishman expecting his son and daughter-in-law? Harp didn't know Mrs. Smith well, but her son, Junior, was a fine boy who enjoyed spending his spare time around the camp's fire. Harp was even teaching the boy how to play the harmonica.

It was too bad about the Englishman. Harp suspected he was more than a little naïve, and now he'd gone missing. That'd be the end of him. *Schade!* What a shame. Granted, he'd always been a bit aloof, but the Englishman readily shared his fine stock of whiskey, and any man who would drink with his hired help was fine by him.

Unlike Terry, the teetotaler.

Harp slipped the small silver flask from his coat pocket, unscrewed the top, and took a quick swig. The liquid burned as it went down, mimicking the anger flaring in his chest. He took another before pocketing the flask again. With a quick eye to see that the wagon was secure and Maybelle content hitched where she was, Harp strolled over to the German homesteaders still arguing over whether to go or stay, frustrated with their indecision. But then Terry's ridiculous hat, more fit for an Independence Day festival than fieldwork, caught Harp's eye. A white pith helmet with a red and blue striped ribbon band, Harp could see it coming out of the Colter Hotel a block away.

"*Entscheidet euch oder geht nach hause!*" Harp snapped at the homesteaders to make up their minds or go home as he stepped past. Blushing in embarrassment at being understood, the couple scurried toward the hotel, passing Terry in the street.

Not wanting to let the wagon and its cargo out of his sight, Harp went no farther, flagging the professor's assistant down. "*Hei!* Over here."

Upon seeing Harp, Terry blanched, as pale as a sun-bleached bone, but instead of joining Harp to help with the unloading, Terry tugged the narrow brim of his hat lower over his forehead and slunk into the alley between the hotel and the Deer Lodge saloon, like a thieving polecat.

"Vhat a *vollidiot*," Harp muttered. "Acting as if he didn't hear me." Shaking his head, he retrieved his flask and took another sip before returning to the wagon to, yet again, do what must be done—alone.

"What do you mean he's missing?"

A chill sliced through the warmth still lingering from her mother's embrace. Stella grasped Lyndy's hand to comfort him; it was slick with sweat.

From the moment she'd arrived in Kentucky a couple of weeks ago and continuing on the train westward, Stella had been restless and on edge, regretting taking Lady Atherly's advice to settle the Kentucky estate first and not head straight to Montana the minute she stepped off the ship. Stella wanted to see her mother again. For days, she'd gone through her father's personal effects and possessions—the paintings, the jewelry, the silver, the stud books—enduring her father's ghost, as tangible as the white dust covers draping the furniture. The scent of Daddy's Havana cigars still lingered in the air. All the while she arranged the sale of the house, the horse farm, and all the horses, Stella had envisioned this happy reunion.

Lord Atherly, please be all right.

"We were prospecting this morning when a big ole branch snapped off and dropped onto Lord A's head." With much gesturing to emphasize a point, Junior launched into the harrowing tale of Lord Atherly's subsequent tumble down a creek embankment and Junior's flight to get help only to return to find Lord Atherly gone.

"We've been out looking for him ever since but had to stop to meet you here." With it being months since she'd seen her and years before that, Stella often dreamed of her mother's soothing voice. But her mother's words were anything but reassuring.

"I say, Katherine. Shouldn't we continue the search as quickly as possible?"

"As soon as we get you and Stella situated, Lyndy."

"No, we're helping with the search too, Mama."

"But you're greenhorns who don't know the country." Junior waved his hand, indicating Stella's tight-fitting royal blue travel suit. "How do you even get around in that getup? Like Lord A, you'd get hurt or killed out there."

Stella winced and snuck a glance at Lyndy. He'd blanched at the truth of her brother's declaration.

"Junior," Mama scolded. "Stella's dressed like the lady that she is." Then abruptly, she waved at someone, shouting, "Mr. Richter!"

She beckoned to a thin man who looked as if he'd been rough-hewn from the wood of a tree trunk; bright, wary eyes set off against his craggy, stubbly face. The man led a feisty sorrel Quarter Horse hitched to a wagon filled with wooden crates. He touched the brim of his slouch hat in acknowledgment. Unlike the man's sturdy but overly beaten attire, the gelding's coat glistened like well-polished copper pans. Here was a man who took better care of his horse than himself.

"You vanted something, Mrs. Smith?" Mr. Richter's strong Germanic accent marked him as one of the millions who'd come from another part of the world and now called this country home. Stella still found it ironic that she'd bucked the trend, going to England to live.

Not that she had a choice.

Stella banished the anger revisiting Daddy's deception always evoked. That was in the past. Right now, it was about finding her father-in-law.

A departing train whistle pierced the air, long and, to Stella's ears, almost sorrowful. She'd never noticed that before.

"I wonder if you've had any news about Lord A?"

"*Nein.*"

"Would you help us look for him?"

Mr. Richter glanced over at the wagon as he hesitated to answer. As he did, the sun caught a glint of something silver in his breast pocket. A battered but shiny harmonica.

"As soon as I unload the fossil crates inside the railway office. We'll meet up at the camp, ya?"

"Yes, thank you." Mama clasped her palms together as if in prayer.

"Seeing as you're all alone, Harp, I'll help you unload if you want," Junior offered.

After a slight nod, Mr. Richter turned back toward his wagon, Junior hustling to catch up.

"Who is Mr. Richter, Mama?"

"He's the hired hand who works for Professor Gridley and Lord A at the dig. He's known around these parts as Harp. Was a homesteader near Helena, from what I hear."

"Friendly sort of chap." Lyndy's sarcasm was understandable. Stella cupped his jaw in her hands, clenched so tight she could see the outlines of his muscles. Lyndy laid his hand over hers, and she felt his face relax. "But shouldn't Papa's welfare take precedence over cargo?"

"We'll find your father. He'll be all right." Stella kissed him, hoping he believed her.

But did she believe it herself?

CHAPTER 3

Lord Atherly noticed the sharp ache in his lower back before the intense throbbing in his head reasserted itself. Something, a pointed rock or a fallen branch or, if he was lucky, another fossil was jabbing into him. Groaning from the effort, he shifted away from the offender, a bleached white woody stem, and remembered where he was—still lost somewhere on the vast Montana prairie. How long had he been asleep? The glaring sun that had caused perspiration to trickle down the back of his neck had been entirely obscured by a thick layer of clouds. The cloud cover gave him some relief from the heat but also created a problem. Without it, he had no sense of time or direction. Slowly, he sat up, gingerly examined the swollen lump on the back of his head, flinching when he met with a tender spot, and took stock of his surroundings.

He was still beside the stream, the same one on which Gridley's camp was being set up, half lying in the shade of one of the Cottonwood Creek's namesakes, the leaves fluttering above him like tiny hands waving in frantic greeting. All he had to do was follow the stream, and he'd eventually make it back. At least in theory. He'd been hiking from where he and Master Smith found the skull. But how far he'd traveled, he couldn't say. And was that today or perhaps even yesterday? Shouldn't he be there by now?

Lord Atherly cradled his head in his splayed fingers, fighting the fog that threatened to engulf him, and tried to focus on the concrete. But concerns surfaced like ale bubbles bursting in his brain. Could he make it back before dark? What if he were to encounter a bear or puma as it drank from the stream's edge? In response, he vaguely recalled having spent a night in a thicket of stubby willow trees. Had that been a dream, or had he already faced these dilemmas? And why had Master Smith abandoned him without a horse, a weapon, or a care? Lord Atherly didn't even have the prize fossil he'd been reaching for when he fell. Had Master Smith taken that, too? The lad struck him as too conscientious, too amiable for such a callous act. How could he have so terribly misjudged him? Or was he still a bit addle-brained after his knock on the head?

Either way, there was but one thing to do. Start moving again.

Lord Atherly licked his chapped lips and decided a quick drink was in order first. After seeking on the ground for his hat without turning his head too much and placing it gently on his head, he crawled the few feet necessary and knelt at the water's edge. Cupping his hands in the cool water, he slurped what he could. The best, aged single-malt Scotch whiskey never tasted this good. He took a few more sips, wiped the excess that had dribbled off his stubbled chin with his soiled sleeve, and sat back on his heels.

As he and Master Smith had driven along the stream, Lord Atherly's mind had been completely bent on the promise of fossils and not the terrain. Now, he noticed the plains stretching out on either side, broken only by the scattered stands of willow, birch, or cottonwood trees growing along the stream's edge, and the distant mountain range that seemed to encircle all the eye could see. Without his lorgnette to aid his vision into the distance, he could distinguish no landmark, no homestead, no sign of civilization to speak of. He had always thought of the New Forest, his home for all of his forty-nine years, with its free-ranging livestock, abundant wild deer populations, and far-reaching vistas of grazing lawns and ancient woodlands akin to the Great Plains of America. But this, this was what true wilderness looked like.

And I'm bloody lost and alone in the middle of it. As if on cue, Lord Atherly's empty stomach grumbled.

Before such an undignified emotion as panic set in, he pushed himself to his feet, allowing his head to stop spinning before moving on. He trekked along the stream bed, avoiding branches, rocks, and holes left behind by animals unseen as fast as his pounding head and the increasing discomfort in his feet would allow. But his pace, spurred by fear at the onset, soon slowed, and his head drooped from the blinding pain. Instead of the vista, he saw the few feet of the ground before him. But what difference did it make? The landscape offered no relief as he hobbled along, growing more conscious of the skin on his left foot rubbing and burning against the inside of his boot. Only his strong sense of self (he was a peer of the realm, was he not?) prevented him from alternating between whimpering and wailing at the mosquitoes, which had grown bolder and more incessant, covering the exposed skin on the back of his neck and hands with itchy welts. He'd not succumb to such humiliation.

Yet he might have a bit of a rest.

He slowed to a snail's pace, but something instinctual urged him not to stop. And as if he'd tapped into the primordial drive for survival that pervaded this place and was rewarded for it, after putting one foot in front of the other for what seemed an interminable length of time, he was rewarded with the sweet, triumphant snort of a horse nearby. Searching the horizon, he could see but a speck in the distance. Could it be Master Smith returning? In his efforts to meet his rescuer head-on, Lord Atherly roamed away from the stream bank and stumbled out into the vast sea of grass. He called out, waving his arms to capture the attention of the approaching rider.

Stella was the first to hop off when her mother parked the wagon, resisting the urge to rub her sore backside. She had never ridden in a buckboard before, and the two- to three-mile journey had given her plenty of time to both admire the landscape and curse their conveyance. The path, little more than a track worn by wagon wheels, wound through an open meadow that stretched across the valley dotted by stone outcroppings into rolling foothills. It was a breathtaking sight—wildflowers and grasses swaying in the breeze, snowcapped mountains rising in the distance, not a single house or barn breaking the pristine vista. But her body registered every uneven patch of ground, every unseen rock, and the wagon's lack of springs. It made for a rough ride.

Lady Atherly would not have approved. Stella's mother-in-law blamed any and every jolt to the body for Stella's inability to get pregnant.

Agreeing to check the expedition's camp for Lord Atherly before splitting up and setting out on horseback, they'd ridden in Mama's farm wagon from town. Lyndy had brooded in the back with Junior while letting Stella sit beside her mother. For a blissful hour, Stella and her mother buried their worries about Lord Atherly and chatted about everything and nothing. As she always imagined. A sore bottom and rattled bones were a price Stella was glad to pay.

While Junior tied up the wagon, Stella greeted the unfamiliar mule at the post, a rangy, testy brown who nipped at her twice. She took in the expedition's camp crammed into a fairly level spot among the hills. Arranged in a square around a central fire ring in a well-trodden yard, it consisted of canvas tents, one three times the size of the others on one side, tables strewn with dirty dishes, soiled hand tools, and a series of buckets sitting between the enormous tent and its neighbors. A small corral housing a few Quarter Horses, its fence posts so recently milled the scent of freshly cut timber still lingered, and a small, one-room cabin made of logs and liberally applied white chinking beneath a small stand of cottonwood trees made up the two other sides. The fourth side was open for fifteen, maybe twenty, yards, sloping down to a large square grid of low-strung rope, its ground partially excavated, that extended toward a thicket of willow shrubs. From the telltale sound of moving water, the willows hid a creek bank beyond. From what Stella's mother had said on the way here, Lord Atherly's expedition had moved from Wyoming a few weeks ago. Yet the camp looked as settled as a homesteader's ranch.

Two men, one with a pith helmet sporting colorful ribbons reminiscent of those she'd seen on boater hats at regattas and the Kentucky Derby, and another nearly hidden beneath the wide brim of a sombrero, squatted among the ropes and the litter of picks, dustpans, various-sized brushes, and a couple of soil sifters reminiscent of the Gold Rush over fifty years ago. Strange mounds of brilliantly white plaster of paris clung to the edge of a shallow trench near the river's edge.

Lord Atherly was nowhere in sight. Stella's heart sank.

"You made it!"

Professor Amos Gridley, the world-famous paleontologist whom Stella had met last summer in England, rose from his knees without bothering to brush the soil from them and, deftly sidestepping the ropes, bounded toward them with an energy belying his fifty-some-odd years. He pushed the sombrero back onto his high, shiny forehead, his eyes crinkling in delight behind his glasses.

"So good of you to visit, Lord Lyndhurst. And you, Miss Stella. How wonderful it is to see you both again."

"I'd agree if I saw Papa here with you." Lyndy visually bristled at the scientist's jovial greeting, adjusting his tie. But it gave Stella hope.

"It's a pleasure to see you too, Professor. Though we wish it were under happier circumstances. And news about Lord Atherly?"

"See for yourself!"

The creak of the cabin door drew everyone's attention. Lord Atherly stepped blinking into the sunlight. But for his sunburned face, he'd never looked so healthy and hale. Relief flooded Stella so intensely she grew lightheaded.

Lord Atherly's face broke into a smile so wide it crinkled his features from forehead to chin. "Welcome to our little camp on Cottonwood Creek."

"Lord A, you're back!" Junior grabbed his harmonica from his pocket and played a fluid run from one end of the instrument to the other.

Lyndy abandoned his usual measured stride and rushed to meet his father halfway. "Jolly good to see you, Papa!" Lord Atherly matched Lyndy's firm grasp with both hands. "We were worried something had happened to you."

"I do apologize for the trouble it caused, but as you can see"—he held out his arms as if to invite inspection, revealing a few singe holes in his sleeve—"I am, but for a lingering lump on the head, unscathed."

But not unchanged. It was subtle, but Stella sensed an ease that had never been there before.

Lord Atherly rested his hand on Lyndy's shoulder. "You're a sight for sore eyes too. Especially after what your mother said happened in Scotland. A bad business, that, eh?"

"Quite." Lyndy patted his father's hand as if to reassure himself his father was still flesh and bone.

"How is your sister?"

"Well. The wedding date is set. But don't you hear from Mother?"

"I wish I didn't. Your mother has a way of scolding one

from thousands of miles away. Would you believe most of what she writes is about her lack of grandchildren?" Stella blushed when his gaze darted her way. "Sorry, my dear. That was most indelicate. How did Knockan Crag get on at Ascot?"

"Won the Coventry Stakes." Lyndy was practically beaming. How he loved that horse.

"Splendid! Splendid! I knew that colt had potential."

"You what? You didn't think he had a chance," Lyndy teased.

Lord Atherly chuckled nervously, dropping his hand from Lyndy's shoulder. "What would your mother think to hear us, gushing like two village schoolgirls?"

The two men retreated a step as if suddenly embarrassed by their open display of affection. Stella took advantage of their separation, pulling Lord Atherly into a tight hug. She didn't want to let go. Taken aback, her father-in-law hesitantly patted her back in response. Holding him at arm's length, Stella regarded him, from Stetson hat to boot heel.

"Are you all right? What happened? Junior said you hit your head but weren't there when he came back with help."

"It's a long story, my dear." Lord Atherly sighed. "One that I'm quite ashamed of, really."

"Let me tell it then." Before his paleontological partner could stop him, Professor Gridley relayed Lord Atherly's wanderings and subsequent rescue by a passerby. "He's lucky to be alive."

"Mind, I've never been on this side of the Continental Divide and had no idea that the stream was flowing in the opposite direction than I supposed." Lord Atherly rubbed a spot on the back of his head. "Or else I would've met Master Smith when he returned with his father. I didn't 'wander off.'"

"It didn't help that I'd accidentally taken his spy glasses with me," Junior offered without conceding Lord Atherly's point. "When Mr. Sullivan first came across you, you couldn't see too far, so you ran. Didn't you, Lord A?"

"Now, now there, my young friend," Lord Atherly chuckled. "There's no need to relate such unnecessary details. Suffice it to say, as bandits and cutthroats are known to roam the prairie, my rescuer had to assure me he meant no ill will before I allowed him to escort me back to camp. Speaking of... Mr. Sullivan!" Lord Atherly's face broke into a wide grin.

A man about Lyndy's age ambled around the corner of the tent, a damp cloth in his hands. Unlike many others Stella had encountered at the depot, strolling the streets of Colter City, or here at the camp, who'd shed the formality of dress coats for more practical attire, this man wore a meticulously tailored checkered cutaway suit, a highly starched shirt, and bright blue silk tie. What looked like a fedora he'd just purchased from the haberdashers sat at a slight tilt on his head. If Stella had seen him in London, she wouldn't have noticed. Here, he stood out like an Indigo Bunting on a snowy winter's day.

"Mr. James Sullivan, this is my son, Viscount Lyndhurst, and his wife, Lady Lyndhurst. This, Stella and Lyndy, is Mr. Sullivan, to whom I owe my life. He's the one that found me out on the prairie."

Lyndy put out his hand. "I'm truly grateful for your assistance, Mr. Sullivan, in finding my father and bringing him back safely." Mr. Sullivan, setting the washcloth aside, shook it heartily.

"Say no more about it, Your Lordship. Say no more. Your father just got turned around is all. And besides, it'll make for a great story."

"Story?" Stella asked.

"My, my. You're American, Lady Lyndhurst."

"I am. I was born and bred in Kentucky."

"Well, isn't that a coincidence? I'm from back east, too. And please," he straightened his perfectly perpendicular tie, "call me Purdy."

"Okay, Purdy. What story are you talking about?"

"Mr. Sullivan is a journalist," Professor Gridley answered. "Recently come west to find his fortune."

"A newspaperman, to be precise. And, yes, Lord Atherly's disappearance and rescue is just the kind of story I'd been combing this valley for." He held his hands wide as if he could see the headline in the air before him: MISSING ENGLISH LORD FOUND. He adjusted the brim of his hat. "And for me to be the one that did the finding, well, that was something else, don't you think?" Purdy flashed a bright smile at Stella and winked.

"Indeed." Lyndy kept his expression carefully neutral.

"Yes, sir. I was just cleaning up before heading back to the telegraph office in town to wire my story." Purdy patted his jacket to indicate the copy was tucked safely in his inner breast pocket.

"You've already written it? How long have you been back?" Mama asked what Stella was thinking.

"Not long, but a man's got to be on his toes. I've been known to write in more unusual positions than on horseback." He winked at Stella's mother this time.

Mama laughed. "Well, aren't you something, Mr. Sullivan."

"Something?" Professor Gridley said, missing Purdy Sullivan's innuendo. "His finding Lord Atherly was an act of sheer providence."

"Well said, Gridley. And I'd like you to dine with us tonight in a show of my gratitude, young man. If that is amenable to you, of course, Mrs. Smith?"

Mama didn't hesitate. "Of course, Lord Atherly. What's one more?"

"Now, that is a very kind offer, but I have plans for this evening." He winked at Lyndy this time as if they were in on a secret. Lyndy tugged on his shirt sleeve in response. "Maybe another time?"

"Then you must return to the dig," the professor offered. "With a proper tour. I'm sure you'll find equally compelling stories to write about."

"Have you found unnamed dinosaurs then?" The reporter,

reaching for the notebook protruding from his jacket pocket, leaned forward.

"Dinosaurs? Pff! Other expeditions might dig for dinosaurs on the Front Range, east of the Rockies, but, like you, we came to this valley, where the rock layer is much younger, for something special—extinct horses."

"Horses?" Purdy Sullivan stuffed his notebook away in disappointment.

"Yes! In fact, Lord Atherly and I may have found the first evidence of *Hypohippus* in Montana."

"The fossil Master Smith and I uncovered before that branch hit me," Lord Atherly explained.

"Well, that's all well and good, but I've got my story, and seeing you here safe and with your lovely family, Lord Atherly"—this time his smile encompassed both Stella and her mother—"is all the reward I need."

"I insist."

"That's kind of you, Lord Atherly, but—" Purdy had been ready with an answer to this point, so Stella guessed he was taking a moment to formulate his response.

"There'll be no buts about it. Our uncovering a *Hypohippus* specimen could revolutionize our understanding of prehistoric horses in this region! It will thrill your readers, I'm quite certain."

It thrilled Stella. Though Lord Atherly's passion for extinct horse fossils wasn't for everyone, she'd never failed to learn something new whenever he talked about it. The newspaperman didn't seem so sure, with his glance darting this way and that as his plastered-on smile waned.

"I'd read about it." Stella held out her hands as Purdy had done. "Lost Lord's Spectacular Find."

"I'll expect you all first thing in the morning, then, shall I?" Lord Atherly nodded as if they'd already agreed. He gestured at Lyndy with a jut of his chin. "Of course, you'll simply want to get your bearings today and rest up a bit. As will I, to be sure. But you two didn't come all this way not to lend a hand at the dig, did you?"

"But . . ." Lyndy protested.

"Of course, they'll help you." Mama did little to stifle her bemused smile.

When Stella asked Mama to invite Lord Atherly to Montana, she never anticipated he'd relocate his excavation there. Lady Atherly had urged her to visit Montana, too, though whether from concern for her husband or hope that another change of "clime" might help Stella conceive (Scotland hadn't done the trick), she wasn't sure. Either way, Stella had eagerly agreed — but she was here to see her mother, not to become Lord Atherly's field assistant.

"And you'll join us, won't you, Mama?"

"We'll all be here with bells on," Mama said, pinning the reporter with her stare. "Bright and early."

"Bright and early," Purdy Sullivan said through gritted teeth.

CHAPTER 4

Stella shifted on the hard stump that was her seat as Professor Gridley built up the fire in the camp's central yard and set the water to boil.

A strong cup of tea and some biscuits.

That's what Lord Atherly recommended they have before setting off for the ranch house. Both Stella and Lyndy were exhausted from their journey and their fear over Lord Atherly's fate, but who was going to deny him?

While Lord Atherly offered to fetch the tea things in his cabin, Lyndy dropped onto the stump beside her, admiring their surroundings. When Mama leaped up to help Lord Atherly, who looked poised to drop the tin cups, the boxes of cookies, and the teapot he was carrying, Lyndy leaned forward, resting his elbows on his knees.

"Looks like Papa is putting your inheritance to good use."

Lord Atherly had nearly bankrupted his family by funding Professor Gridley's fossil expeditions, but with the influx of cash Stella provided when she married Lyndy, he'd been able to not only fund yet another expedition but visit it in relative comfort.

"I'm so glad. He seems happy."

Professor Gridley stirred the embers with a stick. "He is, Miss Stella."

Junior paused in his harmonica playing. It had been a jaunty tune Stella didn't recognize. "And that's despite him getting clobbered and lost and all."

"I admit I've never seen him like this. And offering to fetch his tea tin from his cabin? What would Mother think?" Lyndy chuckled, a mischievous glint in his eye. "But truly, he's a man seemingly transformed by these American wilds. And I heartily approve."

"Pray, of what do you approve, Lyndy?" Lord Atherly asked, passing Stella the boxes of lemon snaps and vanilla wafers. He poured hot water into the pot, followed by a couple of scoops of tea.

"No, no, no, no, no!"

They all turned at the harsh tone. The man in the pith helmet with the colorful ribbons was scolding Harp Richter, who'd returned from town. He'd elected to continue to work even after their arrival. Stella hadn't even met him or seen his face yet. The two men were hunched on the ground among the ropes.

"That's not the way to do it."

"Ever had one of these?" Trying to ignore the men working the excavation site, Lord Atherly handed Lyndy a box of animal crackers.

Stella dipped her hand into the box, grabbing a palm full. She'd chosen a monkey, a camel, a giraffe, and two kangaroos. She bit into the giraffe and savored the slightly sweet cookie.

"Like this. You do it like this!" the harsh voice continued. "If you did it your way, Harp, you'd cause compaction and could ruin whatever we might find below."

"Anyone have time for a quick tour?" Professor Gridley asked as if the belligerent man didn't exist.

Why wasn't the professor saying anything? Why was he allowing Harp Richter to be berated? Stella shared a questioning glance with Lyndy, who shrugged and took a sip of the tea his father had handed him. He wrinkled his nose at the taste.

"I'd love one, wouldn't you, Stella?" Mama sounded overly enthusiastic. And loud. Was she hoping to drown out the man's next outburst? "Lyndy? Are you game?"

After a sip, Stella set her cup on the ground. The watery, tepid black tea was terrible. Stella silently praised Lord Atherly's efforts, but he had no idea what he was doing.

"I would. I'm curious about that enormous tent over there. And I'm looking forward to finding some fossils, too."

The man in the eye-catching pith helmet sat back on his heels, glared over his shoulder, and turned his ire on her. He scratched vigorously at the palm of his hand. "Are you now?"

But for the pair of pince-nez he wore, the man's face, marked by a Roman nose and thick, dark eyebrows, resembled one of those chiseled busts of a Roman emperor Stella had seen in a museum: stark, dignified, and unyielding. His blue bow tie matched his hat.

"I don't know what you think this is, lady, but we don't allow just anyone to root around in our carefully laid-out quarry. If you want to 'find' some fossils for yourself, go somewhere else."

"I say," Lyndy protested, tossing the remnants of his tea into the trampled grass.

In the past, Stella would've worried whether those words were an opening gambit for Lyndy to escalate the argument, but ever since their trip to Scotland last month, he'd been more even-tempered than she'd ever known him to be.

Perhaps time in jail did him some good.

Professor Gridley coughed into his fist and, with a tone of weary patience, said, "Terence, come meet Lord and Lady Lyndhurst. Lord Lyndhurst is Lord Atherly's son, and Lady Lyndhurst is Mrs. Smith's daughter."

The professor's emphasis on Lord Atherly's name got him his intended reaction. Terence immediately erased his disgruntled expression and replaced it with one of contrition. Which made sense. Without Lord Atherly's money, Terence was out of a job. He wouldn't want to appear ungrateful. But Professor Gridley had also emphasized Mama's name. *Why would that be?* Terence removed his pince-nez, tucking the eyeglasses into his breast pocket, and set aside the steel clippers he was holding. Scratching his palm again, he strode the short distance between them.

Professor Gridley made the introductions. "This is Terence Brochard, my assistant from the National Museum. You'll have to forgive his bad manners. He's a promising paleontologist, passionate and protective about his work."

Lyndy sniffed. "Quite."

Terence Brochard, two red marks on either side of the bridge of his nose where his pince-nez had been, straightened his tie before nodding to Lyndy. He touched the brim of his hat at Stella and Stella's mother. "Ma'am," nodding at both mother and daughter, "I meant no disrespect."

"None taken," Stella said before Lyndy could jump in. "I was just hoping I might be able to help."

Terence cast a disparaging glance back toward the excavation area where Junior had joined Harp, clipping away the vegetation surrounding a small patch of woody ground cover. "We certainly could use someone who can follow directions."

Stella stilled her tongue at his implication and shot Lyndy a warning glance. In response, Lyndy tugged on his waistcoat.

"Like your boy, Ma'am," Terence added, touching the brim of his hat at Mama.

"I'm glad to hear it, Mr. Brochard."

"You will find that Miss Stella is as conscientious and cautious as you or I, Terence," Professor Gridley said in her defense. "We did some excavating in a barrow in England, and it was she who uncovered some interesting artifacts."

Terence's jaw shifted from side to side as he processed this new information, a grudgingly updated appraisal of Stella dawning on his face. "Then I'd be glad to have the help. Now, if you'll excuse me. I need to get back to work."

"I hope that goes for me, too," Mama said. "Like Stella, I so want to try my hand at it. Don't you, Lyndy?"

Lyndy didn't answer, intently watching Terence stride purposefully back toward Junior, Harp, and the unwanted woody plant.

"Lyndy?" Stella snuggled up to his arm. "Mama asked you a question."

Maybe she'd been too quick to assume he'd reformed. From the hole he bored into the assistant's back, if Lyndy helped at all, it would be to keep an eye on Terence, not for the joy of discovery. Following Lyndy's gaze, Stella noticed Junior stop clipping to stare at the assistant when he knelt beside him.

"I don't know what else to tell you, Harp," the assistant snapped, giving Stella the impression that she'd missed the start of the conversation. "I can't be everywhere. Just like I can't always be there to secure the corral when some idiot leaves it open."

"I don't know vhat you're talking about. I always latch the gate. It is you, the absent-minded dummkopf, who doesn't even realize what he does."

"Call me that again, and I'll show you what I can do."

"You were supposed to meet me at the depot. I had to have Junior help me unload the vagon," the German said. "Vhat vere you doing, Terry?"

Terence brandished his clippers menacingly at Harp. "For the last time, my name is Terence. Stop calling me Terry!"

Harp shrugged. "I beg your pardon, but it doesn't change the fact that you vere in town but no help to me."

"Because you were hired to help me, Harp. Not the other way around, you slow-witted idiot."

The back of Harp Richter's neck grew as red as a wildfire. "I'm done helping you!" Harp Richter sprung to his feet. "You do it alone!"

He pitched his clippers into the ground like a knife. They stuck mere inches from Terence's feet. Terence launched back, tripping on the nearest rope and landing on his backside, stirring up a small cloud of dust.

"My pleasure!" Terence shouted at the man's back, righting the grid marker before wiping his pince-nez clear with a handkerchief and brushing himself off. "The boy is twice the help you are!"

As the disgruntled worker stormed past, the scent of sweat, soil, and strong coffee followed. "I'll be back later to keep vatch, Professor," Harp said without pausing. "But I vill never help zat blasted man again."

"Very well," Professor Gridley sighed as if resigned to something that Stella suspected had become an all too common occurrence. "And we'll talk about how else you can help us in the morning."

Harp unlatched the corral gate without another word, collected his horse, a young bay gelding, and rode off.

"You forgot to latch the gate!" Terence shouted after him.

"And you forgot these fossils won't work themselves out of the ground, Terence," Professor Gridley chided. "We're lucky he didn't quit outright."

"Good riddance, I say, if he does." Terence turned his back, ending the discussion.

The professor shook his head like a man puzzling a conundrum. When Stella finally caught his eye, offering a sympathetic smile, wondering if he might explain, he said, "Terence is the best field assistant I've ever had, but heaven knows why he has to be so ornery."

Standing among the tables, Stella didn't know where to look first. One table resembled the grid outside but with wooden slats instead of rope. Heaps of fossils and rock, ranging in size from a child's tooth to a large loaf of bread, were piled high inside the wooden squares. Larger fossils, half-encased in plaster of paris jackets, lay on a second table covered with plaster dust and sand-colored soil, and strewn with hand lenses, steel dental picks, cheap wild-boar toothbrushes, half-empty glass bottles, and small wooden-handled pin vise drills.

On the third table, one end contained fossils meticulously arranged in rows, the other stacks of notebooks and field guides and a lacquered papier-mâché pencil box whose colorful, bucolic scene of children playing in a French garden looked as out of place among the fossilized skulls and teeth and finger bones as the bright ribbon on Mr. Brochard's hat. The whole tent smelled like recently applied shellac.

Professor Gridley directed Stella's attention to the far end of the third bench. "Much of what you see, we haven't had time to process. As they say, 'One hour in the field means five hours at the bench.' But we're pretty sure this"—Professor Gridley laid a light touch on the skull still partially encased in plaster in front of him—"is a *Miohippus*."

"A mio what?" Mama laughed. "Sounds awfully important, Professor."

"Trust me, Mrs. Smith. It is."

"And that's significant why?" Lyndy poorly stifled a yawn. Lyndy had never been as interested in his father's pastime as Stella had been.

"Because *Miohippus* is an early form of horse," Stella answered. "And I'm betting it's never been found in the area before either, has it?"

Lord Atherly, staring into a microscope set up on a sturdy desk commandeered from somewhere to hold the precious equipment, looked up, a twinkle of sheer joy in his eyes. "You have been paying attention, my dear. Gridley found several in Wyoming. That's what *that woman* tried to steal." Lord Atherly might never get over Jane Cosslett's attempt to discredit the professor by stealing his specimens. "But as far as we know, only Earl Douglass has found *Miohippus* this far north. And now, with the tooth I found, us." He patted his waistcoat pocket.

"Is that tooth the culprit that's to blame for you going missing then?" Lyndy said.

"No, that is." As Professor Gridley pointed out a sharp jaw fragment with a row of intact teeth, Lord Atherly rubbed the spot on the back of his head again. Stella couldn't tell if it was out of habit or because it still pained him. "And I don't regret it for a moment. It may be the most significant find to date."

"Couldn't agree more," Professor Gridley said.

"What is it?" Stella had to ask.

"Our possible *Hypohippus* specimen, my dear." Lord Atherly beamed with pride. "Suffice it to say that if we find nothing else and it proves to be what we think it is, I can die a happy man."

Stella cringed at his choice of words. She and Lyndy had seen too much death since they'd known each other.

"A rather poor choice of words, Papa," Lyndy chided as if reading her mind. "We just spent the day worrying that you'd done just that. Besides, Mother . . ."

Lyndy's scolding abruptly ended when the sound of the tent's heavy canvas flap rose, and a young woman ducked in.

"Lord A! I'd heard you'd gone missing." The woman approached, grinning at Lord Atherly with the recognition of a friendly acquaintance. "I was so worried you wouldn't be okay."

"Well, my dear, that's quite kind of you, but as you can see—"

Mama cut him off. "Well, Miss Letti Landstrom. What are you doing here?"

Stella's peer in age, the woman had blonde hair piled on her head in thick braids and the palest skin Stella had ever seen—even her eyebrows looked nearly white. If it weren't for her dusty, brown split skirt, trail-worn boots, and the enormous camera she cradled between her hands as if carrying a baby bird, Stella would've thought the woman had just stepped out of a Renaissance painting.

Miss Landstrom tapped her camera with pride. "Professor Gridley hired me, Mrs. Smith."

"Letti is our local photographer. And Letti, this here is my Stella," Mama threw her arm around Stella's shoulders. Despite the warm, stuffy air in the tent, Stella relished how their hips bumped each other. She'd never felt so close, literally or figuratively, to her mother before. "And her charming husband, Lyndy."

"I am pleased to meet you both. I've got a studio in town if you ever want to get a family portrait done while visiting." Letti offered her hand first to Stella and then Lyndy, her pumping handshake strong and assured. "I've heard so much about you. Especially you, Miss Stella. Your mother can't stop talking about you."

"Ah, now, Letti," Mama said, catching Stella's eye. "Don't go embarrassing me in front of my girl." Despite her words, nothing but pride and love gleamed in her mother's gaze.

"Stories of her as a child, perhaps?" Lyndy ventured, his

mischievous grin spreading as Stella squirmed under everyone's curious gaze. "Do tell, Miss Landstrom."

"Well, she mostly told me about your and Miss Stella's wedding, about her living in England now and her being a viscountess, but... did Stella ever tell you about the time she managed to get a pony in her bedroom when her father told her it was impossible?"

"Mama!" Stella was simultaneously pleased that her mother remembered and mortified that she'd told a stranger the story.

Egged on by Stella's reaction, Letti continued. "Or how, at the age of four, Miss Stella bribed a groomsman with cookies every day until he agreed to teach her to ride against her father's wishes?"

"Really?" Lyndy chuckled, confirming the tales with a glance at Stella's mother. "Stella, my love, you have always been this persistent?"

Mama laughed. "Lyndy, you have no idea."

Stella needed to change the subject and quickly. "What do you do in here again, Lord Atherly?"

Lyndy laughed at her transparent attempt, but it did the trick. Lord Atherly eagerly took the bait.

"This is where we can process and store the specimens we've discovered out of the weather."

"Ah, Lord Atherly, you don't do it justice." Professor Gridley threw his arms straight before him, guiding everyone's attention to the tent. "Except for where we do the actual digging, this is the most essential aspect of this camp. This is where the magic happens." His eyes gleamed with wonder, bordering on fanaticism. "This is where we begin to discover what we've truly found."

"And here I thought it was just a tent full of tables covered in plaster and bones." Letti laughed.

"I say, Miss Landstrom!" Lord Atherly, half-joking, half-not, said, "You of all outsiders should know it's more complicated than that. You've seen for yourself all that we've found already."

She laid a hand on his arm for a moment. The familiar gesture got Lyndy's attention. He muttered his excuses to Stella's mother, arched an eyebrow, and then turned to Stella with a questioning look. Stella shrugged.

"I know, Lord A. I was joking."

"Of course you were, my dear." He patted her hand.

The tent flap rustled, and Terence strode in, carrying a specimen in his palm. To Stella, it looked like seashells were embedded in the rock. He scanned the contents of the nearest table as if looking for something, then eyed Miss Landstrom with suspicion. "Where are the brachiopods you found, Lord Atherly? I want to add these."

When Lord Atherly shrugged, Terence set his specimen on the nearest table. "Who is she?"

"Letti Landstrom." She shoved her hand out, then pulled it back when Terence stared at her, scratching at his palm instead. With her thumb and forefinger, she pinched the end of her nose.

"Our photographer," the professor said. "I've hired Miss Landstrom to document the site and the specimens as needed."

Terence crossed his arms across his chest. "We have a male cook. We have male field hands. When did we resort to hiring women for anything?"

"I say, Terence, that's no way to speak to Miss Landstrom. Her work is quite invaluable. Already, she has taken photographs of everything from the fossils to the creek bed." Turning to Stella and Lyndy, Lord Atherly explained, "It's important when we are no longer on site for reference, you see."

"Thank you, Lord A." Letti grinned shyly but tweaked the tip of her nose again.

"And you expect me to lug that contraption around, I suppose? Give her access to everything?"

Professor Gridley took out a handkerchief and wiped his brow. "I do."

"Unbelievable." Terence threw up his hands.

"Now, now. We are a team here, as you well know, Terence. None of our work would get done if we didn't all pull our own weight. Everyone is needed and necessary."

"Then why do you always get to be first author?"

"Excuse me?" Professor Gridley sputtered. "What does that have to do with . . . If you have grievances or a problem with the arrangement, we agreed upon . . ." He hesitated, indicating his guests. "This is not the time or place. But I'm saying that if Harp needed help unloading the crates, you should've been there. If Letti needs time in the tent to take pictures, we give it to her."

Terence had spurned the professor, walking to the far table instead of staying to listen. He was focused on choosing a notebook from the stack when he scoffed, "I have more important things to do, thank you."

Professor Gridley gestured toward Miss Landstrom before facing him head-on. "Let me put it this way, Terence. We need Miss Landstrom's pictures as much as your notes."

Terence, his mouth agape, wordlessly slammed the notebook onto the table, rattling the fossils at the other end, and stormed off, purposefully knocking shoulders with Professor Gridley on his way out. Stella winced at the reckless display of temper. It reminded her too much of her father.

"I say," Lyndy whispered, leaning into Stella until their shoulders touched, the lemon from the cookie he ate still lingering on his breath. "I half expected a shoot-out."

"Because you've read too many of those dime novels," Stella teased, grateful for Lyndy's attempt to lighten the mood. She'd had enough tension for one day.

"Is your assistant always like that, Professor?" Mama asked.

"Terence? He'll be fine." He hadn't answered the question. "Now." He clapped his hands as if he'd forgotten the incident and was ready to talk more about his work. "Where were we?"

As Professor Gridley sought something specific from another table, Stella glanced at the one nearest her. She wanted to study the rock with Terence's fossilized shells. But it was gone.

CHAPTER 5

The surrey's wheels crunched on the weed-ridden gravel drive, kicking up more of the sweet-dry scent of prairie grass. With Stella and her mother's farm wagon in the lead, Junior steered the surrey toward the ranch house. Distant cattle lowed. Lyndy finally loosened his grip on the rail. Being driven by a boy of twelve was just one in a long line of oddities Lyndy was adjusting to.

At least I'm bloody well trying.

Seated in the back beside Lyndy, Professor Gridley superfluously announced, "We're here."

The ranch, which had been in sight for much of the trip, came into stark focus. The home of Lyndy's mother-in-law wasn't grandiose like Morrington Hall or stately like the Kendrick home in Kentucky. Still, the sprawling yet squat two-story building with its simple rectangular design, white-washed clapboard siding, green shutters, and surrounding white picket fence spoke of prosperity against adversity. In the side yard, chickens clucked and pecked below a steel windmill creaking with every turn. Lyndy found it charming indeed. Set against the backdrop of the nearby foothills, distant mountains, and endless sky, the house was just one building among many spread out over at least a half dozen acres. There were barns and bunkhouses, a blacksmith and stables, a carriage house and chicken coop, a granary and ice house. In pure size, the ranch dwarfed his father's estate. And yet, it was but a speck on the landscape, a vastness that could make anything and anyone feel small, and like the town, it lacked the history and permanency that his ancestral home had. Here, those qualities belonged to the land.

"I've dined at the Ninebark several nights and still find it remarkable," Papa said over his shoulder. And as if he'd read Lyndy's mind, he added, "To think not one of these structures existed fifty years ago."

When they finally pulled into the stable yard alongside the Smith wagon, Lyndy alighted before the wheels of the surrey came to a halt. After a challenging day of fretting over his father, an hour and a half bumping across the prairie plagued by Papa's and Gridley's unbounded enthusiasm—first to the dig, where they endured the workers' acrimony, and then here—Lyndy's head hurt as much as his backside, and he couldn't wait to escape. Besides, the Thoroughbreds had arrived.

With the horses tied to the fence, Lyndy joined Stella in inspecting the half-dozen Thoroughbreds they had brought on the train from Kentucky. They nickered softly in greeting, their lips soft and warm as they gently scooped the peppermint bit from his palm. (He'd learned from Stella to keep extras in his pocket.) As the groom that accompanied them stood by, he and Stella carefully looked them over. But with their coats shining, their eyes and ears alert, not one horse seemed worse for traveling nearly two thousand miles by rail. The groom had done well. Lyndy paid the groom and watched him mount his own horse before Stella waved her mother closer.

"We have a surprise for you, Mama." The truth of it shone from Stella's face. "How do you like them?"

"They're beautiful."

"They're Thoroughbreds, aren't they?" Junior's voice broke, evidence of his excitement.

"Magnificent creatures," Papa said. "From your horse farm, my dear?"

"We sold everything else, but I couldn't part with these." Stella patted the nearest one fondly.

"Nor could we risk taking them back to England," Lyndy added.

They'd wanted to. Hadn't Stella and her father sailed with Tupper, Orson, and Tully on board? But they'd been lucky from what he'd since learned, even taking all precautions. Horse traders they'd spoken to on the voyage confirmed they often lost many of their animals. Neither Stella nor Lyndy were willing to take that risk.

"So, wanting to ensure they found a good home, we thought we'd bring them to you, Mama."

"Running a horse ranch—" Lyndy began.

"We've got plenty of cattle, too," Junior interjected.

"Yes, well, either way, we felt certain your husband could find a use for them," Lyndy said.

Speechless, Katherine threw open her arms and beckoned everyone into them. Another embrace? Lyndy resisted but was tugged forward by several encouraging hands. Squished between Stella and her brother, with Professor Gridley's spectacles mere inches from his face, Lyndy caught Papa's eye.

He stood apart as if he'd anticipated this absurd predicament, chuckling at Lyndy's discomfort as Katherine squeezed harder. "Welcome to America, my boy!"

"And," Lyndy's mother-in-law opened her arms to encompass all they could see, "welcome to the Ninebark Ranch."

"We've actually been on ranch land the whole time." Junior began collecting the reins after Katherine directed him to take care of the horses before washing up for supper. "Pa's got over a couple thousand acres, and the camp is on the western edge."

"I can't believe I'm finally here." Unable to contain her delight, Stella squeezed Lyndy's arm. Lyndy would never know how her face didn't ache after so many hours of smiling. "You'll have to show me every inch, Mama."

Perhaps it was his fatigue or an unwarranted frustration he couldn't put a cause to, but Lyndy loathed the thought of aimlessly roaming the outbuildings spread out as if land were never an issue. He wanted nothing more than supper and his bed. But for Stella's sake, he masked his growing irritability with silence.

Two men emerged from one of the many buildings and approached. One, a nondescript fellow in a slouch hat, strode directly to unhitch the wagons. The other, a tall man with gaunt cheeks and gray speckling his bushy mustache, stopped midway to meet Junior, leading the Thoroughbreds toward the stables.

"By golly, are these fine animals!" The older man greeted the horses with reassuring whispers, running his hand along each one's long back. What he pulled from his vest pocket and offered to each, Lyndy could only guess. When he stepped back to allow Junior to proceed, he lightly slapped the nearest mare on her haunch. "Fine animals indeed."

"Well, if it isn't Miss Stella at long last." The newcomer swiftly covered the ground between them in long, deliberate strides.

"How'd you know?"

"Because you're the spitting image of your ma."

Lyndy resisted raising a skeptical eyebrow. His mother-in-law was a handsome woman, even at her age, but his Stella was the very definition of beauty, even with fatigue and dust from their travels evident on her lovely features. But when Mrs. Smith and Stella beamed at the new arrival, most likely for very different reasons, it demonstrated to Lyndy that the man had gotten some of it right. Their smiles were identical.

"And this is Stella's husband, Lord Lyndhurst, Clem. Clem's my brother-in-law."

Clem Smith was everything Lyndy envisioned in a cowboy,

from his Western calf-high boots to the black Stetson hat on his head that he tipped back with a finger before offering Lyndy a firm handshake. He was dressed in trousers made of denim, wore a loosely knotted scarf around his neck instead of a tie, and smelled of leather and horses.

"Do call me Lyndy." He was quite pleased to be able to fit the ideal to a name.

Dime-store novels, indeed. This man could've walked off the page.

"Will do. I'm pleased to meet you. And, of course, Katie's beautiful daughter. I've heard much about you, Miss Stella."

"Mama's told me about you too, Uncle Clem."

"Uncle Clem?" He rubbed his stubbly, pointed chin and stared up toward the white wisps of clouds. "I'm not sure I like the sound of that. I'm Junior's uncle, sure, but hearing a lady like you say it just makes me feel worn out and old."

He flashed Stella a toothy smile and poked Lyndy in the ribs with his elbow. "You are one lucky man there, Lyndy." There was no flippancy, no jealousy in his tone. It was said with all the straightforward sincerity Lyndy expected from a man who ranched the American West. Besides, it was apparent from his stolen glances that he preferred his sister-in-law's mature beauty to that of Stella's spring freshness.

"Indeed, I am."

"Lord A, Professor," Clem acknowledged Papa and Gridley with a tip of his head. "Are y'all here for supper again?" His tone was teasing, eliciting an amused scoff from Lyndy's father.

"As if I would refuse such fine cooking. As I've stated before, I've never eaten more succulent beef than at your table."

Lyndy regarded his father with renewed respect. *Who was this man who bantered with cowboys and complimented frontier cuisine?* Lyndy was beginning to be quite fond of this version of Papa. Imagining what Mother would say, Lyndy inwardly chuckled.

"I hear from your pa, here, Lyndy," Clem tilted his head toward Papa, "that you're a man who loves a fine horse."

"My wife and I both do."

"Then we'll have plenty to talk about. I'm not only Ned's brother but also responsible for the draft and saddle horses on the ranch. Love to show you around sometime."

"Thank you. I'd quite fancy that."

Clem laughed and slapped Lyndy on the shoulder, nearly jarring him into taking a step forward.

What had he said that was so amusing?

Lyndy had spent a couple of weeks in America, and its people's behavior still baffled him. Is this how Stella felt when she arrived in England? Yet again, his appreciation and admiration for his wife and how well she'd adapted to her new life grew. She'd proven more than worthy of him amongst his countrymen. Lyndy vowed to try to do the same.

"You saw those Thoroughbreds Junior was leading to the stables," Katherine Smith said. "Stella and Lyndy brought them from Kentucky."

"I see you don't mess around. Bringing your steeds all the way from Kentucky. They are some of the finest I've ever seen."

"I don't think you understand, Clem. Those Thoroughbreds are a gift. Stella and Lyndy brought them here for us."

"For us?" Clem's eyes widened with unseen possibilities.

"Stella thought you'd find a good use for them," Lyndy said.

"And I sure will." With his mind still on the horses, Clem headed unceremoniously up the stairs that led to the porch. When he glanced over his shoulder, catching a quick glimpse before the Thoroughbreds disappeared into the stable, he beckoned, seeing no one had followed. "Well, don't be shy. No need to mill about in the yard. Come on in."

When Papa and Professor Gridley followed Katherine up the stairs and into the house, appetizing aromas drifted through the doorway. Lyndy's stomach grumbled in reply. But for the biscuits, he'd not eaten since breakfast.

Up on the porch, Clem continued to scrape mud off the bottom of his boots on a horizontal wrought-iron bar fastened to the flooring beside the front door. "Lord A and the professor take a drink before we eat. I bet you could use a stiff one after your trip, too, Lyndy?"

It was music to his ears. "Shall we, my love?" Lyndy offered Stella his arm. She was still craning her neck, trying to take it all in.

"Isn't it everything you hoped for?" With the temperature dropping, she shivered in the cool evening breeze.

"It is," Lyndy said, his attention fixed on her. She noticed and rewarded him with a spirited laugh as they ascended the stairs. "Still could use that drink, though."

When Lyndy and his lovely wife stepped inside the ranch house and into the short, uncluttered hall, constructed of painted boards and containing a not-so-grand stairwell, there was no butler to take their hats, no footman to show them to their room. Instead, Clem tossed his Stetson onto the brass hooks that lined the wall by the door and disappeared into the small room to the right. As the door briefly opened, Lyndy glimpsed a man hunched over a rolltop desk strewn with papers. The man stifled a hollow cough with his fist. Could that be Mr. Smith, Stella's stepfather and owner of this impressive ranch? If so, why had he not been there to greet them? The two men's voices murmured, their words indistinct through the door, but there was no doubt they were arguing. With Papa and Professor Gridley preoccupied with hanging their hats and discussing the implications of striations on a particular fossilized bone, Lyndy shared a questioning glance with Stella as she leaned her ear closer and closer to the door.

"What's all that about?" he asked, hanging his hat among the others.

"Something about an unexpected drop in horse sales." She held out her hat and leather handbag for him to hang.

"You must be Miss Stella." A woman in black—black dress, black shoes, black hair pulled loosely into a bun—appeared abruptly at the end of the hall drying her hands on her stark white apron.

Stella straightened like a coiled spring and, nervously tucking a stray strand of hair behind her ear, replied, "I am."

"And you must be her husband, Lord Lyndhurst?" Not young nor old, the woman in black had a timeless serenity to her. If hard-pressed to say what part of the world she hailed from, Lyndy wouldn't have been able to guess. "I'm Maria. It's so nice to meet you finally."

"And you, Maria. Mama's told me so much about you."

"Not all bad, I hope."

She and Stella shared a chuckle, Maria's deep and melodic, reminiscent of a cello, in contrast to Stella's violin. Who was this woman with an accent he couldn't place? Another member of the family? Certainly not the housekeeper she appeared to be.

"What delights have you prepared for us tonight?" the professor asked, rubbing his hands together. Lyndy couldn't imagine any meal creating such a reaction. But then again, if the paleontologist was used to eating around that fire ring, anything cooked properly might sound like a treat.

"You know I don't make anything fancy, Professor. All the same, I was beginning to wonder if you'd make it in time. Supper will be ready in ten minutes."

Ten minutes? They barely had time to wash the soot and soil from their hands, let alone dress for dinner.

Papa must have noticed the distress on his face, for he leaned over his shoulder and whispered, "I've yet to see them dress for dinner here. It's quite freeing, really."

"Can I help?" Stella offered.

"That's kind of you, but not tonight. Tonight, you're a guest."

Maria's implied response caught Lyndy off-guard. What did

Maria assume Stella was offering to do? Polish the silver? Stir the soup? Bring the dishes to the table?

As if none of this was out of the ordinary, as if expecting a viscountess to sweep the kitchen floor was not a humiliating insult, Maria added, "I'll show you where you can wash up," and led Stella, Lyndy, Papa, and Professor Gridley through a large sitting room, the connecting dining room—both far more similar with their oak furniture, lush decor, and walls adorned with paintings (though here, instead of dour ancestors, they were all of horses) to Morrington Hall than the plain hall would suggest—and into the kitchen. Lyndy had stepped across the threshold prepared to voice his objection (who expected lords and lady to cleanse their hands in the kitchen?) but stilled his tongue at the whistle of a kettle boiling.

He'd never been in a kitchen before. This one was dominated by a wrought-iron stove accented with shiny copper pans and drying herbs hanging above. A long central wooden table held baskets of biscuits and rolls, bowls covered with linen tea towels, and a wash basin steaming with hot water. The enticing aroma of the succulent beef Papa had mentioned mingled with the scent of the freshly baked bread. Were kitchens all this homely, welcoming, and snug? Had the kitchen at Morrington Hall resembled this in the days before it was fitted with running water? Did it always smell this good?

Having used the rough sacking towel to dry his hands, Lyndy passed it to Papa. A man, obviously related to Clem but stockier, clean-shaven, and fair-haired, strode into the kitchen, the spurs on his boots tinkling like tiny bells announcing his arrival.

"There you are," Katherine Smith said. It was the gent Lyndy had seen at the rolltop desk. *The one arguing with Clem.*

"Good evening, Lord A, Professor. Seems I'm the last one to this party. You must be Stella and Lyndy."

How many times had he heard this? Evidence, along with their gracious smiles and hardy handshakes, that not only had the family been expecting them but welcomed their visit. Lyndy internally blanched at the memory of how Stella had been greeted the first time she'd arrived at Morrington Hall. Who was he to be offended by an invitation into their kitchen? He tugged at the cuff of his sleeve, hoping to keep the shame burning his chest from revealing itself on his face.

"Welcome to my humble abode." The newcomer greeted Lyndy and Stella as he leaned in to kiss Katherine Smith's cheek. He showed no signs—no scowl, no sullen posture, no inflamed cheeks—of having argued with his brother moments before. Did they argue so often he could shrug it off that easily? Or had it been of little consequence? If only Lyndy knew what it was about.

"Eugene Edward Smith. But everyone calls me Ned." The man greeted Lyndy with a bone-crushing handshake. Once released, Lyndy could not help but try and shake the effects off.

Ned grimaced. "Sorry about that. Too used to manhandling the cattle and equipment."

When Ned Smith didn't offer his hand to Stella, she embraced him like a long-lost relative. "Whoa, little lady. I'm still covered in dust."

Stella backed away but didn't back down. "As if I care. I'm just thrilled to finally meet the man who makes my mother happy."

Ned colored beneath his sun-tanned cheeks. He strode to the water bowl, which Maria had pitched and replenished while they'd been talking. "I do try." He coughed into a fist, then plunged his hands into the hot water, turning it brown again.

"It's getting a bit crowded in here. If you don't object, Mrs. Smith?" Papa indicated the dining room beyond, where Maria was setting a platter of fish fillets on the table.

"No, by all means, Lord Atherly, Professor, please take a seat." She then turned her attention to her brother-in-law filling the doorway. Surprisingly, removing his hat did nothing to diminish his stature. "What do you have up your sleeve now, Clem?"

Clem Smith had stepped aside to allow Papa and the professor to pass, a sly smirk curling his lips and lighting up his expression. He, too, seemed little disturbed by the argument. *It couldn't have meant much.* "I've got a surprise for Junior."

He whistled three quick notes in short succession, and almost immediately, the scrape of multiple clawed feet scurried toward them. Before Lyndy could imagine what they could be, furry, fuzzy balls of energy, yipping and biting, bounded into the kitchen.

Wolf pups!

"Bloody hell!" Lyndy exclaimed.

One broke off from the pack, scampered toward him like his trousers were made of venison, and pounced on something behind Lyndy's shoe. Something's tail still dangled from the pup's mouth when it leaped on Lyndy's leg. Stella squatted to pet its gray, mangled fur.

"That one likes you," Stella laughed, unfazed by the wild animals roaming the kitchen.

"And he's a good mouser." Unfazed, Ned continued drying his hands.

"Get them out of my kitchen!" Maria cried, echoing Lyndy's silent plea. The wildest animals he'd ever been this close to were New Forest Ponies, and all their names were listed in the stud book. Maria tried shooing the pups from the kitchen to no avail.

Stella joined the chase, giggling as the wild critters dodged and ran from her attempts to catch them. She wasn't really trying.

"Like this," Clem instructed, snatching one up harmlessly

by the scuff of its neck. The pup's little legs dangled like a marionette's.

Stella tried again, and Clem grabbed up a second in his other hand. Watching his technique, Stella cornered the third, disregarding its show of pointed fangs, and snagged the creature by the scuff.

Stella hoisted the docile pup, cooing, "Now, this isn't so bad, is it?"

With the wild creatures still clasped in both fists, Clem turned to Lyndy. "Ready for that drink?"

"Indeed. I thought you'd never ask."

CHAPTER 6

~~~

Harp let the last note of "After the Ball" fade into silence before dropping his harmonica back into his pocket. He poked the fire, setting bright yellow sparks sizzling toward the darkened sky before taking another swig from his flask. Professor Gridley had insisted he stay sober while guarding camp, but Harp held his liquor more than most, and it took more than a few sips of rye until Harp even began to feel its effects. Besides, no one was here. The British noble and the professor had gone with the newcomers to the ranch house, and Terry had left without so much as a say-so.

"What a dummkopf," Harp muttered before taking another sip. A coyote howled in the distance and was answered by yips and barks much closer to camp.

The night was calm, clear, and almost chilly. Harp preferred the cool to the heat, but without enough distraction, nights like this brought Helga and his homestead to mind. As if he was standing in his yard, he could picture Helga and the baby rocking on the porch in the sole piece of furniture Harp ever made by hand, the rocker creaking in rhythmic time with the squeak of the loose board he never seemed to get around to fixing. How Helga enjoyed the crisp, fresh air. So different from the acrid, sooty stuff they used to breathe back home. It was diphtheria that took his wife and son within hours of each other. Why Harp survived, he'll never know.

Harp took a long draw and emptied his flask. "Better not to have."

Life had been nothing but a struggle since. The great drought took his crops and lost him the homestead. Then days, weeks, months spent stripping the Claxton mine of every last ounce of gold until there was nothing left. Now, he worked for the odd pair of Atherly and Gridley. Some would say he was lucky. But digging for fossils wasn't much different than digging for gold. The heat, the mosquitoes, the pay were the same. And although he had nights like tonight when he could play his mouth harp to his content and drink the bottle of rye he got the last time he was in town, he also had to put up with the likes of Terry Brochard, a loudmouth, complaining, know-it-all who didn't know a thing.

Harp snorted in disgust. *As if going to college made him better zan me.*

The rustling of heavy canvas yanked Harp out of his reverie. He was supposed to be alone.

He reached for the shotgun set against the pile of freshly cut wood he'd been leaning against and launched to his feet.

"Hallo?" No answer.

Outside the limited ring of light from the fire, all was dark, and Harp aimed his shotgun into it and waited. Nothing. A horse snorted, and he jerked the shotgun in that direction. What was he thinking? Had he had too much to drink after all? He lowered his gun but strained to hear something, anything that would confirm he hadn't imagined it. The distant coyotes calling to each other pierced the silence, and Harp flinched. He reached for his flask but remembered it was empty.

There was the sound again. It came from the research tent. Who or what was that? Bears were uncommon in the valley but not unheard of. And, of course, coyotes, cougars, even a raccoon or skunk could've wandered in. Harp didn't want to face any of them.

"I know you're in there," he called, not noticing the slur of his words. "Come out now, and you von't get hurt." No response. He'd have to scare it off.

Harp raised his shotgun toward the sky and blasted a warning into the darkness. The boom shattered the silence, startling the horses into a chorus of frightened squeals. Fossils clattered, and books crashed moments before something large hurried out of the tent. Could be a bear or a man bent low. Harp stood his ground, hoping whoever or whatever it was, predator or rustler, would scram before Harp had to shoot again.

"Zat's right," he shouted. "Hightail it out of here!"

Harp stepped to the edge of the fire's light, hoping to catch a glimpse of what was out there. As his vision adjusted, the sharp crack of wood and the stomping of feet alerted him to the horses kicking open the corral that Harp had built. And then, before he could react, the horses were upon him. He leaped out of the way as they bolted past the dying fire and into the dark.

"*Zum Donnerwetter!*" Harp cursed, slamming the butt of his shotgun into the ground. "That *arschloch* left the gate unlatched again. I'll kill him ze next time I see him!"

With little time to decide, Harp abandoned the camp to who or whatever, hoping the intruder had been as frightened as the geldings, and took off in the direction they had galloped. The British noble and the professor might argue their bones were treasures, but everyone knew nothing out here was more valuable than a horse.

After a leisurely and delicious supper, the diners dispersed: Lord Atherly and Professor Gridley headed back to their camp,

Lyndy and the Smith brothers went outside, and Stella followed Mama and Maria into the kitchen, where the scent of freshly brewed coffee and huckleberry stacked cake still lingered. At Morrington Hall, she was a lady and expected to allow the staff to do their jobs. But here, out on the prairie, it was painfully apparent that Maria and Stella's mother managed everything themselves—from the kitchen tasks to the garden, even milking the cows each morning. They could do with the help. But they'd shooed Stella out of the kitchen. As their guest, just like at Morrington Hall, she was expected to respect the rules. Guests, even if they are your daughter, don't help dry the dishes.

At loose ends, Stella joined Lyndy outside. She hesitated near the kitchen door as Ned's voice through the window reassured Maria about the pups. He hadn't sounded so accommodating when he and Clem had been arguing earlier. What had that been all about? In the stable yard, Clem was teaching Lyndy to lasso in the circular pool of light cast by the gas lamp. Whirling the circle of rope high, Lyndy flung it toward the post he was practicing on. He missed. He pulled the loop toward him and tried again and again. She was impressed. When had Lyndy ever been so persistent despite facing such repeated failure?

When he was courting me. Stella stifled the chuckle she couldn't suppress behind her hand. Then, the loop settled perfectly over the post.

"Bloody hell, I got it!" Lyndy pushed his Panama hat, suddenly seemingly out of place, back from his forehead and allowed a broad grin to take over his face. Stella couldn't resist planting a kiss on his cheek.

"My cowboy," she teased.

"Well done, Lyndy," Clem said.

"Keep at it," Ned advised. "It's one thing to lasso a post that's standing still. It's a whole other when you're roping a calf from horseback."

Eager to prove himself, Lyndy tried again with renewed vigor. His next wild toss sent a passing chicken running and clucking away in distress.

Ned laughed as he strolled toward the paddock. A horse nickered. He grabbed a pitchfork leaning against the hay-filled wagon parked beside it and pitched some over the fence. Distracted by the already plentiful piles of hay scattered around the three-acre enclosure, several horses, a mix of Morgans and Quarter Horses, were getting acquainted with the Thoroughbreds at a safe distance from each other. Leaving Lyndy to his lassoing, Stella joined him. What better opportunity to get to know her mother's husband better?

"I heard you offered Clem and me your Thoroughbreds." Ned rested his elbows on the paddock fence, his gaze fixed on the horses, his tone squelching a million questions Stella wanted to ask.

"They were my Daddy's horses, and I wanted you and Mama to have them."

"But those are full-blooded Thoroughbreds. Some of the best I've ever seen. And as you know, your mother and I met in Kentucky, so I've seen some fine horses. They must be worth—"

"A great deal, but that's not the point," Stella interrupted. "Lyndy and I didn't want to chance bringing them back with us to England, and with you breeding horses on your ranch, I thought—"

It was Ned's turn to interrupt. "That's fine, Miss Stella, but you don't understand. Clem and I do breed and trade horses, but we can't afford these beauties."

"No offense, Ned, but you don't understand. I'm not selling them to you. They're a gift."

Ned shook his head, avoiding looking her in the eye. "I can't accept them."

"Why not?" Did he loathe that they once belonged to his wife's former husband? Or was it simply a matter of pride?

"Mama wrote that you were thinking of breeding a new kind of horse, and I thought these might be just what you were looking for."

"It's too generous."

"Too generous to give to my mother and her family? After all she's been through on my account?" Stella still couldn't let herself dwell on the sacrifices her mother had made, which her father demanded, to ensure Stella inherited her father's estate. "It's because of her that I can be generous. Please, let me be."

"On behalf of your mother and Junior, then," he accepted grudgingly.

"Thank you."

To cover the awkward tension between them, Stella clicked her tongue, and Daisy Chain, a gentle chestnut filly, approached to sample the newest pile of hay. Stella climbed two fence rungs, leaned over, and stroked Daisy's shoulder. As Ned approached, the filly sidled away skittishly but continued to graze. Stella jumped from the fence and brushed off her skirt.

"You talk about impressive horses. Those of yours certainly aren't knock-kneed nags."

"No, you're right. They aren't as fine as the ones you brought, but they are hardy and strong and came almost as cheap."

Though more familiar with Thoroughbreds, Stella knew a quality horse when she saw one. "I think whatever you paid was more than worth it. Look how effortlessly they move, so athletic and graceful, with their well-arched necks and well-defined muscles, especially in the shoulders and hindquarters. And I can see the gloss of their coats from here. They're beautiful, Ned. And a stallion, too."

"Well," Ned offered a self-deprecating grin. "I can't take credit." He coughed into his fist, a chill growing in the night air. "Clem got them for a song from a homesteader selling up and going back east just this morning. Man wanted to offload them quick." Ned tapped the fence rail like a single, decisive drumbeat before stepping back and reaching for the pitchfork again. "Who knew when this family woke up this morning what a lucky day we'd have."

And it wouldn't be the last if Stella had anything to do with it.

Clutching the notebook to his chest, Dr. Aurelius Moss pocketed the wrought-iron key after locking the door behind him. Although the chambermaid had serviced his hotel room earlier (there was no mistaking that mix of carbolic soap and wood polish), he couldn't afford any risks. It was imperative he not be disturbed. Moss tossed his hat onto the bed, yanked the thick curtains across the room's one window to block out the night, and settled into the wingback chair. He pulled the floor lamp closer, casting a direct light on the notebook in his lap. Too absorbed with the implications of his newest possession, he failed to appreciate how the thick curtains, the chair's rich damask upholstery, the quilt folded neatly at the foot of the brass bed, and the stained-glass panes of the lampshade matched the verdant hue of his name.

He pulled the monocle from his waistcoat's breast pocket and fitted it impatiently, bringing the fine writing and diagrams on the first page into sharp focus. He sought a dinner mint from a glass dish on the side table and popped one into his suddenly dry mouth. The stiff new pages rustled with every turn as he flipped through the notebook. There would be time enough to study every diagram, map, and illustration later. As he flipped faster and faster, the illustrations seemed to dance off the pages, almost causing him to overlook it—an unfamiliar curve, striations he had never seen before leaped out at him. He peered closer as if proximity alone could clarify what he was looking at.

Could it be? Before him lay a carefully crafted and well-labeled illustration of a fossil he'd never encountered.

Moss had organized a dig in Wyoming, like many before him, but when Amos Gridley pulled up stakes for Montana,

Moss had to wonder why. And then the telegram came. Moss couldn't leave Wyoming fast enough. He'd wired countless landowners in the area until one granted Moss permission to establish his operation. It could've been anywhere—a farmer's homestead covered with wheat and barley—miles from any fossil bone yard. Only providence explained how he'd managed to set up less than two miles up creek from Gridley's camp. It had been costly and time-consuming, and Moss wondered what devil possessed him to do it. But here, he thought, smoothing his hand across the thick paper as if he could feel the fossil, was his reward.

He lifted the open notebook against his chest, cradling it like the newborn infant he never had time for, while a sly grin crept across his face.

"I've got you now, Gridley," he whispered. "I've got you now."

CHAPTER 7

With Mama too busy with chores to join them after all, Stella had been reluctant to leave her. However, with the fossil campsite in full view, Stella now itched to get her hands in the dirt and discover something new. But that meant kneeling and bending and squatting until her thighs were sore. And already her muscles were tired. Kept up by the exhilaration of being under her mother's roof and Lyndy's amorous attention, she'd risen before sunrise to help, trying her hand at milking the cow, collecting herbs and vegetables from the garden for breakfast, and making up her bed. The trip across the open meadow hadn't helped. Instead of sitting up properly, balancing and adjusting to the bumpy trail, she'd snuggled against Lyndy, bracing and straining not to fall out. The day had barely begun, and she was exhausted. Was finding a fossil worth all this?

Lord Atherly would think so.

As Lyndy passed the makeshift cabin and pulled into the camp's central yard, Stella stretched to work the cramp out of her neck and shoulders and then stopped, her fatigue forgotten.

"Where is everyone?" Stella whispered as if there were some danger in disturbing the silence.

The camp was empty and quiet, too quiet. No rustling, no whispers, no footfalls, no soft *tap, tap* of steel on fossilized bone or rock. Only the sounds of nature prevailed: the whisk of their horse's tail, the occasional *pop* and *hiss* from the dying fire, the constant murmur of the flowing river beyond.

"Hello?" Stella called. No answer but the flap of canvas as a gust of wind blew through.

"Papa insisted we arrive early." Lyndy lifted his watch from his waistcoat pocket. "It's gone near eight o'clock. Surely, they aren't all sleeping? Good morning!" Lyndy shouted. No response.

"Lyndy, no one's here. Look, all the horses are gone." The corral stood empty, the gate hanging crooked and half-open.

"Right!" Lyndy jerked on his waistcoat. "They were expecting us, but we know how single-minded Papa and Gridley can be. They must've set off, what did Papa call it, prospecting for fossils and simply forgot to meet us."

"Maybe," Stella said, though the knot in her stomach told her otherwise. She jumped from the wagon and ducked into the research tent while Lyndy hitched their horses temporarily to a post.

"Anyone about?" he asked when she reappeared.

Stella shook her head. They split up and searched the other tents and the makeshift cabin. All empty. Stella strode to the quarry site. Brushes, picks, and small dustpans were strewn haphazardly. Lord Atherly might be absent-minded, but Stella got the impression that Professor Gridley's assistant, Terence, was a stickler for method and order. He'd never leave these just lying around.

"I don't like this, Lyndy." When he joined her, she pointed to the abandoned tools. "Perhaps we should get the wagon and see if we can find them."

Together, they took in the vista, the rolling hills, the sweeping valley, and the distant snow-capped peaks. They could see for miles, but Stella couldn't spot a surrey or men on horseback anywhere. How would they know which direction to take? She and Lyndy had followed the already well-worn track between the dig and the ranch house and hadn't passed anyone. That still left three directions to choose.

"I hate to say it, but we aren't any more equipped to navigate the unfamiliar terrain than Papa was," Lyndy said. "Perhaps it would be best to wait here to see if anyone returns. Or go back to the ranch house and get help? Or—"

Stella continued to gaze intently at the landscape before them, hoping the view might hold the answer. Her attention was drawn to the sun's reflection glistening on the dark waters of the distant creek. Although the nearest reaches were hidden by the willows bordering the quarry and the curving hillsides, the creek wound its way far into the distance, snaking across the valley.

"The creek bed!" Stella snapped her fingers excitedly.

"What about it?" Lyndy's voice rose in concern as she pulled the pin from her hat and tossed it onto the ground.

"It's the one place hidden from view."

Without waiting to see if Lyndy followed, Stella plunged into a thicket of willow, pushing and shoving the branches, snagging her skirt and hair to peer over the edge of the hill. Here, the slope was relatively gentle, but it grew steeper downstream as the creek widened and carved its way between two hills, rounding a bend. She'd half expected to see the missing men below. Why, she didn't know. It wasn't that deep of a ravine that they wouldn't have heard them earlier.

"See anyone?" Lyndy called above his loud thrashing through the brush.

"No. But I think that's where they might be." She pointed downstream.

Joining her, Lyndy slapped his leaf-littered Panama hat against his pant leg. Stella stifled a nervous chuckle. She hadn't noticed before, but he looked like a tourist out here. They both did. No wonder Maria had raised an eyebrow as they'd left this morning. Attired in a frilly white linen day dress more fit for a garden party than a fossil dig, Stella vowed to ask her mother's advice on what best to wear. Better yet, ask her to take her shopping in Colter City.

Where I'll get Lyndy a new hat.

"I'm not sure why they'd need the horses, but you're right," he said. "Perhaps they went prospecting around that bend?"

"It's worth a look."

Together, they skidded, slid down the bank, and followed the narrow creek bed, the mineral scent of wet stone rising from the rushing water. Lyndy set the pace as if his legs had been given free rein, like a stabled horse that had never been beyond a paddock. Too many times, she'd seen him restless like a caged animal, and here he'd been set free. She'd come to Montana to see her mother and all the good that would do, but she hadn't known how Lyndy would react. He'd dreamed of cowboys, cattle drives, and glorified gunfighters, and she thought he'd be disappointed. The open range was closed, the buffalo all but gone, and the stories from his dime novels were just that, mostly stories. Yet they'd been here for less than a full day, and already he was embracing all he could from her mother's lifestyle: learning to lasso, eating supper "family style," driving a farm wagon himself. How little he resembled the haughty noble she'd first met. She grasped his hand, and they traversed the distance together. When Lyndy paused to kneel and scooped up water in his cupped hands, Stella couldn't help bending over to kiss the back of his sun-burned neck. Seeing him so uninhibited was as refreshing as the cool creek water.

"Ahhh!"

"Who was that?" Stella straightened at the sound of the echoed cry as Lyndy sat back on his heels.

"I didn't recognize the voice."

Lyndy bounded to his feet, grabbed Stella's hand, and they ran, scrambling over the damp, pebbly creek bed, the hem of her skirt occasionally trailing in the water until they rounded another bend. Standing beside the rushing water, a steep incline to their backs, were the missing men. All save one. He lay face down at their feet, one arm floating in the creek, one shoe missing, his weathered jacket and dark, rumpled hair sullied by dirt, leaves, and sand.

"What the bloody hell happened?" Lyndy called.

"We were looking for the horses that got out last night and instead came across him," Lord Atherly explained.

A chorus of protests erupted as the men tried to discourage her from getting closer, Terence even trying to block her view with his body. Cotton gauze was wrapped around the palms of his hands, or he probably would've grabbed her. She side-stepped him through the frigid water.

"From the look of him, he's been out here awhile," Professor Gridley said. "Though not long enough for animals to find him, thank goodness."

A quiver of disgust ran along Stella's spine. She tried to suppress the images of a body ravaged by predators by focusing on the man as he was, but that offered little relief. Only then did she notice the hideous, impossible angle of his neck. She had to look away.

"Then who screamed?" Lyndy wanted to know.

"That was me," Purdy Sullivan explained sheepishly, chewing his pencil. He'd been scribbling furiously into a small pocket notebook since they arrived. Was this death to be fodder for his newspaper readers? Why was he even here?

"But who is it?" Stella asked, impatient to know.

"We're not sure," Gridley admitted.

Before she could object and explain why they shouldn't touch him, Terence used the heel of his boot to flip the man over. His body splashed water on them, like the sprinklings at a baptism, as more of him landed in the creek.

"You shouldn't have done that, Mr. Brochard." Stella peered into the familiar face.

The man's mouth twisted into a permanent scowl as if he, too, objected to the rough handling, his unblinking stare accusingly fixed on them. Harp Richter would never play his harmonica again.

CHAPTER 8

Stella reached her hand out. "Can I have your handkerchief?"

Lyndy gave it to her without question. Stella covered the dead man's face, making both the professor and Lord Atherly blanch, though Lyndy showed no surprise. Purdy flipped to a fresh page of his notebook as if he needed to record what she'd done, and over the scratching of pencil on paper, Stella stated the obvious.

"We have to tell the police."

"Must we involve the sheriff, Miss Stella?" Professor Gridley said. "Surely this is an accident."

"Accident? I thought we assumed the man took off with the horses," Terence said.

"No, you assumed that," Professor Gridley corrected. "Lord Atherly and I never once considered Harp to be a horse thief." Lord Atherly agreed with a slight nod.

"Gridley and I arrived at camp after dark last night, having done a bit of prospecting on our way back from dinner," Lord Atherly explained, as if he needed to clear his conscience. "We noticed the paddock stood empty, the gate splintered and open, and Harp nowhere to be found, but we thought not much could be done. We'd assumed Mr. Richter had gone after the horses. If we had known." Lord Atherly gestured toward the body, unable to say more.

"Either way," Terence said, apparently not willing to concede Harp's innocence, "it's obvious the man had been drinking." Stella, too, had noticed the faint scent of whiskey. "I told him more than once Demon Rum would be his undoing. He must've stumbled off drunk and fallen down the ravine." Terence curled his lip. "That is, if he wasn't stealing the horses."

"He wasn't," Professor Gridley said. "He was as honest a fellow as they come. Do you think I would've asked him to guard camp if I thought he'd steal from us?"

"Then what do you think happened?" Stella asked.

"Didn't Harp notice the corral hadn't been secured properly yesterday?" Lyndy offered. But Stella had seen the gate. It looked more trampled than left open. "You, Terence, you argued with him about it."

"What if I did?" Terence snipped.

"If I remember, Harp blamed you, and you blamed him."

"What are you getting at, Lord Lyndhurst?"

Stella could feel the tension between the two men rising, though Lyndy's posture and tone didn't worry her. He was provoking the man without sparking his temper. But it emboldened Stella to ask what she'd been thinking.

"Where were you, Terence, that Harp had to stand guard?"

"That, Lady Lyndhurst, is none of your business."

Her new title had rarely been said with such contempt. It stunned her. A man was lying dead, and Terence didn't seem to care. A tiny, petty voice in her head wanted to remind him that her inheritance was funding his explorations, but honoring the control it was taking Lyndy not to raise his fists, civility won out. Everyone reacted to death, especially tragic death, differently. Perhaps this was Terence Brochard's way of dealing with what he couldn't explain.

Or maybe he's hiding something.

"Well, at least you can tell us if you left the gate open before you left. It would explain how the horses got out."

"I don't have to tell you anything."

"That's enough, Terence," Professor Gridley said. "My God, Harp is lying dead in this ravine, and Miss Stella is just trying to get to the bottom of what happened."

"Why? Unless I'm supposed to take that watch pin on that dress of hers for a badge," Terence muttered.

"No, you're right," Stella said as Lyndy, his fists clenched, his patience wearing thin, took a step closer. "That's why we need to tell the sheriff. So he can investigate."

"But that would mean answering questions." As if Lord Atherly couldn't think of anything more intrusive. What did he have to hide?

Stella dismissed Lord Atherly's complaint as a mere objection to inconvenience rather than something more worrisome, keeping her focus on Terence to gauge his reaction. "Yes, Lord Atherly, it would. But then we'll know, one way or another."

Terence didn't blink. He crossed his arms deliberately as if issuing a silent challenge.

"I'll get the sheriff," Purdy Sullivan suddenly declared, holding up his pencil to accentuate his announcement. She was so caught up in the argument with Terence that she'd almost forgotten he was there. She noticed the multiple teeth marks at the tip of his pencil—a nervous habit, maybe? Why was he there at all? Had he visited the camp as he'd promised yesterday, or was he in the ravine when the others arrived? Before she could question him, he was making good on his offer and scrambling up the embankment.

"Mama and Ned need to know about this." Stella hated to admit it. Stella envisioned explaining to her mother that she'd come across yet another dead body, and this one on her ranch. *What will Mama think?* Stella's visit was supposed to strengthen her bond with her mother, not embroil her in more death and possible murder.

Lyndy wrapped his arm around her shoulder as if sensing the cause for her hesitation. "Shall I ride back to the ranch and tell the Smiths what's happened?"

"While I'll make sure nothing gets disturbed until the sheriff arrives." And in the meantime, she could take a good look around.

"Let me know what you find," he whispered as if he'd read her mind and knew what she was up to. Stella planted a big kiss on Lyndy's cheek.

After Lyndy headed off, Stella searched the creek bed and embankment for any signs that Harp's fall was anything but an accident. However, with all the trampling and clambering, any evidence was long gone. There was no hope of answering the questions bubbling in her mind like a pot of boiling water. She looked around his half-floating body, struggling to ignore how he bobbed like a fishing lure. Again, she found nothing. She attempted to search his clothes, but the moment her fingers brushed the cold, sodden fabric of his vest, a wave of nausea surged up her throat, making her feel like she might be sick. If only they could drag him onto the sandbank. But she'd leave that to the sheriff's men. Seeing the body as it was found might be all the evidence left.

She turned to her father-in-law and the two paleontologists. "Why was Purdy here?"

"Why else?" Lord Atherly replied. "He wanted to see our possible *Hypohippus* jaw. The discovery, if we can confirm it, will be most scintillating to his readers."

Stella didn't want to disillusion her father-in-law. Newspaper reporters don't rise this early to glimpse a fossil. After submitting his heroic rescue of Lord Atherly, would his newspaper even accept such a follow-up? Could Purdy have had something to do with Harp's death? An assignation gone wrong?

Stella regretted how suspicious she'd become. She wanted to see the good in everyone, but her and Lyndy's multiple encounters with murder had jaded her, making her question everyone and everything.

"Shall we wait for the law enforcement in camp?" Lord Atherly said. "I could use a cup of tea."

"By all means," Professor Gridley said.

Surveying the scene, assuring herself that Harp's body was secure and in no danger of slipping any farther into the rushing water, Stella accompanied the men toward a gentler slope in the creek bed.

As they pushed through the willows that lined the creek's bank, Terence broke their silence. "I wonder if any of you realize what Harp's death means for our work?"

As they passed by the quarry, with its patchwork of deep and shallowly dug square holes, Stella spotted the rounded hump of a partially uncovered fossilized bone. She shivered. She hadn't sensed any similarity between this and a graveyard. Until now.

"I'll find you another field hand, Terence," Professor Gridley grumbled. "Though the way you treat them, I doubt they'd stay for long. Harp, God rest his soul, put up with you the longest. How, I don't know."

"It's not that, Professor," Terence said. "His death threatens the project."

"Why?" Stella asked.

"As *if* you don't know."

"What do you mean by that?" Stella's ears burned with frustration. Like Lyndy, her patience with this man was waning.

"We all know your mother was the force behind allowing us to excavate on her husband's land. With the pall of a dead man, especially with her daughter involved, hanging over us, she's certain to withdraw her support. The rancher was never that keen on us being here in the first place. He'll use this as an excuse to evict us." Why hadn't Stella learned of her mother's involvement and Ned's reluctance before? What else didn't she know? "We could've avoided all that, but Lady Lyndhurst had to send for the law, and Lord Lyndhurst just had to inform all of Ninebark Ranch."

"What would you have us do? Bury Harp without ever telling the sheriff or the Smiths he died in Cottonwood Creek?" Gridley demanded, forgetting that he, too, wanted to keep the sheriff out of it. "Harp taught young Junior Smith how to play the harmonica, for goodness' sake. The boy, at least, will be more than sorry to hear of this."

Terence shrugged. "Failed homesteaders up and leave all the time. No one needed to know. But thanks to you, Lady Lyndhurst, all we've worked for and done here is finished. Ruined."

Stella bristled at his turning it around to blame her. "A man's dead, and all you can think about are ancient animal bones?"

"Those ancient animal bones, as you put it, are why we are here. They are everything. The reason we get up every morning. The reason we can sleep at night. How do you think I'll get to be a museum director or acquire a position at a university without them? I'm a paleontologist. It's what I do."

"He has a point, my dear," Lord Atherly said in a condescending tone Stella could do without. "We all regret what happened to Harp, but none of us wishes to jeopardize the dig."

Stella dug her nails, dirtied with the sand, soil, and leafy branches of this morning's traipsing around, into her palm, curbing her frustration. Passion was one thing. Willful apathy and selfishness were another.

"I don't want you to lose access to your fossil beds any more than you do. I was looking forward to finding some myself. And I will speak to my mother and see what I can do." She hoped her relationship was strong enough for her to have the influence the men might need. "But don't you see? Getting kicked off my mother's rangelands could be the least of your problems. If Harp Richter's death wasn't an accident, all three of you are potential suspects in his murder."

Purdy Sullivan launched from the saddle and flipped the reins around the crowded hitching rack with the air of a man who'd just won the table and made himself an easy hundred bucks. His mule whinnied softly, and Purdy patted him on the shoulder before striking out for the telegraph office down the street. He tipped his hat at every woman he passed, whistling "Maple Leaf Rag" in step with the clack of his boot heel on the wooden planks until he remembered where he'd heard the tune last. Harp Richter had been playing it on his harmonica yesterday. Purdy swallowed hard, put his head down, and picked up his stride.

The small, narrow telegraph office, with a room in the back, sat wedged between D.W. Fabius Hardware and the Commercial Hotel's dining room. Purdy slipped inside, the scent of ink and oil spoiling the aromas wafting in from next door. With his pointed chin tinged by the jaundiced hue of his bright yellow bow tie, Horace Poole bobbed his head in acknowledgment and tapped the telegraph machine key without skipping a beat. A large, plain paper calendar, courtesy of the Colter City Banking and Trust Company, hung on the wall behind him. When he'd finished sending the telegram, he stood and approached Purdy, leaning against the wooden counter.

"Back so soon, Mr. Sullivan?" In the short time Purdy had been in town, he and Horace had become acquainted.

"You bet, Horace. News breaks fast around here. And my editor won't believe it. I've got something even bigger this time."

"Bigger than rescuing that British lord?" Horace slid his notepad closer, licked his finger, and poised his pencil over the paper. "I'm ready when you are."

Purdy told him in one short, sweet sentence what he wanted

his publishers to know. Horace's eyebrows lifted at the news, but he didn't voice his surprise. He learned secrets in this job, and was only still employed because he knew when to keep his mouth shut.

"Will that be all?" the telegraph operator asked.

"Isn't that enough?" Purdy nervously chuckled.

He straightened his tie, the green silk one he'd bought the day of his first byline, before pushing the door open and ambling back onto the wooden sidewalk. His fingers itched to feel the typewriter beneath them—what a story it would be to write—but that would have to wait. He promised that fine Kentucky lady he'd fetch the sheriff. And why not? There couldn't be a better way to guarantee the scoop. Whatever the sheriff learned, Purdy would know. And Purdy had to know. His life depended on it.

CHAPTER 9

~~~

From the cover of his wide brim, Hank Becker stole another glance at his audience before lifting the handkerchief covering the dead man's face. He'd seen it all: gunshot, stabbing, hanging, stampede, bear mauling, mine collapse, snakebite, and drowning, just to name a few. He'd been sheriff of this county for well on nine years and seen every way a man can die. And this fella wasn't any different. What was, were the interested parties: a renowned paleontologist, his assistant, an English earl, his daughter-in-law, who also happened to be the ranch owner's kin, and a reporter from out east. Well, maybe the reporter wasn't so unusual. His kind always did seem to root out trouble, like a pack of bloodhounds on a scent. But the others?

Only time and careful consideration would tell.

Becker was a reasonable man, a cautious man, some would say too cautious, but with this death, he'd have to step mighty lightly indeed. He didn't want to create an international incident, did he? Or find himself on the wrong side of the newspaper reading public? It was an election year, and he would prefer to keep his job.

Out of habit, Becker picked up a perfectly flat skipping stone nearby, pocketing it as he rose from his crouched position next to the body. He'd learned all he could by simply looking. His broad shoulders continued to shade the dead man from the sun, but Becker welcomed the warmth after the chilly morning ride. He'd barely had time to finish his first cup of coffee. Brushing off his pant leg, he addressed the man in charge.

"You were telling me, Professor Gridley, that Mr. Richter worked for you and was left alone at camp last night while you and the others visited the Ninebark Ranch. Is that right?"

Becker knew the Ninebark, though he'd never been to the house. The brothers, Clem and Ned Smith, were good, solid folks. Horse and cattle ranchers. Becker had never had any call to trouble them, and they'd never given him any. Becker's wife, Amanda, was in a literary club with Ned's wife.

"Yes, every one of us but Terence."

Becker would get to the assistant in a minute. "And after you left the Ninebark?"

"Lord Atherly and I—" the professor began.

"Mr. Sullivan!"

Becker let his cool stare linger on the newspaperman leaning against the nearest shade tree until he slipped the notebook out of sight. Becker had hoped to shake the reporter back in town, but the pest clung to him like a burr. Now, despite Becker's warning, he'd tried to jot down his notes as if Becker couldn't hear his pencil scratching ten feet away.

"I warned you. You keep quiet, out of the way, and stop that scribbling, and I just might let you stay." Sullivan opened his mouth as if to object but snapped it shut, having thought better of it. "Pardon me, Professor. You were saying?"

"Lord Atherly and I did a bit of prospecting on the way back, unsuccessfully, I might add, and arrived after dark. Harp, I mean, Mr. Richter was gone. Along with the horses."

Becker retrieved the smooth skipping stone and weighed it

in his hand. Was Richter trying to steal the horses and accidentally fell? Or was he chasing the thief? Or did the horses have nothing to do with it? "Then what did you do?"

"We thought it best to wait until daylight," the earl answered. "We retired for the evening in hopes of getting an early start."

"And you can vouch for one another?"

The earl straightened his shoulders in indignation. Lucky for Becker, he kept his retort to a minimum. "Of course."

That seemed all right. For now. Becker turned to the assistant, though out of the corner of his eye, he caught sight of Katherine Smith's daughter, biting the skin from her dry, ruby red lips, just about bursting with something to say. She was a beauty—silken brown hair, porcelain complexion, bright, intelligent gaze—and wildly out of place. What was she doing here? And who did she remind him of? Evelyn Nesbit. That's who. Her railroad baron husband murdered an architect in Madison Square's rooftop garden in New York City. Her photo had been plastered on the front page of the newspapers for weeks. But Lady Lyndhurst, as she was introduced, had none of the actress's artifice about her. And to her credit, she waited to say her piece.

A mosquito buzzed in Becker's ear before landing on his neck. He killed it with a swift slap. "And where were you, Mr. Brochard?"

The professor's assistant adjusted his pince-nez, shoving it with one finger up the bridge of his nose as an act of defiance. "If you must know, I was in town, having supper and visiting a local doctor." He raised his hands. His palms were wrapped in white cotton gauze.

The dead man's neck had been broken. He could've fought his killer first. Were those bandaged hands a way to hide injuries Mr. Brochard got while murdering the fella?

"And when I came back, Lord Atherly and Professor Gridley were also just returning. And as they said, Harp and the horses were nowhere to be seen. I think Harp stole them, myself."

Becker weighed the skipping stone in his palm again.

"And the name of the doctor?"

"Why? What difference does that make? And every moment you waste asking us useless questions is time not spent excavating."

"Indulge me if you would, Mr. Brochard."

The assistant rolled his eyes. "How am I to remember?"

It didn't matter. Colter City wasn't big enough for Becker not to know each doctor on a first-name basis. It would be easy enough to check.

"Is there something you'd like to add, Lady Lyndhurst?" Becker couldn't ignore her any longer. She was poised to speak whether he was ready to talk to her or not.

"Please call me Stella." When Becker agreed, she added, "It's important you look in the research tent. Something is off about it. I looked around while we were waiting for you. I can't put my finger on it, but—"

As Becker wondered what the research tent half a mile from where they found the body could have anything to do with anything, Lord Atherly interrupted Lady Lyndhurst's sentence and Becker's train of thought.

"Nothing more was stolen, was it?"

"Something was taken?" Becker asked.

"Only a cluster of minor brachiopod shells. Fortunately, the fossil thief didn't know what they were about."

"There is no such thing as minor fossils, Lord Atherly," Terence Brochard sniped. "I would think you of all people—"

"When was this?" Becker interrupted the assistant's grumblings.

"Yesterday afternoon."

"And this morning, I discovered something else is gone." The professor paused. "And I'm sorry to say it is far more important than the brachiopods."

"Not the *Hypohippus* jaw!" the earl cried, his breathing suddenly short and shallow. Miss Stella stepped forward as if bolstering her father-in-law, reassuringly touching his arm.

"No, no, Lord Atherly," the professor cut him off, waving his hands as if to stop the flow of words. "Not *that*."

"Thank goodness. I'd keep it about me if I could." From his breast pocket, the earl plucked a tooth. It trembled in his hand. And folks thought Becker's toting skipping rocks around was odd. "I don't think I could survive a repeat of what happened last year."

Leaving what happened last year to another time, Becker wanted to know more about what was taken today and yesterday. He started to speak, but the earl continued as if Becker had ceased to exist.

"What was stolen?" Miss Stella asked before Becker had the chance.

"Not any fossil this time but a vital notebook of data and drawings," Professor Gridley said.

"I knew it," Miss Stella said. "It was the green duck cloth one, right?"

"That's the one," Gridley confirmed. "It had been in a stack with the others. I didn't notice it until this morning. But it's gone and many months of hard work with it." Becker was impressed. Miss Stella had a sharp eye on her. What else could she tell him? "I didn't have the heart to tell you, Atherly," the professor said. "But as you say, thank goodness they didn't get any fossil specimens."

"When did you notice it missing?" Miss Stella asked, again before Becker could.

"This morning. They must've taken the notebook after poor Harp left the camp."

"Do you think Mr. Richter could've taken it, Gridley?" the earl asked the professor.

"That's what I thought," Terence Brochard chimed in.

The professor retrieved a handkerchief from his pocket,

wiped the sweat from his shining brow, and then rubbed his spectacles clear. "I wouldn't have posted him to watch camp if I'd thought like you, Terence."

"You're too trusting by half, Professor," the assistant said.

"But we didn't find the notebook," Miss Stella said, "and between the sheriff and me, we've searched everywhere near Harp's body." When had she done that? And why? Becker couldn't fathom a pretty young woman surveying the area around a dead body. But then again, he was quickly learning this was no ordinary lady. "Unlike Harp's whiskey flask."

Miss Stella pointed to it hidden among the sedges a few feet away. Becker hadn't noticed it earlier. He strode over and picked it up. Engraved with the man's initials on one side, a dent marred the inscription on the other—LOVE, HELGA. Becker rattled it. It was empty.

"Can we get back to work now?" the assistant moaned.

"His harmonica," Miss Stella said, "is still in his breast pocket." That at least Becker had noticed earlier. "So, if Harp did take the notebook, what did he do with it?"

"A very good question, Miss Stella." Becker flipped the skipping stone from one palm to another. She'd given him a lot to consider. But she wasn't finished.

"Granted, he smelled of whiskey and could've simply fallen," she continued. "But even assuming he was drunk, why was Harp at the edge of this tall ravine at night in the first place? Part of his job was to guard the camp. And when did the horses escape, before or after he left camp? And I'm assuming you noticed he'd left his shotgun behind." Becker hadn't had time to visit the camp yet. "Who in their right mind does that in this country?"

When she finished, every face turned to Becker in anticipation. Miss Stella had thrown out some tricky questions the others now expected him to answer. As she was the one who asked, Becker ignored the men and answered the little lady.

"In my experience, no one. Out here, even drunks keep their shotguns handy."

Lyndy didn't like Elmer Claxton the moment he met him. When he arrived at the Ninebark Ranch house with the news of Harp Richter's death, Lyndy had found the man in Ned Smith's study, leaning back and cradling a pungently strong cup of coffee on his protruding stomach as if it were a shelf. He'd pulled out a bottom drawer of Ned's desk and had propped his dusty boots on it, forcing Ned to move his chair to accommodate him. The desk was strewn with the papers Lyndy had noticed before (but couldn't decipher from the doorway), and despite Ned's hearty introduction, Claxton was reluctant to allow Lyndy's arrival to divert his attention from them. He pinched the brim of the stiff, high-domed hat he didn't bother to remove in greeting, the same tight-lipped smile that had been plastered on his face, and motioned to Ned with a wag of his meaty finger to gather up what they'd been looking at. Ned plopped the papers in the opposite bottom drawer and locked it. It was then that Claxton invited Lyndy to share what he'd come to say. Claxton rose swiftly enough after that, slurping up the last of his coffee and kicking the drawer closed. As it turned out, he was the coroner of the county and the man legally in charge of suspicious deaths. Within minutes, he and Ned were following Lyndy back to Papa's campsite.

With the sun glinting off the six-pointed star badge pinned to his vest, the sheriff was waiting for them.

"Claxton." After offering first Ned and then Lyndy a grim smile, a firm handshake, and his thanks, Sheriff Becker stuffed his hands deep into the pockets of his sack coat and greeted Claxton as if saying his name tested his ability to be civil. "You managed to come mighty quick."

"He happened to be at my place when Lyndy arrived," Ned

explained. *But why?* When Stella's silent expression asked him the same thing, Lyndy shrugged.

The sheriff introduced the others to the coroner with a brief overview of how they knew the deceased. Terence scratched at his bandaged palms while Papa and Professor Gridley stood as silent and unreadable as statues.

"Just bring me up-to-date, will you, Becker?" Claxton snapped his suspenders and eyed up the others without addressing them. "And just the known facts. No speculation on your part. I like to make up my own mind."

"Best if we do it in the creek bed."

"Why would that be?"

Becker rolled his eyes and blew his breath out in frustration. "Because I'm assuming you'll want to get a close-up look at the body first?"

Claxton agreed but immediately threw out a halting palm as Stella took steps to accompany them. "Just Sheriff Becker, if you don't mind."

Lyndy tugged at his waistcoat. More time in this man's company didn't improve Lyndy's impression.

"But—?" Stella started.

Claxton cut off Stella's objection. "And what is he doing here?" He jabbed a finger in the direction of the reporter.

"We invited Purdy to do a write-up about our excavation," Professor Gridley explained.

"I will not have the press interfering with an official investigation, do you hear, Sullivan?" Claxton warned.

"I've got rights, Claxton, and you know it. Familiar with the freedom of the press? It's in the Constitution. Oh, that's right. You aren't a lawyer. You're not even a medical expert. Why in heaven's name you were elected coroner, I'll never know."

"Just don't get in my way." Claxton bristled. He turned his back on Purdy and impatiently gestured to Sheriff Becker to lead the way. The pair disappeared into the willows.

"Mr. Claxton might object to us joining him." Stella grabbed Lyndy's hand. "But he can't stop us from watching and listening from above."

Stella led Lyndy along the top of the embankment until they had a clear view of the men making their way along the creek bed. Purdy Sullivan followed them to the edge while Papa, the professor, and Ned remained in camp with Terence, who had been scratching at his bandaged hand and itching to get back to work since Lyndy arrived.

Lyndy found himself sandwiched between Stella and Purdy, the scent of the reporter's overly starched shirt making his nose twitch as they stared into the ravine. Purdy held his notebook and chewed pencil at the ready, reminding Lyndy of a particular constable from back home. Stella leaned as if preparing to launch herself down the steep embankment at any moment. At the bottom, Becker and Claxton approached Harp Richter's dead body, scaring off an opportunistic raven who abruptly fluttered into a tree a few yards away.

Lyndy shuddered to think what the bird had found to eat.

Carried by the water and echoing off the steep, curving embankment, Sheriff Becker's dispassionate telling of what he'd learned reached those above. He'd examined the site, interviewed Stella, Papa, and the others, and concluded that Harp Richter's death was worth investigating. Too many questions remained unanswered. And all the while, Elmer Claxton was treading semicircles around the body, avoiding getting his feet wet but carving a path in the gravel. When Becker concluded, Claxton grabbed the sheriff's arm to steady himself as he clumsily lumbered to one knee, leaned in close to the dead man, and then pulled himself up.

"I can see why you wanted me down here," Claxton said. "It's obvious the man was drunk and fell in the dark."

"That may be, but why leave his shotgun behind? And maybe he didn't fall on his own accord but was helped?"

"Pushed, you mean? Don't be ridiculous, Becker. It's an open-and-shut case. This man's death was an accident."

"But what about the horses?" Stella shouted. "And the missing notebook?"

Becker's head shot up, empathy replacing surprise on his face. Claxton ignored her.

"Arrange to have the next of kin notified and the body buried, will you?" Claxton brushed the wet pebbles from his hands and trouser leg, signaling the discussion was over and he'd made up his mind. He didn't wait for Becker's response before trudging upstream.

Lyndy and Stella, with Purdy on their heels, were waiting for him when he reemerged from the creek bed. So, too, was Terence, who'd stopped sifting through a pail full of dirt to ask, "Will there be an inquest?"

"Of course, Mr. Brochard, but I have no doubt the jury will come to the same conclusion I have. There's no need for you to do anything more, Becker. I have all the evidence I need." Becker pulled a stone from his pocket, weighing it in his palm.

Bloody hell. He's going to throw it at him.

But Lyndy was wrong. The sheriff slipped it away as he said, "It's your call, Claxton. Doesn't mean I agree with it."

"Good thing you don't need to. I'll set the date and see you at the inquest, Becker. Coming, Ned?"

As Claxton climbed into his carriage, Lyndy was content to see him go, but beside him, Terence was scratching ceaselessly at his palm, his focus flitting from Claxton to Ned unhitching his bay, Whiskey, from the post.

"You heard him, right, Mr. Smith? This was just an accident, nothing more."

Stella sniffed indignantly, an almost perfect impersonation of Lyndy's mother. "How can you say that, Terence? A man died."

"By accident," Terence reiterated. He turned to Ned again. "It's no fault of ours. You won't kick us off your land now, will you?"

"I haven't decided," Ned said, dropping into his saddle. He turned his head to the side and coughed. "Like Miss Stella said, this is an awful thing. If it proves to be something worse, having y'all around could be bad for business."

Terence fired a glare at Stella, cold and menacing like a spray of buckshot. Lyndy took a warning step toward him.

"But you can't stop the dig," Terence insisted. "You just can't."

Claxton steered his team toward them, driving a wedge between Terence and Ned and compelling everyone to step back. Leaning down, he said to Terence, "It's his land, son. He can do whatever he wants."

Redirecting his outrage from Stella to Claxton, Terence took his aim at the back of the retreating coroner. If "looks could kill," as they say, Elmer Claxton would've slumped from his carriage seat and tumbled dead to the ground.

CHAPTER 10

Stella squatted to see where the line of boot prints led and blew the stray hair impeding her vision away in frustration. Only a few feet away, the prints disappeared into a trampled mess of horseshoe imprints. At the sound of rustling willows, she paused what she was doing and stood as Sheriff Becker, standing easily six and a half feet tall, shouldered through the shrubby tree line.

With Terence refusing to help, insisting the "fossils won't unearth themselves," and Purdy preoccupied documenting the occasion in his notebook, the rest of the men had had the sad, onerous task of retrieving Harp's body out of the creek bed. Stella had spent the time studying the corral gate, with its unbroken rope latch but freshly splintered wood, and looking over the research tent, hoping to find something to explain what happened to Harp and the horses. She was partway into a sweep of the ground, starting at the fire ring and circling out, when Lyndy, the sheriff, and the other men emerged and entered the camp.

And what a waste of time. Stella hadn't found a thing.

"Now, what's this?" Sheriff Becker puffed heavily under the strain of carrying a dead man. "What's that lady photographer doing here?"

As Lyndy and the sheriff hoisted the makeshift hand litter they'd rigged out of a canvas wagon cover, the fabric giving off a familiar, usually comforting musty scent, and its heavy burden into the back of the wagon they'd driven, Stella followed his gaze to see Letti Landstrom arriving in a dogcart, her gray mare shaking her harness. A sudden pang of sadness washed over her. Letti's horse reminded Stella of Tully, her beloved horse left behind in England. She hadn't realized how much she missed Tully until now.

"I invited her," Purdy explained. "Thought she could take pictures of the dead man and the spot where we found him."

"We don't need photographs," Becker said. "You heard what the coroner said. It was an accident."

"Is that him?" the photographer asked, craning her neck to peer in the wagon even as she started to unload her camera equipment from the back of her dogcart.

Lord Atherly swiftly flipped over the excess canvas to shield Letti from witnessing Harp's broken body. "I'm afraid, Miss Landstrom, it's not a thing a fine young woman like you should see."

Stella had seen more than her share of dead bodies. What must her father-in-law think of that?

"Now, Lord A," Letti said, dismissing his concern but flashing her appreciation with a smile. "You have no idea what a woman like me has seen in my short lifetime."

What did she mean by that? Intrigued, Stella opened her mouth to question the photographer further.

"I heartily agree." The sheriff unwrapped the horse's reins from the post and held them toward her. "It's not a sight a woman should see." His eyes flickered in Stella's direction. For a moment, his tone, almost apologetic, hinted less at recrimination than regret. He snapped his attention and admonishment back to Letti. "Now, Miss Landstrom, you can go right ahead and put your camera back where it was."

Letti's smile evaporated in an instant. "But Purdy, you said you needed my help. I canceled a family portrait sitting for this. Now, how am I going to get paid?" She tweaked the tip of her nose.

"I know. I know," the reporter said, rolling his eyes and clenching his pencil between his teeth. "Who could predict the sheriff here would be so objectionable? I planned to pay you out of what I got from my newspaper. For back east, you see, if a reporter has photographs to accompany his story, it might make the front page."

"And as you can see, we're a long way from home, Mr. Sullivan, and if it were up to me, you'd find yourself on a train back there tomorrow." While Becker berated the reporter, Stella sidled up to Letti as she packed up her camera again.

When Purdy took his cue and was on his horse and riding away before the sheriff could confiscate his notebook, Stella whispered, "Just wait a few more minutes, Miss Landstrom. You can take your photographs when the sheriff's gone."

Whether the sheriff overheard or suspected what she was up to, Stella couldn't guess, but his expression as he regarded first her and then Letti over the buckboard's rails told Stella he knew. And yet he didn't object, climbing without a word into his wagon, the springboard bench sagging under his weight.

"You will tell us if there are any developments?" Professor Gridley said.

"I have no cause to investigate further," Becker said. "But of course, I expect the same courtesy. If one of you learns something that should be brought to the coroner's attention, I want to hear of it first."

Becker made a show of regarding each one of them as he hitched his horse to the back of the wagon. But he'd lingered a split second longer when their eyes met. Was that a slight nod he'd given her? With Mr. Claxton tying his hands, was Sheriff Becker giving her permission to keep digging? After all, he hadn't been entirely convinced Harp's death was an accident, and they agreed the coroner had been too hasty to say so. There were so many unanswered questions. As Sheriff Becker climbed into the wagon and then flicked the reins, encouraging the horses to move out, Stella had already decided, whether he intended to or not, he was asking for her help. And since Letti was already here, that meant having the photographer document everything—the corral gate, the research tent, Harp's tent and his belongings, the spot in the ravine where the flask was found, where Harp's body had lain, all of it—in pictures to peruse or use as need be. Before anything else changed, was trampled or destroyed.

If only we'd had a photographer on hand after every murder.

"Now, what's this all about, Lady Lyndhurst?" Letti asked when the sheriff was out of earshot. They were alone but for Lyndy, the others having moved to the quarry, eager to return to work.

In this rustic setting and after the humbling tragedy of Harp's death, the title, which she was proud to bear for Lyndy's sake, sounded absurd. Even Lord Atherly had tolerated the locals calling him "Lord A."

"Please, call me Stella, and if you'll get your equipment, I'll explain."

Stella grinned at Lyndy with grim satisfaction as the creak of the buckboard's wheels faded into the distance, and Letti headed to fetch her camera.

The camp was eerily quiet. With the coroner and Ned returning to the ranch house, Sheriff Becker carting Harp's body back to town, Purdy dashing off to write his article, and Letti promising to have the photographs developed by the end of the day, Stella and Lyndy found themselves sitting by the last vestiges of this morning's fire alone, cradling tin cups of the warmed-up coffee Professor Gridley had made hours ago. It was black, lukewarm, filled with grounds, and very, very strong. At least she was drinking it. Lyndy feigned taking sips, his face scrunching up at every attempt. Behind them, over in the quarry, Lord Atherly, the professor, and Terence worked in silence. The cadence of gently clattering pebbles as they sifted dirt through a sieve, searching for the tiniest fragments, or the swish of brushes uncovering a more significant find should have been soothing, but Stella's mind was a jumble, questions and emotions swirling together like a whirlpool where everything was blurred or distorted. She wanted to discuss the eventful morning with Lyndy but didn't know where to start.

"Stella, Lyndy, you came this morning to help, did you not?" Lord Atherly called from the quarry site.

"We did," Stella agreed.

"Then let me give you your first lesson on how to tell fossils from modern bone fragments, compacted soil, and the like."

Lord Atherly was right. Stella needed to do something besides stew in her thoughts. She slapped her thighs and stood. "Care to join me?" She held her hand out, offering to help Lyndy.

"If I must." He took her hand, drew her to him, and kissed her before bounding to his feet. They strolled to the quarry hand in hand.

"Now, let me explain," Lord Atherly said, transforming from the man who hid in his study, letting his wife run the estate, to an enthusiastic expert willing to get his hands dirty. He was all business. "We call it the four *s* identification system: shape, shade, structure, and stick." Lord Atherly ticked them off on his fingers. He crouched and scooped up a palm full of dirt and pebbles. Sifting through it, he illustrated what he meant by each *s*, even licking his thumb, sticking what looked like a spongy stone to it, and waiting to see if it held for five seconds or more. It did.

"I thought we'd be finding bones like that," Lyndy grumbled, pointing to the circular fossilized bone emerging from the ground Terence had been carefully unearthing. "Not tiny fragments."

"You might uncover something easily identifiable. We all hope you do." Professor Gridley rose and thrust two dustpans and brushes at them. "But we collect everything. You've heard the phrase 'no stone left unturned'? This is 'leave no fossil behind.'" Professor Gridley's smile crinkled his eyes. He, at least, was enjoying himself.

"That's quite good, Gridley." Lord Atherly chuckled. "Quite good indeed."

Stella wished to share their lightheartedness, but something the professor said started her mind racing again. *Leave no stone unturned.* As if subconsciously, he, too, thought something unresolved.

The professor directed them to one of the untouched squares in the quarry and instructed them to start on the surface, brushing the soil into their dustpan, inspecting it for fossils, and then sifting it to ensure they'd gotten everything. It was slow, tedious work, and Stella, who'd enjoyed helping in the barrow in the New Forest last summer, was soon conscious of the hard ground against her knees, the thin layer of dirt that stuck to the sweat on her skin, and her wandering mind. She'd thrown aside a pile of soil she'd sifted through before realizing she hadn't noticed a thing about it.

So much for no fossil left behind. She would have to start again.

Beside her, Lyndy, lying on his side, was diligently cutting away at a stubborn mat of hairy, grayish-green leaves spread across the upper right corner of the square. He was biting his lip in concentration, oblivious to the smudge of dirt on his cheek or her watching him. Perhaps it was more satisfying to snip and clip than the brushing and sifting Stella was tasked with.

She picked up her brush again, this time in pretense, and whispered, "How did Mama take the news about Harp?"

Lyndy glanced up as if he'd forgotten she was there before jabbing his shears straight into the soil and the heart of his vegetal nemesis. "Of course, she was saddened but was more stoic about it than I expected. And when I said so, she remarked how accidents were common occurrences, that they 'come with the territory.' On the other hand, Junior flew out of the house in tears."

Stella's chest tightened at the image of Junior grieving. Of course, he'd be upset. Hadn't Harp taught her little brother how to play the harmonica? They must've been close.

"Do you think Mama's right? Harp's death was nothing more than an unfortunate accident?"

"That Claxton said so. The sheriff seemed to agree."

"That's what they said, but Sheriff Becker seemed open to investigating further until the coroner showed up and shut it all down. I can't help thinking we should—"

"We should what, my love?" Lyndy said.

"I don't know. Get answers, maybe? You must admit there are still so many unanswered questions about it."

"Indeed, you're right."

"And maybe I imagined it, but I think the sheriff was putting on an act about Letti taking those photographs. Lyndy, I think he wants our help."

"I didn't get a chance to tell you." Motioning for Stella to get closer, Lyndy leaned in and whispered so Stella could barely hear, let alone Terence working a few yards away. "Becker implied in the ravine his regrets that he couldn't investigate further."

"If that's true, why doesn't he just do it?"

"He didn't say precisely, but I believe it has something to do with the dynamics between him and that coroner."

"Or the politics more likely. They are both elected officials, after all."

"And obviously not from the same party."

"But even if Harp's death was an accident, the sheriff could look into the circumstances surrounding the missing horses and notebook."

"And I said as much. When I pressed him, he said he'd be happy to have me pursue it. I don't think he was being flippant. I think he was expressing his desire."

"Where should we start first?" The prospect of unearthing answers energized her every muscle. She truly wanted to help Lord Atherly find fossils, but with a possible murderer on the loose, this took precedence.

Lyndy shrugged, a crooked half smile spreading across his face. "Isn't that more your forte, my love?"

Stella's mind whirled, but she caught ideas and possibilities this time before they slipped away. "Letti said she'd have the photographs ready later this afternoon. Why don't we go into town to get them, and while we're there, we can visit the doctor?"

"Stella," Lyndy jerked upright, enveloping her hand in both of his, concern, fear, and hope flashing alternatingly across his face like a magic lantern. "Are you ill? Oh, my love, you're not—?"

He stopped short of asking if she was pregnant, but his tone said what he hadn't. Suddenly, her ears burned with embarrassment and frustration. Lyndy's innocent assumption had blindsided her. She hadn't expected to have to think of it, not here, not now. Caught up in questioning Harp's death, she'd banished her concerns and dreams of having a child to the furthermost corner of her mind. She wasn't prepared to let them loose right now.

"No, nothing like that." Flicking them away like the pebbles pressed to her palms, she indicated Terence with a jut of her head.

Lyndy sighed; whether in relief or resolution, she couldn't say. He stood, brushed himself off, and offered Stella his hand.

"And after you've checked up on my alibi, which he will confirm, by the way," Terence said, guessing what Stella had in mind and commenting as if he'd been a part of the conversation the entire time, "perhaps the doctor will have time to check you over. And if you are with child, then—"

"Shut the bloody hell up," Lyndy protested as Stella let Lyndy haul her to her feet.

"Let's go, Lyndy."

Terence shrugged and continued—despite Lyndy's tightening jaw, his stiffening shoulders, and the snarl curling on the edge of his lips—seemingly unfazed by the growing threat. "And then, if you want to make yourself useful, go to the ranch house and convince your stepfather not to evict us off his land."

Stella caught Lyndy's arm as he raised it back, his fist clenched so tight his knuckles were white. *Not this again.* He'd been controlling his temper so well. But their childlessness had hit a nerve. After experiencing elevated hope and crushing disappointment in the span of a few seconds, who could blame him? Her anger was just as close to bubbling over. She tugged on his jacket, urging him to come away from the quarry, and reluctantly, he backed off.

Striding toward Lord Atherly's surrey like a pair of parading horses, Stella clutched Lyndy's hand and kept going, ignoring Lord Atherly as he called after them. She'd make some excuse later, but right now, she needed to find answers, calm down, and put as much distance between them and Terence Brochard as possible.

CHAPTER 11

The brass nameplate beside the door, tarnished and slightly corroded with patches of bright green along its edges, read W. St. George, Physician and Surgeon.

This was the fourth doctor's office they'd visited, having learned there were five. The first three physicians had never treated any patients named Terence Brochard or matching his description the day before. Had Terence lied, not expecting them to check his alibi? But then why mention it? That's why Stella insisted they visit all five of them. Surprisingly, Lyndy hadn't objected. She'd expected him to want to accuse the assistant paleontologist after the first two doctors denied treating Terence. But Lyndy seemed content to stroll arm in arm as she peeked in shop windows, reading signs painted on buildings advertising everything from five-cent cigars to the Commercial Hotel (complete with directions) and observing the many different people going about their lives. When parking Lord Atherly's surrey, they'd even run into Purdy Sullivan heading to the telegraph office.

As they passed a livery stable, an American Indian with two

black braids trailing from under his brimmed hat and down his striped shirt and vest led a sorrel Mustang stallion into the street. He bit into a hard-boiled egg before returning Lyndy's greeting. In front of one of the butcher shops, they nearly got run over by a distracted cyclist who steered with one hand while holding onto his bowler hat with the other. Outside one of the smaller hotels, a newspaper boy hawked his wares by announcing headlines about the murderer Harry Thaw, the continuing aftereffects of the San Francisco earthquake, and political news from Helena. Lyndy pressed a generous dime into the boy's hand and took a paper. Together, they scanned through it quickly. There was no mention of Harp Richter's death. Yet.

Stella knocked.

"The door's open!" a man shouted from inside.

"Dr. St. George?" Stella asked as she and Lyndy stepped into the small office. The sharp smell of antiseptics, disinfectant, and medicinal herbs made Stella's eyes water.

A large, mahogany secretary desk with cupboards stocked with drugs in paper boxes and glass-stopper jars dominated the far wall. Bookshelves and filing cabinets lined the opposite wall. In the middle of the room was a leather examination chair, a sheen reflecting off it from the electric lamp that hummed directly above. A small pedestal sink stood in the corner, with steel medical instruments soaking in a tray on a side table beside it. But for a well-worn copy of *The Complete Dramatic and Poetical Works of William Shakespeare* tossed onto a desk chair, it looked like every other physician's office they'd visited.

A short, gray-haired man, his shirt sleeves rolled up to his elbows, shook excess water from his hands into the sink basin and reached for a hand towel. "That's me. What seems to be the trouble?" He squinted first at Stella and then at Lyndy.

"Actually, we just want to ask you a question," Stella said.

He shrugged, then carefully folded the towel and laid it to dry on the edge of the sink. "Shoot."

"Do you know Mrs. Katherine Smith from the Ninebark Ranch?"

"I sure do. I treated young Eugene Jr. for the croup last winter."

"Well, I'm her daughter, Stella."

"You don't say?" He scratched the top of his head. "Well, pleased to meet you, Miss Stella. I didn't know Ned and Kate had a daughter." Not wanting to explain the family dynamics, she didn't correct him. "What can I do for you?"

"Have you heard about the fossil excavation on my Mama and Ned's land?" Stella had learned from the first two doctors that despite having over ten thousand people, Colter City was the type of town where everyone knew everyone. *And everything about them.*

"Sure, sure. A different group of folks heads out there quite often. I thought of joining them one of these days. Some English lord and a famous professor are in charge of it, aren't they?"

"I'm that English lord's son," Lyndy said.

"Well, now that I hear you talk, I couldn't doubt it as otherwise." Dr. St. George laughed. "But what's all this got to do with me?"

"Did you treat a man named Terence Brochard yesterday? He had something wrong with his hands?" Stella described Terence.

"Sure, that paleontology fellow with the sensitivity to plaster of paris? Ironic, isn't it? Couldn't stop himself from scratching. Why do you ask?"

Lyndy cursed under his breath, clearly disappointed. Terence hadn't lied. Stella half hoped he had, too. But just because a man rubs you the wrong way shouldn't be cause to suspect him of murder. Should it?

"A chap who worked for my father and Professor Gridley died last night or early this morning," Lyndy said.

"Was it an accident?"

"The coroner, Mr. Claxton, thinks it was," Stella said. "But we're not so sure."

"Did Sheriff Becker put you up to this?"

Why would the doctor assume that? Stella asked as much.

"In all the years I've known them, those two have never seen eye to eye. But Elmer Claxton has a lot of clout in this town, and Hank Becker risks losing his job if he's seen working against him. So, it just wouldn't surprise me if our good sheriff asked the pair of you, being outsiders and all, to do a bit of quiet asking around for him."

Neither Stella nor Lyndy satisfied his curiosity. They didn't want to get the sheriff in trouble.

"We fancy getting some questions answered, that's all," Lyndy said.

"You think the man I treated was involved?"

"Possibly."

"Will you help us?" Stella asked.

"If I can."

"Do you recall what time you treated Terence?" Lyndy asked.

"Couldn't say. I had an early supper, and it was after that I saw the paleontologist gentleman, but I had two patients before him and didn't pay attention to the time." Although vague, it put Terence in town in the evening, as he claimed.

"Did he have any injuries, cuts, or scratches other than on his palms?" Lyndy asked.

"Anything to indicate he'd been in a fight, you mean?" He pulled at his ear. "No. Of course, I only dressed his hands, but I didn't see anything like you're thinking."

"How did he seem?" Stella said, grasping for anything. "Was he agitated or upset?"

"A tad rude, if I recall, but that's how I'd describe many of my patients. I don't tend to see folks at their best."

Having run out of questions, Stella thanked the doctor and headed for the door. However, just as Lyndy was opening it for her, Dr. St. George stopped them with his own question. "By any chance, did the man who died suffer from a gunshot wound?"

Goosebumps tingled across Stella's skin. "No, he seems to have died of a broken neck. What made you ask?"

"I had a patient this morning who'd been camped out on the prairie last night. Said he'd heard a gunshot just as he was bedding down. He doesn't carry a gun or rifle and is not from around these parts. He thought there might be bears or other predators he needed to worry about. From his description, he was just beyond the barbed wire marking the southern border of the Ninebark Ranch, no more than a mile from where the fossil dig is."

Stella locked eyes with Lyndy, and he was clearly grappling with the same question. If Harp died of a broken neck, who shot the gun and why?

Professor Amos Gridley waved as the surrey rumbled away from camp. He stood rooted to the ground until the night grew quiet again. Too quiet. He hadn't realized what comfort he'd always taken from the small noises the horses made. A wolf howled in the distance as if reading his thoughts, making Amos shiver. He'd organized excavations for years now. He was no stranger to the vast western sky or the wild sounds in the night. But he'd always had company, whether man or friendly beast. They'd never found the runaway horses. He hoped they were safe.

With Harp's death, they were down to the three of them. Amos had volunteered to guard the camp from animals and marauders while the others went to town for the dance. Terence had offered, but Amos had no stomach for frivolities tonight and insisted Terence indulge in some. The fellow sure could use it. Besides, staying behind would give Amos some much-needed time to catch up on the work he'd been too distracted to do this morning. Or so he thought. Amos stared into the sky, not dark enough to see even one star.

What happened to you, Harp Richter?

Amos was a man of science. It had guided him throughout his life, coloring his earliest childhood memories. Then why did he feel that perhaps he wasn't alone after all? That Harp's ghost hovered over him, demanding answers? Or was that his innate curiosity calling him out, demanding he do something?

But what could he do? Amos was masterful in solving ancient mysteries locked in rock and soil. Let the authorities and the likes of Lord and Lady Lyndhurst deal with those of the human kind.

The wolf howled again, breaking the spell, and Amos strode into the research tent. The oil lamp had burned down, filling the tent with the acrid odor of burning kerosene. The mail Harp had retrieved from town yesterday was still lying in a pile on the nearest table. Collecting it up, Amos adjusted the lamp wick, settled into one of the ladderback chairs, and sifted through it. Letters from colleagues back east made up the bulk of it—requests for fossils, clarification on a point he'd made in a fossil description, or his opinion on a fossil baffling a friend. He left for last the hefty packet containing issues of academic journals with the latest findings in paleontology. He'd arranged before he'd left Washington to have them shipped from the museum and relished the nighttime reading of what the rest of his scientific community was up to.

But he never got to the journals. The last letter he sliced open with his pen knife contained a short correspondence from Charles Walcott, a friend and respected colleague, stapled to Walcott's copy of the latest issue of the *American Journal of Science*. The note read, "*T. brevicornus*. Wasn't that the name you ascribed to the short-horned *Triceratops* you discovered and planned to publish on this year?"

Amos ripped the note off the staple and flipped through the journal until he found the paper Walcott was referring to—"A New Species of Short-horned Triceratops from Wyoming." His breath caught when he read the sole author's name at the top: Dr. Aurelius Moss.

Moss was no stranger. He was no friendly colleague either. They'd trained together at Yale. Moss was always taking short-cuts. He was careless and conceited. He cared more for the accolades of describing a new species than the thrill of its discovery. Amos and Aurelius Moss had been at odds almost from the beginning but had kept it civil until they'd vied for the same prestigious position at the National Museum. Amos got the job, and Moss had never forgiven him. He'd been disparaging Amos's work ever since.

What was the vainglorious fool up to this time? Amos scanned the paper's words, figures, and conclusion. Almost to the letter, the work Moss claimed was Amos's own.

"Underhanded thief, more like!" he growled. But how had Moss gotten the data? The exact location information? The diagram originally sketched in Amos's hand?

Amos's gaze swept deliberately from the words on the page to the lamplight, casting flickering shadows across the stack of notebooks nearby. There was one less notebook tonight. Did Moss have a spy in Amos's camp? Was that where the missing fossilized shells and notebook went? Did Moss or one of his cronies kill Harp?

Amos, not one to succumb to irrational fears, pushed back

from his chair, his anger crystallizing into action. He fetched the rifle leaning by the open tent flap, faced the chair toward the door, and plopped himself back down. After a moment's thought, he cocked the gun. If Moss or his accomplices returned, they would find Amos Gridley prepared and waiting.

CHAPTER 12

The jaunty string music washed over Stella like a salve as it bounced between buildings, filling every man-made crevice before it escaped into the night. When her mother had sprung on her and Lyndy that they were to be guests of honor at the town dance, neither had been keen to go. Despite having attended more social events in the past year than she had in her entire lifetime, making small talk with strangers wasn't how Stella wanted to spend her second night in Montana. Especially after the day they'd had. She'd been looking forward to a quiet evening at the ranch with Lyndy and her mother. But now that she was here, she could shed her questions and concerns like the soiled day dress she'd been wearing and enjoy herself.

As the couples danced on the makeshift platform set in the middle of the street, a swirl of color and sheen of cotton print skirts and dresses of rich fabrics to rival the lavender satin and lace gown that Stella had packed just in case, Mama paraded Stella and Lyndy through the crowd, introducing them to her friends. And Mama had a lot of friends! Between meeting the mayor and the wives of seemingly every leading businessman and shopkeeper, Stella spotted a few people she already knew—the coroner, Mr. Claxton, stood among a cluster of men checking his gold pocket watch, Sheriff Becker was surrounded by a posse of women who Stella assumed were his wife and teenage daughters, Letti Landstrom, who'd set up a photograph booth (Lord Atherly was her current customer), and Clem Smith skillfully twirling a pretty brunette in a bright yellow frilly cotton dress. Even Terence Brochard weaved past, a glass of honey-sweetened lemonade clutched in his hand. As Mama said, "everyone who was anyone" was there.

Not Harp Richter.

The macabre thought passed as swiftly as it had arrived, and as the evening wore on and the raucous music grew louder, Stella began tapping her feet, eager to join the dancers.

"We usually hold dances in Cottonwood Hall, on account of the cold," a Mrs. Thompson was explaining. Stella hadn't heard how the conversation began. "But we never miss an opportunity to dance under the big sky if we can help it. First time in Colter City, Lord Lyndhurst?"

"First time in Montana."

"And what do you think of our fair state? Any plans to visit the glaciers up north? I can imagine you have nothing like them in England."

"We were hoping to go to Yellowstone National Park."

"That, sir, is in Wyoming," Mrs. Thompson huffed.

When Lyndy, overly dressed in a black suit and white tie, tugged on his waistcoat, Stella stepped in. "Why don't we all go dance?"

While Stella was accomplished enough not to embarrass herself, Lyndy was a divine dancer, whether from years of expensive lessons or because he channeled his pent-up energy into it. She didn't know, but she loved to feel his strong arms expertly guiding her, leading her in a whirlwind around the floor. When was the last time they danced? Stella couldn't remember.

"Yes, let's."

Lyndy led her toward the dance floor, and her mother and Lord Atherly, who'd recently joined them, followed. Ned, declaring his clumsiness, stayed back to strike up a conversation with Mr. Claxton. But before they could join the revelers stomping to "The Preacher and the Bear," Sheriff Becker approached.

"What is it, Sheriff?" Stella asked, not sure she wanted to know.

"Has there been a development?" Lord Atherly added, an edge to his voice. Lord Atherly, like Lyndy, looked every bit the part of an English earl in his black suit and white tie. A far cry from the dirty camel-colored canvas-like duck pants and vest he'd been wearing this morning. But British noble or not, he was worried.

Privately, Stella's father-in-law had confided in Lyndy (who'd subsequently told Stella) how troubled he was that Harp's death might jeopardize the future of the dig. Lord Atherly mourned for the man and had offered to pay for a proper burial, but he hadn't traveled across an ocean and a continent to have his dreams crushed by a hired man's drunken fall. Would Ned Smith evict them off his land? Lord Atherly had suggested offering Ned a financial incentive to let them stay, but Lyndy discouraged it, believing it would worsen the situation. Besides, when they'd talked it over on the ride back to the ranch, Stella had reasoned that Ned had already agreed to let them stay if Harp's death was ruled an accident. As a man of the West, Ned understood that accidents happen. Murder, on the other hand...

"Not of any consequence, Lord Atherly," Sheriff Becker said. "The inquest is still set for tomorrow, and the outcome is all but assured. Claxton's chosen jurors, without fail, deliver the verdict he's decided ahead of time." Was the sheriff insinuating the coroner was corrupt or highly perceptive and good at his job? From the tone, Stella suspected it was the former. "I can almost guarantee it will be ruled an accident."

"That would be a relief then." Lord Atherly's posture reflected his words as his shoulders relaxed, and he offered to take Stella's mother onto the dance floor. Mama happily agreed.

"We know you aren't investigating Harp Richter's death," Stella prefaced cautiously once her mother and father-in-law had left, "but we have learned a few things that might be related to it. If you're interested."

With a flick of his finger, Sheriff Becker asked them to follow him away from the crowd to the quieter refuge of the nearest alley. They ventured just a few feet into the narrow space, rank with the stench of urine, as the dim glow of the street lantern barely illuminated their way.

"What did you learn?" the sheriff asked with the eagerness of a town gossip.

"That Terence Brochard did visit Dr. St. George in town, as he said," Stella explained, "but the doctor couldn't pinpoint the time. Sometime after the doctor's early dinner but before dark."

"That doesn't tell us much, does it?" The use of the word *us* was not lost on Stella. She'd read the sheriff right. He had hoped for her and Lyndy's help.

"No, but what is intriguing," Lyndy added, "was the doctor's comment about a gunshot being heard in the direction of the dig that night."

Sheriff Becker was already nodding his head before Lyndy finished. "That would be consistent with what I found. Before leaving the camp, I looked at the rifle Gridley said was used to guard against predators and the like. It was missing a cartridge. I never got a chance to look around for it."

"I did," Stella said, "and I didn't find anything like that."

"Doesn't mean someone didn't find it first."

Lyndy was right. Anyone in or near the camp could've picked it up the next morning. Anyone like the person who stole the notebook.

"I can't help thinking about the missing notebook. Do you

think Harp could've caught the thief in the act and shot at them?"

"I don't know, Miss Stella. I haven't learned of a man suffering from a gunshot wound, so it's just as likely Harp Richter shot at an animal if it was his shot that was heard in the first place."

Stella couldn't argue. "And I didn't find any blood anywhere."

"Why would Harp have used the rifle?" Lyndy asked.

"Again, assuming it was him," the sheriff said. "Many ranchers, cowboys, and the like have firearms."

"Regardless," Stella said, "it could explain why the horses bolted. A blast like that would be enough to spook them."

"And with the latch not secured . . ."

"They would've easily gotten out," Stella said, finishing Lyndy's sentence. They shared a sheepish smile.

"And if Harp Richter chased after the horses unprepared with a lantern, he could've missed seeing the ledge of the creek bed," the sheriff said.

"Especially if he'd been drinking," Lyndy added.

"Doggone it!" Sheriff Becker swore. "It seems Claxton's right. It was an accident."

"Except none of that explains the missing notebook," Stella reminded him. "And why is Claxton so determined to rule it an accident? Just to be contrary?"

"Don't you know? They're opening up the ceded Crow land. Claxton stands to make a fortune from the wave of homesteaders coming in. He'll do what he can to keep them coming. And murder investigations have a way of scaring folks off."

Before Stella could ask how Claxton thought to gain from the land sales, Mrs. Becker appeared at the end of the alley, her hands on her hips.

"There you are, Hank." A solid, plain woman nearer forty than not, she had a round open face and broad smile that made her all the more appealing for her lack of conventional beauty.

She projected common sense and safety, both having high value in this unpredictable landscape. "That's enough monopolizing our guests of honor's time. If I'm right, these young people haven't even gotten the chance to dance."

Mrs. Becker's persistent shooing was not to be ignored, so Stella and Lyndy left the discussion of Harp Richter's death at that and finally joined the dancers. Stella was thrilled at the firing up of her muscles and giving in to the joy and romp of the music. Yet by the time the last bar had faded, a question like a pesky weed in her mother's garden popped into her mind.

Could it be a coincidence that Harp happened to fall to his death the same night an essential notebook went missing? Stella shook her head in silent response to her internal question.

"You want to keep dancing then?" Lyndy shouted over the musicians, who launched into the next song in response.

"Yes, please!"

Lyndy misunderstood her gesture, and Stella missed what he'd said. But it didn't matter. The dancing kept the questions at bay as if the swirling in her head stilled for as long as her body was in motion. It didn't make sense. But then again, neither did someone wanting to steal a notebook with descriptions of fossilized bones in it.

Breathless but happy, Stella finally agreed to sit out the next dance while Lyndy and Junior fetched them some lemonade. They had danced five Virginia reels in a row. A whoop and a hollering from the dancers as the music crescendoed almost made her regret it. The energy and joy were invigorating, and she couldn't wait to dive back in. But she had promised Lyndy to wait for him, so she moved off to one side, not far from a cluster of matronly women in their Sunday best—lacy, embroidered dresses, bejeweled broaches, and fine straw hats. Their watchful gazes took in everything and everyone. But Stella was no stranger to being watched. She smiled in greeting and returned to tapping her foot to the beat of the music, watching her mother and Ned stomp the boards. Had Stella ever seen her mother so happy? Certainly never with her father.

Although the music drowned out what the women were saying, the matrons were undoubtedly gossiping. In England, they hid behind fans, but not needing them under this cool, open sky, most of these women used their hands instead. Neither the women's fans nor their hands could shield their admiring eyes as they tracked the path of a man sporting an impeccably cut, charcoal, tailored suit, a crisp new brimmed hat, and a meticulously trimmed beard as he ambled by. And how could they not stare? Gifted with striking features that exuded confidence, privilege, and charm, he stood out like a shiny new penny among the weathered cowboys, ranchers, store clerks, and tanners. Of all the men there, only Lyndy rivaled him in appeal. His cologne, as he passed, reminded Stella of green wood and old books. Oblivious, he passed without a nod, a smile, or a tip of his hat in recognition of the fervor he'd created among the ladies.

Who is he?

"I don't know," her nearest neighbor said in a breathy tone when Stella asked, "but I'm gonna make it my business to find out."

"Allow me," Stella said and winked. The woman giggled and gratefully agreed.

Stella stepped away, following the man, who seemed too preoccupied to notice. But he slipped through a crowd of men, sneaking whiskey and gossiping as much as the ladies, and Stella lost him. She approached a solitary building with wrought iron spanning the length of the second-floor balcony, set off by itself half a block away, its white-washed brick glowing like a ghost in the lamplight. Across the building's plain façade, a wooden sign read in block letters: COLTER HALL. It was quieter here, and Stella paused, wondering how she'd let her curiosity pull her away from the fun. Sometimes, like this morning, she let it get the best of her. The coroner declared Harp's death an accident. Why did she have to push it further and, instead of spending time with Mama, check up on Terence's alibi? Then again, if they hadn't, they wouldn't have learned about the gunshot.

But what could she possibly learn by following this stranger? Stella turned back.

"What were you thinking?" a low, deep voice grumbled as if reading her thoughts. Stella swiveled on her heel to answer, but no one was there. "You almost got caught."

Stella cautiously approached the corner of the building from where the voice emanated, her wary gaze circling the street. Few others were around, but most of the festivities were not far away. Feeling secure knowing Lyndy was less than a block away, she inched closer until she leaned against the wall.

She'd missed the reply but knew there had been one when the man added, "I'm aware of that, but you weren't fool enough to kill someone, were you?"

Stella could've sworn her heart stopped. Was he talking about Harp? How could he not be? How many men had died prematurely today?

"Never mind. I don't want to know," the man continued. "Just stick to the plan, and no one else gets hurt. Well..."— here the man's deep, throaty chuckle echoed—"at least no one that doesn't deserve it."

Stella didn't wait to hear more. She scurried away like a squirrel with a prized nut toward a small group of boys, crouched barefoot under a street lamp, the light gleaming off the object of their intense focus—a scattering of swirling multicolored glass marbles. As she loitered beside them, as if interested in their game, one and then another of the boys squinted or scowled at her before dismissing her as harmless and returning to their game. Over her shoulder, Stella watched and waited to see who might emerge from around the side of Colter Hall. A minute went by and then another, marked by the soft clinking of marble against marble. Would the man ever come out? Or had he left by another way? And what of the person he was talking to?

A sharp, loud clunk of glass jolted Stella from her musing. A marble, hit too hard, had careened against the window of the millinery shop, leaving a chip in the glass. With no regard for her, the boys scattered like the precious marbles they left behind. As Stella studied the damaged window, she caught the reflection of someone behind her, his hand on the crown of his hat as if expecting a sudden gust of wind to carry it away. It was the stranger she'd followed.

Stella stood her ground as if admiring what she could barely see in the unlit window. Her insides were nothing like the calm she projected as the reflection of the man drew closer. Then, he turned to stroll down the middle of the street, artfully dodging fresh horse piles and weaving drunken cowboys, until he was eventually enveloped in the crowd again.

Stella turned around, squatted to retrieve a sizable, chipped green and yellow swirled marble, and clenched it in her hand. "I'm definitely going to make it my business to find out who you are now," she promised him.

CHAPTER 13

With blood and music pounding in her ears, Stella scouted the crowd for Lyndy's familiar form. She finally spotted him on the far side of the dance floor, chatting with the Smith brothers and Lord Atherly. He still held two full glasses of lemonade. She started to weave through the crush of people but never seemed to make any progress. Someone was always stopping her, eager to meet and chat.

Then, she noticed the stranger lingering at one end of the refreshment table. With Mama at the other end. Stella beelined it to her mother, apologizing for her haste as she went.

Stella eyed the stranger, and then the array of fruit pies sliced and plated—just waiting for her to take one. Stella chose a slice of the cherry. It smelled and tasted delicious. She indicated the stranger with her fork. "Mama, who is that man? The handsome one in the charcoal suit."

Mama squinted, sizing up the man over the rim of her glass of lemonade. "Well, I don't know, Sweet Pea. I don't reckon I've seen him before. Why?"

Stella hesitated to tell her mother about her suspicions or the content of the overheard conversation. Did she want to involve her mother in something as sinister as murder? She had been back in York, but that was an accident. But wasn't this Mama? Couldn't she tell her anything?

"He was arguing with someone. And he mentioned a killing."

Mama's eyes flew wide and then sharply narrowed with the shrewdness of someone who understood both the implications and the risks. "You're talking about Harp Richter, aren't you?"

"Could be. I don't know. That's why I want to know who he is. I could be completely wrong. What he said may not have anything to do with what happened to Harp."

"Or, as you suspect, it does. When have you ever been wrong about these things?" Stella inwardly cringed, knowing she'd been wrong a few times. But her mother didn't need to know that. "Let's see what we can find out."

Mama grasped Stella's hand as if she were a child and led her through the crowd, deftly avoiding conversations and slipping through the spaces between people like water. As they walked, Stella committed to memory the texture, the strength, the curves of her mother's hand, basking in the pressure, the reassurance, and the security it represented—things she'd lived so long without. When Mama let go, Stella felt the absence more keenly than she could have guessed.

"Here now," Mama said. "If Elizabeth Claxton doesn't know who he is, no one does. Elizabeth!" Mama called out, gaining the attention of the coroner's wife.

Elizabeth Claxton, who wore her dark blonde hair in a similar style as Stella, a voluminous bouffant on the top of her head, and sauntered toward them in an elegant dark blue silk and lace gown too form-fitting to allow for dancing, had to be at least ten years younger than her husband. As the wife of one of the town's most prosperous citizens, she graced the event with her presence and her benevolent smile. How could she be married to Elmer Claxton? She and Stella had met briefly before, but her husband had escorted her away. He had no intention of encouraging his wife to form an acquaintance with a woman who'd not blanched on seeing a dead body. He'd even said as much. But his wife, alone and free from her husband's influence, greeted Mama with all the warmth of the friendly neighbors they seemed to be.

"Katherine." Mrs. Claxton held her hands toward Mama as if to a long-lost relative. The lilt of her voice gave away her British origins, but her accent was slight, making Stella wonder how long Mrs. Claxton had been in this country. "I was wondering when I would get more time to chat with your lovely daughter."

"How about inviting Stella and me to tea? Then you can chat all you like." Mama laughed. "My friend here hosts the best tea parties in Montana," Mama boasted to Stella. "But seriously, Elizabeth," she continued as Mrs. Claxton feigned humility, "we need a favor." Mama's conspiring tone immediately pulled Mrs. Claxton closer.

"You know I'd do anything for you, Katherine. What do you need?"

Stella was touched by the genuine affection the woman had for Stella's mother. Throughout the evening, Stella had seen similar sentiments from all sorts, from toothless old men to hardy homesteaders' wives; Katherine Kendrick Smith was a beloved member of this community.

How could Daddy have mistreated her? The troubling thought gnawed at Stella, compelling her to seek out Lyndy. He was still engrossed in a lively conversation with Ned Smith, who'd lured Mama away from Daddy. Stella had her answer.

"It's nothing much," Mama was saying. "I just wondered if you knew who that was?" She tipped her head toward the handsome stranger. "Don't look so closely, or he'll notice we're talking about him."

"But why ever shouldn't we?" the coroner's wife teased. "He's a handsome devil. He'd expect it."

Mama conceded the point, and Stella noted that Mrs. Claxton was more insightful and possibly more cunning than she had expected from the wife of a man Stella found to be close-minded and superficial. Stella was grateful she and her mother were allies.

"Then go ahead and gawk all you want," Mama said with a lighthearted smile. "Just tell me if you know who he is."

"I most certainly do know." Mrs. Claxton waved to the gentleman, who nodded politely. "That's Dr. Aurelius Moss. He's a paleontologist from a museum in Chicago, and he's setting up a fossil finding camp, just like the one you have on yours."

"Really?" Stella stammered, the news coming as a complete surprise. "Do you know when he got here? Or where his camp is?"

"He arrived yesterday. And you'll laugh, Katherine"—Mrs. Claxton gently tapped Mama's arm with the end of her folded lacquered wood and lace fan—"but I think we've started a trend among the ranchers akin to the ornamental hermit craze back in England."

"What are you talking about?"

"I'm talking about how you have a famous paleontologist in residence on your land, and now I have one on mine. Soon, every rancher will want one." Her high-pitched laugh resembled wind chimes.

Stella vowed to ask Lyndy about the hermit craze, but for now, she settled for a simple clarification. "Dr. Moss's camp is on Mr. Claxton's ranch?" Mrs. Claxton confirmed it.

"What a coincidence!" Mama declared.

"I'd say. And who knew mine would be so fetching?" Mrs. Claxton spoke as if she were describing a toy poodle or porcelain doll.

As the two other women burst into a bout of girlish giggling, Stella's world grew silent, the music, the chatter, the laughter fading into the background as her eyes fell on Dr. Aurelius Moss.

A rival paleontologist arrives the day before Professor Gridley's notebook goes missing, before Harp Richter mysteriously falls to his death, and is overheard complaining to someone about a killing.

Coincidence?

Not likely.

"Where have you been, my love?" Lyndy asked as Stella took his proffered glass of lemonade. His kiss on her cheek was warm and welcoming.

"Talking to Mama and Mrs. Claxton," she said. It was true, although not the whole of it. She had so much to tell him. But not in front of the others. "If you'll excuse us, gentlemen, I want to have a private word with my husband."

"Of course," Lord Atherly said, answering for all of them before resuming his conversation with Ned about the differences in harvesting hay in Montana compared to back home in Hampshire.

As she and Lyndy strolled beyond the crowd back toward the relative privacy near Colter Hall, Lyndy leaned close. "You've learned something." Arm-in-arm, he held her so close their hips were touching. As if he, too, sensed the menace still lingering in the air.

"How did you know?"

"You've got that glint in your eye."

"You're right. I've found out quite a few things." As she recounted all that she'd learned, she watched a cluster of heavy clouds move toward them, so dark they stood out against the night sky. She paused mid-sentence, while expressing how she suspected the timing of Dr. Moss's arrival was no coincidence, to say, "That doesn't look good."

A pair of mules hitched to an empty carriage and tethered to the post advertising Colter Market nearby, who'd been languidly waiting for their owner's return, suddenly stomped and snorted in protest of their restraint.

Lyndy followed her gaze. "Lord, no. It doesn't."

A gust of wind fluttered the street's awnings, swirling dust from the road. Stella rubbed at her eye as a speck lodged itself in the corner.

The musicians had seen the approaching storm, and the music suddenly stopped. The whistling, almost keening rush of the wind filled the silence. Suddenly, rain and hail bigger than the marbles the boys had played with pelted them. Musicians, dancers, and dignitaries alike skittered toward safety like disturbed ants on an anthill. One hailstone hit Stella's elbow and burned like a bee's sting. Stella clutched Lyndy's hand as they ran toward shelter while a man's camel-colored high-domed hat soared past them. Like a beacon, the door to Colter Hall flew open, shadows of those already safe and dry flickering in the dim light. Men and women, holding on to their hats, shouted and waved, and babes in arms wailed as their families joined Stella and Lyndy in the dash toward the hall. But the rain and the hail drenched them before they could make it. Water rained off the brim of her hat and dribbled down her back. With her hair plastered to her face, she could barely see. Jostled by the stampede, Stella clutched her skirts in one hand to keep from tripping while gripping Lyndy with the other. What would happen if she let go? She didn't want to find out. Just steps from the door, Letti Landstrom pushed past Stella, bumping into her as she tried to escape the storm.

"Sorry!" the photographer shouted above the din, not slowing.

Stella rubbed at the pain where they'd collided, but it wasn't Letti's hip that had left her side stinging. The photographer was clutching a new leather handbag, which had come between them. Or, more specifically, something bulky and unyielding inside it.

Was that what she thought it was?

Once in the hall, Stella breathed in the scent of damp, sweaty bodies mingling with floor polish as she picked out the outlines of stacks of folded chairs, bare wooden tables lining the wall, the thick velvet drapes on either side of the unlit stage as she stumbled toward it. She looked for Mama, the Smith brothers, and Lord Atherly as Lyndy guided her through the clusters of people gathering on the hall's vast, highly polished wooden floor to a space of their own, snatching up a chair as he went. She didn't see any friendly faces and hoped they found shelter elsewhere. Stella shivered as he gently pressed her into the chair. Her soaked gown clung to her like a second skin, and after taking an admiring glance, Lyndy threw off his jacket and draped it across her shoulders. The outside fabric was wet and musty, but the jacket retained some of Lyndy's warmth. She pulled the jacket closer around her. But she couldn't keep her eyes off Letti Landstrom as the photographer found friends to wait out the storm with. Amid the hushed murmurs of those gathered around her, the pale woman laughed. Stella shivered again.

"Stella. Are you all right?" Lyndy brushed a lock of hair sticking to her wet cheek. Usually, Stella would've relished the intimate gesture, but this time, she hardly noticed. "Who are you looking at?" Lyndy craned his neck, following her gaze over his shoulder.

"That photographer, Letti Landstrom."

"What about her?"

"She bumped against me as we ran."

"It was a bit of 'catch as catch can' out there." Lyndy snorted, and then, registering the intensity in Stella's gaze, added, "Are you hurt?"

"No, I'm fine, but I think Letti Landstrom is hiding a gun in her handbag."

CHAPTER 14

If Stella weren't so much on edge, the plodding, rhythmic swaying of the horses clopping down the street would've lulled her back to sleep. She hadn't slept much last night, and rising at dawn to be in town on time hadn't helped. As they passed a block of businesses, all advertising in English with Chinese characters beneath, Stella regretted that this wasn't a pleasure trip. It would be fun to wander in and see what exotic offerings she could find. And what unusual aromas! Stella breathed in what was wafting into the street. Even the laundry smelled different. Wouldn't it be interesting to compare it to what she'd seen in Scotland? But such an adventure would have to wait. The inquest into Harp Richter's death started in less than a half hour, and she couldn't miss it. Today, they'd learn if Mr. Claxton would rule it an accident, stopping any future investigation, or rule it suspicious, causing Ned to ask Professor Gridley to pack up camp and leave.

Stella couldn't decide which verdict would be worse.

Seated on the back bench beside Lyndy, Stella leaned forward and rested her cheek against her mother's back. Her mother, upfront with Ned, swiveled in her seat and gently patted Stella's knee.

"I'm so glad you're here, Sweet Pea."

"Me too, Mama."

"What are they doing?" Ned cut in.

In front of them, Professor Gridley, with Terence driving, had parked the surrey along a stretch of road crowded with two-story brick buildings. Stella sat upright to read the signs on the nearby storefronts: WALSH'S MEAT MARKET, LABLANC'S FURNITURE, THE COLTER CITY GAZETTE, SALMONSEN'S DRUG CO.

"The inquests are held at the courthouse." Ned stifled a cough. "That's two blocks that way." He pointed down a tree-lined street lined with the homes of some of the town's most prosperous families.

"Maybe they need to pick up something beforehand?" It was a wild guess.

They'd met with the pair on the outskirts of town and agreed to attend the inquest together. Clem had stayed back at the ranch. As Ned explained, someone had to do the work. Clem, Stella understood, but why had Lord Atherly volunteered to stay behind at the dig? Wasn't it Terence who was always so eager to get back to work?

"Well, maybe we should stop too, Ned," Mama said. "See if there's something wrong."

Ned had to drive another block to find a suitable place to park the wagon. As he tied up the horses, Stella assured Mama she and Lyndy would find out what the professor was up to.

As their shoes clomped the wooden planks of the sidewalk, Stella said, "So, you still think we should keep quiet about Letti's gun?"

"Until we know more, I do," was Lyndy's immediate reply.

Snuggled into their bed, warm and dry after returning from

the dance, Stella and Lyndy had discussed everything—Dr. Moss, his argument, even Letti bringing a gun in her handbag. Lyndy, having read more about the American frontier than Stella ever thought to, insisted everyone probably had a gun hidden on them somewhere. Stella had laughed, telling him he'd read too many dime novels. Most people couldn't afford a gun. She'd hurt his feelings, but he found a way for her to make it up to him. She'd been more than happy to oblige.

But she couldn't dismiss Letti having a gun so easily. Stella had felt the barrel of the gun in Letti's handbag and, from what little she knew, guessed it was about the size of the pistol that Stella's Uncle Jed had stolen, the one that was claimed to have belonged to Jesse James. The same one that almost killed her and Lyndy last Christmas. Lyndy insisted they bring it to the States. A gift for Junior, maybe? They hadn't decided. It hadn't left the case it was packed in.

But Letti carried one around with her. Why? It was small enough to fit in her handbag but big enough to kill someone. Yet Harp hadn't been shot. He'd died of a presumed broken neck. But the question remained—Lyndy's wild ideas notwithstanding—why would Letti have it in the first place? And why bring it to the dance? Dr. Aurelius Moss's intense, chiseled features flashed into Stella's mind.

"But if it turns out to have something to do with Harp's death?" Stella asked.

"Then we'll tell Becker," Lyndy agreed. "There's the professor."

With Terence on his heels, Professor Gridley disappeared through a door across the street, halfway down the block. Stella and Lyndy stepped into the street, dodging a one-horse dogcart whose driver refused to slow, and hurried into Horton Mercantile, a large, warehouse-like store with a cornucopia of everything anyone could imagine needing from crockery and cutlery to flour, feed, and small pieces of furniture. From what Stella could see, Sears & Roebuck had nothing on Colter City's Horton Mercantile.

Lyndy drifted away to look at the copious display of Western-style cowhide boots. He'd been envying those of Clem and Ned and coveted getting a pair of his own. After ordering a couple of split skirts on her mother's advice to replace the borrowed one she was wearing, Stella found Terence and Professor Gridley near the wrought-iron stoves and ranges. Nearby was an impressive sampling of agricultural implements on one side and a display of personal cast-iron safes on the other. What could they be looking for?

"I don't know what you want with one of those," Terence was saying when Stella approached.

Gridley indicated one of the safes to the shop clerk, a fresh-faced youth in a stiff striped apron, who opened it so Gridley could examine its decoratively etched, fireproof interior. "Because I'm determined not to lose one more line of data, one more drawing or description."

"But what about the fossils?" Terence scoffed. "You can't put them all in there."

"No, you're right. I wish they had ones big enough to fit the larger fossils, but at least we can lock up any that a thief could carry away."

"I'll guarantee no one is going to carry this away," the clerk boasted, caressing the edges of the steel box like something precious. "This here safe weighs several hundred pounds. Remove the wheels, and it's not going anywhere."

"See there." Professor Gridley rubbed his hands together in satisfaction. "That's exactly what we want. How much to have all three of them delivered?"

The clerk patted the safe three times, a spontaneous smile bursting across his face. "All three?"

"Three safes, Professor? Don't you think you're overreacting?"

Why was Terence objecting? He'd been furious when the small fossil Lord Atherly dismissed as unimportant was taken. Didn't he want to ensure whoever kept stealing from the camp couldn't take anything else?

"No, Terence. I am not," Professor Gridley responded when he'd finished arranging the sale and shipment with the clerk. He took off his spectacles and wiped them with the same handkerchief he often used to wipe his sweaty brow. "For you see, I'm not just buying this store out of safes to protect all our vital research but to send a message. One that everyone gets." With a tilt of his head, he indicated the clerk, who'd returned to the counter and was slyly pointing them out to another customer. "News has a way of spreading."

Having abandoned the boots, Lyndy strode toward them, glancing several times as the three safes were wheeled past. "Did I hear you bought all those safes, Gridley?" he asked.

"You see," Professor Gridley gloated, winking at Stella. "First, everyone in the store and then everyone in town." Terence tsked in annoyance. "I did indeed buy those safes."

When he purposefully projected his voice so that all could hear his response to Lyndy, several heads raised to see who spoke. Professor Gridley winked at Stella again.

"But what message are you trying to send?" Stella asked.

The professor's genial countenance hardened, a sudden distant look in his eye. He pinched his lips together. "That no one is going to steal from Amos Gridley ever again."

"Well, that's a relief," Mama sighed as the men of the jury scraped back their chairs, and the din in the crowded chamber rose. The inquest, for what it was worth, was over.

With the fossil expedition having piqued the curiosity of locals ever since Lord Atherly's disappearance, the inquest into the death of one of its members was enough for half the town to close up shop or put off chores to find out what happened. Unsurprisingly, Purdy Sullivan was among them, busily scribbling notes. Being two of the few women in the paneled chamber, which was so new Stella swore she could still smell the scent of paint, Stella and her mother chose to sit in the last row of benches, hoping not to bring attention to themselves. Lyndy and the other men opted to sit up front. Dr. Aurelius Moss was there, too, but on the opposite side of the room. It was apparent there was no love lost between the two paleontologists. Neither the distance nor the proceedings stopped Moss and Gridley from shooting venomous glares at one another.

After a call to order, Elmer Claxton had presided from behind a highly polished, oversized mahogany table on a raised platform, the coroner's jury in the rows of chairs to his right, and on the left the portraits of President Roosevelt and Montana Governor Toole hanging prominently on the wall. Throughout the proceedings, the coroner appeared dwarfed by the auspicious surroundings. But Stella wasn't fooled. The man got the verdict he'd predicted.

He'd begun by stating that he had seen Harp's body at the site of his death and that the men of the jury had been allowed to witness the state of Harp's body in the office of the medical examiner. He'd called the medical examiner, who verified Harp had been drinking whiskey, had sustained injuries consistent with a fall, and had died from those injuries. The jury heard Sheriff Becker's testimony, which included a detailed description of the creek bank. Several jurors gave knowing nods, indicating their familiarity with the place. Having found Harp's body, Professor Gridley and Terence were also called to testify. The jury took a vote, and as Claxton and Sheriff Becker had predicted, they concluded Franz "Harp" Richter's death was an accident due to a fall caused by darkness and his intoxication. The whole proceeding took less than twenty minutes.

Stella was hoping for more.

"Ned really didn't want to upset Lord A and the professor," Mama said, as she and Stella stood, waiting their turn to exit the extended bench, "but to have a murder associated with the ranch . . . He couldn't afford that. It just would've been bad for business."

Stella ran her hand along the smooth cap rail. "I know. That would've been hard."

But her relief and understanding were tainted by frustration. Frustration that Claxton had instructed the jury to ignore the missing notebook and the stolen brachiopod shells since neither was found near Harp's body, choosing to focus on the flask instead. He also dismissed the sheriff's suggestion that Harp might have been defending himself with the shotgun, calling it pure speculation. Stella hated loose ends, and the verdict was anything but neat and tidy.

"Though I shouldn't be surprised," Mama said. "If Elmer Claxton says something is going to happen, it happens."

"Powerful man, is he?"

Mama leaned in to whisper in Stella's ear. "As the biggest banker around, he owns half the mortgages in the county." That explained his interest in selling the Crow land, Stella realized. "People do or vote as he says. He was mayor before he was coroner."

Stella knew of doctors, undertakers, and even sheriffs being coroners, but a banker? This was a first. She asked her mother about it.

"I think it's just another stepping stone to something bigger. Elizabeth Claxton hinted one day over tea that her husband had his sights on Helena."

Claxton wanted to be governor?

"But why coroner? And why be so involved in the investigation?"

"Maybe he likes the power of judgment it brings?" Mama shrugged. "And an unnatural death is like a train wreck that stirs everyone's curiosity. As the coroner, he sees everything—the blood and gore—firsthand. Something, he likes to brag, not everyone gets to do."

Stella cringed. It wasn't something she'd ever choose to do. "Does Mr. Claxton own the mortgage on Sheriff Becker's house, too?" The sheriff did as the coroner dictated but didn't like it to the point of secretly defying him by getting Stella and Lyndy to help.

"No, in fact, Hank makes it known he owns his house free and clear."

"Then why does he do as Mr. Claxton says?"

"Because Hank likes being sheriff. Elmer would ensure he didn't get reelected if he were too contrary. However, Elmer also knows Colter City has never had such a good sheriff, and the town's never been so safe. So, most of the time, the two grumble at one another but ultimately let the other do as he pleases."

"Unless they disagree on whether a man's been murdered or not."

"As far as I know, that doesn't happen very often. Usually, they bicker because they don't like each other, not because they disagree."

By the time they reached the end of the bench, Lyndy was already waiting in the aisle. Together, they joined the spectators streaming out of the chamber into the more expansive hall. There, causing the crowd to part around them, stood Dr. Moss and Professor Gridley, toe to toe, with Dr. Moss towering half a head taller. Terence stood apart, observing the confrontation but making no attempt to intervene.

"Who knew you'd let your safety standards slip to such depths, Amos?" Dr. Moss said. "At this rate, you'll be out in the field alone, your hired hands either working for me or dead."

Prof. Gridley's face flushed crimson red. "You, you . . ."

Ned laid a staying hand on the professor's shoulder. "Time to go, Professor." When neither man budged, Ned ordered, "Step aside, Dr. Moss."

Dr. Moss showed no signs he would oblige, continuing to goad Professor Gridley as if Ned and the others weren't bearing down on him to give way. "And they'll all be working for me because I've found something groundbreaking, Amos. Something really big."

"Found something? Don't you mean you stole something?" the professor countered. "You came to our camp and stole the notebook, didn't you? You sneak thief, you . . ." The professor stuttered with fury. "When I prove you've stolen our data, I'll see you thrown out of the Philosophical Society. I'll see you humiliated. You'll never publish again!"

"As if you can prove anything," Moss quipped. The once devastatingly handsome man grew repulsive and sinister in front of her eyes. They had to get Professor Gridley away.

As if sensing her urgency, Lyndy entered the fray. "Ned said to step aside, Moss." He inserted himself between the paleontologists, forcing Dr. Moss to move out of the way. Seeing a gap open, Ned swiftly guided the fuming professor past. Stella grabbed her mother's hand and pulled her along behind them.

After he passed his rival, the professor shouted over his shoulder as if trying to resist Ned's restraint. "Seeing how low you'd stoop, I wouldn't doubt that you had a hand in poor Harp's death!"

Why would he think that? Stella hadn't even told him about the argument she'd overheard.

"I had nothing against your hired hand, Amos," Dr. Moss scoffed, examining his fingernails as if he couldn't be bothered to face Gridley or his accusation head-on. "Besides, I do not need to get my hands dirty."

Even with Lyndy, Ned, and Terence insulating him from the bystanders who had hung back to watch the exchange, Professor Gridley swiveled around, his finger jabbing in repeated accusation, "For once, we agree, Moss. Even in the field, you get someone to do the dirty work for you."

With that, Lyndy and Ned hustled the professor out of the building, leaving Stella and her mother scurrying to keep up.

CHAPTER 15

"This is so much more fun with you here, Mama." Stella licked her thumb to see if the rock in her hand would stick and grimaced at the taste. At least it stuck. After taking instructions from Terence, who'd given them in a condescending monotone, Stella and her mother returned to the same square she and Lyndy had worked, kneeling on the ground and brushing away the soil. Stella put the fossil fragment in the pile with the others. "I'm so glad you decided to come."

After the inquest and a quick meal in town, Professor Gridley and Terence were eager to return to the dig site. The altercation with Moss seemed to have ignited a new spark in them—as if they needed more motivation. The professor had urged everyone to join him, but when the men bowed out—Ned having plans to inspect a gold mine he'd recently bought and Lyndy jumping at the chance to see it—Professor Gridley turned to Stella and her mother. When her mother surprisingly agreed, putting off the chore of roasting coffee she'd planned to tackle that afternoon, Stella enthusiastically agreed, too. With Junior tasked with picking up supplies during the inquest and rounding out the party, Stella was as eager as the paleontologists to head out.

"Seems I wasn't the only one wanting to try my hand at it." Mama brushed her brow with her forearm and gestured toward the camp.

A crowd of gawkers clustered about ten yards away—*tourists* was the polite word Professor Gridley used. These were the people from town, men and women, who occasionally came out to watch them work. There had been two or three since Stella arrived, barely enough to notice, but this group bordered on disruptive. There had to be at least two dozen. According to Lord Atherly, people had started arriving within minutes of the inquest ending. But Stella's father-in-law had it in hand, engaging them, answering questions, and, most importantly, keeping everyone at a distance. He was charming, his accent and manners captivating the crowd probably more than his lecture on the differences between extinct horses and the living ones eating a fresh pile of hay in the corral. Yet still, they craned their necks to see past him, whispering and gossiping behind their hands.

"You'd think I'd be used to it by now." Stella sighed.

"Used to what, Sweet Pea?"

"All the scrutiny." As Lady Lyndhurst, Stella had been at the center of attention at countless balls, dinner parties, and social calls for almost a year. She did her duty—and her best—but she still didn't enjoy it. Who knew she'd have to deal with it here?

Trying to ignore the sightseers, Stella bent her head to her work. But as she did, Junior pulled out his harp to serenade them, bringing Harp Richter to mind.

Was it an accident or not? Did Dr. Moss have anything to do with it?

"Put that damn thing away," Terence growled under his

breath. The harmonica squealed off-key as Junior, surprised by Terence's vehemence, quit playing mid-stanza.

"Pray continue, lad," Lord Atherly called. "I believe our audience was quite enjoying it." He received several affirmations to his claim.

"I was, too," Professor Gridley said.

"Go ahead, Junior," Mama said. "You keep playing."

"It's distracting," Terence argued. "Stop. Now."

Stella planned to stay out of it. She wanted to support her brother but had to admit that the music and its obvious homage to the dead homesteader were making her melancholy. But then Terence forcibly snatched the harmonica from Junior's hand as her brother raised it to his lips. Stella threw her brush, kicking up dry soil that tickled her nose, and sprung from her knees.

"What's wrong with you? Harp taught him to play. Can't you see he's just trying to honor his memory?"

"Can't you see I'm trying to work?" Terence sputtered. "Leave it to a woman to—"

"She's found something!" one of the bystanders exclaimed, pointing excitedly, cutting Terence off. "It's big enough. I can see it from here."

Everyone's attention dropped to Mama as she brushed clumps of dirt from the large chunk of rock before her. Stella dropped to her knees, rested her elbows on the ground, and leaned closer to admire Mama's find. Darker than the soil around it, the fossil was a gradually revealed mosaic of smoothed ridges, bumps, and indents. *What could it be?* Stella gently traced its contours as if that alone would unlock its secret. Her breath caught as a surge of excitement and awe quickened her heartbeat. Unearthing this fossilized fragment of a long-extinct creature, hidden for thousands, if not millions, of years, was both humbling and exhilarating. And Stella hadn't even been the one to find it.

No wonder Lord Atherly loved this so much!

Terence suddenly loomed over them. "Brush around there," he said, his tone firm but almost reverent as he indicated a spot on the ground an inch away. Within moments, more fossilized bone was revealed. "Yes, keep at it just like that."

Professor Gridley abandoned his square, and Lord Atherly his role as gatekeeper and guide, to stand shoulder to shoulder with Terence. With Lord Atherly no longer holding them back, the bystanders rushed to get a better look, their long shadows stretching almost to mother and daughter kneeling on the ground.

"What's that she's found?" someone whispered with the reverence reserved for the hush of a church.

"I'm not sure yet," Professor Gridley said. "We'll need to reveal more to know."

"Jolly good work, Mrs. Smith," Lord Atherly said.

"What were you saying about leaving it to a woman, Mr. Brochard?" Mama carefully swept the fossil clean of debris and soil with the same precision as painting a delicate watercolor.

Their heads bent together, Mama caught Stella's eye and winked. A lighthearted laugh burst from Stella; she couldn't have said it better.

Stella sat back on her heels, unable to ignore the ache in her knees from the hard ground any longer. For several minutes, maybe more, no one spoke. The gently rustling willow leaves and the equally gentle swish of Stella's mother's brush filled the silence as Mama revealed the fossil beside her inch by excruciating inch. The townspeople, too, inched closer, though still at a respectable distance, as captivated by the emerging fossil as the paleontologists. Though Mama was a study in patience, Stella resisted the urge to grab a pick and start digging. There had to be a faster way than this. Suddenly, a commotion broke out. A man was trying to shoulder his way through forcefully. But the tightly knit group of onlookers wouldn't part so easily, and those with the best views objected loudly, throwing curses and elbows to prevent his passage. But he wasn't to be stopped. Shoving and shouting, he emerged, off-balance and stumbling, as if rejected, spit out of the crowd, breaking the invisible line between the camp and the quarry.

"Those there are my horses," he claimed, glaring at the townspeople behind him and adjusting the well-creased hat on his head.

Although he stood not two feet from her, Stella could make out nothing unusual about him — average height and build, a bit of shaggy brown hair, the usual cowboy or homesteader attire — except for the puckered scar that ran straight across his cheek.

"I say," Lord Atherly said, as if offended more for being caught disregarding his duties as gatekeeper than the intrusion, "what's the meaning of this?"

"Like I said. You've got some of my horses, and I want 'em back."

Almost as one, heads turned from the fossil protruding from the ground to the corral where the man was pointing. Inside were three horses: the one who'd driven Lord Atherly and the professor to the ranch the night Harp died, and the two Clem had sold to Professor Gridley as replacements for those that bolted that same night. Sadly, despite their best efforts, the original pair was never recovered. Lyndy had told Stella he'd envisioned they'd found a band of feral Mustangs living wild and free. Stella hadn't contradicted his fantasy but knew they'd be lucky to find water. Or better yet, find their way to Clem's herd.

"Those are our horses, Mr.?" Lord Atherly drew up to his full height. The frontiersman who slept in a cabin and sat by a campfire evaporated in a haughty haze, leaving the eighth Earl of Atherly rooted in his place.

The man hesitated as if weighing his chances against this suddenly formidable opponent, then barreled ahead, his words coming out as a challenge. "It's Drucker. Onie Drucker. And I've had horses stolen from me, and you've got two of them in that there corral. See."

He strode toward the corral, the townspeople parting immediately this time, their curiosity drawn from the fossil to this potential crime. Stella leaped to her feet after Lord Atherly, with Professor Gridley following close behind. Terence and Stella's mother barely looked up as they were abandoned to their task.

Onie Drucker hooked a heel into a plank and swung his other leg over it. He was over the fence before anyone could stop him. He pointed to the crooked, indecipherable symbol on the bay's hip. "See here. It's got my brand." He then pointed to the same symbol on the chestnut mare.

"I assume you have proof, Mr. Drucker?" Lord Atherly asked as he insistently waved the cowboy back over the fence. The cowboy complied, albeit reluctantly.

"Of course I do. Just have a look here." Onie Drucker shoved a hand into his front pants pocket and produced a well-creased yellowed paper. He unfolded it and handed it to Lord Atherly, who passed it on to the professor. The professor pushed his spectacles onto his forehead, peered at the paper, and shook his head.

"I don't understand. I bought those horses fair and square from a reputable seller. I'd never be involved in buying stolen horses. Goodness, I've never even stolen a grape from a grocery stand."

"Of course you didn't know." Stella glanced over the professor's shoulder, grateful he hadn't mentioned the Smiths by name. The paper was certified proof that the brand on those horses belonged to Onie Drucker. Clem had gotten a bargain for them. Now she knew why. "I'm sure whoever you bought them from didn't know either."

But the brand was clear. Whoever stole them did. Stella wouldn't entertain the thought that either Ned or Clem stole the horses, but she couldn't deny the dilemma Onie Drucker represented. How did the Smith brothers come by stolen horses?

"Can you tell us more about the theft, Mr. Drucker?" she asked.

"Yes, ma'am, I can." He slipped the hat off his head and held it, rolled and bent, in his hand. "As you can see, I ain't a rich man, but I had me six fine horses. And then, one day, thieves snuck in and took five of them from my homestead a few miles outside Laurel. Would've gotten all six if I hadn't ridden to the creek and gone fishing that day. Not that I caught much, mind you. Who knew the one day I decided to take off, that would happen?"

It was a good question. "Who did know you'd be gone?" Stella asked.

The homesteader shrugged. "Could've been any number of folk."

"If your homestead is near Laurel, how did you end up here?" the professor asked. "That's over two hundred miles away."

"Like I said, all my riches are tied up in them horses. I've been scouring the state, making my way west looking for them."

"And you just happened to stumble on us?" It came out more of an accusation than Stella intended. But it was hard to believe. Did he know more than what he was telling them? Besides, what else could she do but discredit him? If Ned thought a murder at the dig would tarnish his reputation, being arrested for horse theft would ruin him. *And Mama.*

"Now, that ain't right. I'm the one that's been done wrong here." Onie Drucker slapped his hat back on. He was done being polite. "It's true. I did just happen to hear about this fossil bone dig while quenching my thirst in town. But who wouldn't want to see what all the fuss was about? Lots of folks."

He pointed to the cluster of townspeople milling about between the corral and the quarry, their curiosity split between the two.

"I didn't come here imagining I'd find two of my stolen

horses, that's for certain. But now that I have, I'll be taking them back."

As Onie Drucker reached to unlock the gate, the heart-stopping sound of a gun lever cocking stayed his hand.

"Stop right there!"

Like a tableau vivant, everyone froze in place. Stella squeezed her eyes shut, forgetting to breathe and counting the seconds before the blast. It didn't come. As if moving through water, Stella dared to look behind her. Terence stood not ten feet away, pointing a rifle at Onie Drucker.

"Oh, Terence. Put that thing away," Mama scolded from behind him in a disapproving tone Stella knew all too well from her childhood. Mama, raised on her knees with her hands planted on her hips like sturdy branches, looked as rooted to the ground as the fossil she was uncovering. Was she thinking about the time Stella waved a branding iron like a sword almost too heavy to hold or when a man pulled a gun on them in York? Or maybe experiences in Montana now ran through her mind? Regardless, she appeared fearless, far calmer than Stella.

"Now, see here," Onie Drucker raised his hands as he purposefully backed away from the gate. "You have no cause to threaten me. Those horses are lawfully mine, and I mean to take them with me."

"You will be doing no such thing, Mr. Drucker. If that's even your name. Those horses were bought and paid for and belong to this expedition now."

"Terence," Professor Gridley said through gritted teeth. "Put the rifle down."

"Ah, Professor. You just don't get it, do you?"

With that, he raised the barrel and fired. Stella covered her ears and flinched as the loud blast exploded directly above Onie Drucker's head. The startled horses in the corral tore away, bucking and snorting in fear, desperate to escape. If Stella had doubted why the horses bolted the night Harp Richter died, she had no doubt now.

The thrill seekers, getting more than they bargained for, scattered and dashed for the safety of their wagons and buggies, finding a fast retreat harder with their horses skittish and scared. But as the camp emptied of idle onlookers, Terence kept his focus, ignoring the havoc he'd created, and lowered the gun at Onie Drucker again.

"Get out of here."

Terence advanced steadily toward the homesteader, backing him first into the corral fence and then scrambling out of the line of fire to the hitching post. Onie Drucker untied the reins of his anxious, hard-eyed sorrel, then fumbled and dropped them twice before slinging himself into the saddle. All the while with the barrel of the rifle aimed at him. He shook his fist.

"You won't get away with this. Next time you see me, I'll be with the sheriff. Those are my horses, and I want them back."

"And I want to get back to work." Terence shot again in the air, spooking the sorrel, which raced off with Onie Drucker cursing and trying to find the second stirrup.

"I say, Terence," Lord Atherly said, watching the homesteader and his horse grow to the size of a speck on the horizon. "I appreciate your passion for the work, but running that man off at the point of a gun? A bit much, don't you think?"

Stella, overwhelmed by the scent of gunpowder, would've laughed at the earl's knack for understatement if the situation hadn't been so scary. Instead, she let out a small sigh of relief.

"Perhaps," Terence conceded, leaning the empty rifle against the hitching post. "But our specimens have to be shipped back east, and as you know, we need two horses to haul the crates into town."

"But to intimidate him in such a manner." Lord Atherly bristled. "Now we'll have the sheriff to contend with again."

"You're right, Lord A. I hadn't thought of that." Terence shrugged as if he hadn't just threatened a man's life. "All I could think of was getting that specimen out of the ground and to the museum."

"Even I'm not that fanatical," Lord Atherly quipped with a hint of nervous laughter.

The professor shook his head in disbelief. "All he could think was . . ." The professor's whisper died on his tongue as Terence turned his back on them and strolled to Stella's mother and the fossil awaiting him.

Stella's stomach clenched. Was her mother safe working side by side with him? Were any of them? If Terence had been that quick to raise a gun on a stranger in front of plenty of witnesses, how easily could he have forced Harp Richter off that embankment?

CHAPTER 16

～∽～

Well, bloody hell. Isn't this frustrating? Lyndy unbuttoned his collar, yanking it open at his neck.

When Ned had invited him, Lyndy had jumped at the chance. Wouldn't his mates back home be impressed that he'd rolled up his sleeves and found gold? Lyndy had read many stories about men making their fortunes or breaking their backs over it. Gold was the stuff of legend. But the journey to get there soon grew tedious. Lyndy tried to engage Ned in conversation about the mine. Ned freely shared that he had acquired the mine as part of a recent land purchase to expand his ranch. But when Lyndy continued, questioning how the mine worked, how much the mine had yielded, how much they might expect to find today, getting Ned to talk was as taxing as finding water in the desert.

Hoping to draw his stepfather-in-law out again, Lyndy tried shifting the conversation to how Ned and Katherine met, how long he'd been in Montana, and whether the stories about renegade outlaws hiding in the hills were true. Stella's influence had given Lyndy's natural curiosity free rein, but when Ned mumbled, offering monosyllable answers, Lyndy's decades-old habit of keeping mum took over. The two men soon drifted into silence.

Listening to the rhythmic creak of the bench springs and the wagon wheels, Lyndy gazed across the landscape, growing increasingly steep and rocky, the mountains looming ever closer. He marveled again at the vastness beneath a sky so blue it almost hurt to look at, breathing in the crisp, clean air. A man could get lost in that sky. *Or lose himself on this endless prairie.* That had been Papa's plight. He and Ned were alone in this wilderness with a horse, four wheels, and the few supplies tucked in the back. Papa hadn't even had any of those. He'd wandered, injured, on foot.

Something bright and white, like a lighthouse beacon in the night, glinting in the sun caught Lyndy's eye. As they rumbled past, Lyndy leaned over to see it up close. It was a sun-bleached carcass, picked clean of any skin or meat.

"Dead calf," Ned explained. "Winters can be hard out here."

Could that have been Papa? To stave off a sudden melancholy that Lyndy was neither familiar with nor prepared for, he pulled out the small lasso he'd taken to carrying with him, swiveled in his seat, and practiced on the barrel of water they hauled with them. Despite the rocking and bumping of the wagon, he only missed occasionally. He was becoming quite good.

"Is all this yours then?" Lyndy asked. They'd left the ranch well over two hours ago.

"It is." Ned tilted his head aside and coughed. "Doesn't mean much, though. Takes a lot of land to raise horses and cattle. And even then, there's no guarantees." It was the most Ned had uttered in an hour. His hope rising, Lyndy opened his mouth to ask something else. "You really do like to lasso, don't ya?"

Clamping his lips together, Lyndy stiffened. He let the rope drop and drew it onto his lap. What was he to say to that? As a viscount, Lyndy wasn't used to having his actions questioned or mocked, except perhaps by his mother.

"And what if I do?" Lyndy scoffed, purposefully tossing the lasso into the air, spinning it to reaffirm how little he cared for Ned Smith's opinion or anyone's else's. That he was entitled to do whatever he pleased.

But it felt wrong. As did any haughty demonstration of his superiority or his disdain. The longer he was married to Stella, the more he thought about his actions, the consequences, and how he could make things better.

"Suit yourself." Ned shrugged and fell into a strained silence again.

Lyndy let the rope and his gaze drop into his lap. The tiny frayed wisps along the length of the rope reminded him of the silky threads of hair near Stella's ear. She'd made him a better man, and his petulant outburst made him cringe.

Can't a man lasso if he wants to? Lyndy sighed, feeling a pang of self-pity.

But that was just it. He was just a man here, wasn't he? And isn't that what drew Papa here? Shedding the title, the rules, the expectations, and being simply William Searlwyn for once? Now that he'd been given the same chance, Lyndy wasn't sure he liked it. Who was he if not Viscount Lyndhurst? Stella's husband? A dutiful son? (One who has yet to produce an heir.) A punter who spends too much time reading the racing forms and drinking whiskey?

A curiosity. Here, at least, that's what he was—something for the locals to gawk at. At the dance last night, he had a full dance card, but every single woman simply wanted him to speak so they could giggle at his "funny" accent. They demanded to know if he lived in a castle, had met His Majesty the King, and attended endless parties. Not one of them asked him about himself or his impressions of America. No one cared what he thought. Lyndy looked up and stared into the depths of the never-ending blue.

In the short while since he'd spent time in jail, facing the hangman's noose, he'd been more introspective than in his entire life. He'd thought the adventure to America would be something frivolous, fun, and exciting. He didn't know he'd end up contemplating his place in the universe.

"Getting lost, are ya, sonny?" the older man said, saving Lyndy from the musings that hurt his head.

"A big sky has that effect on some. Come on. We're here, and I'll show you around."

Grateful to have arrived, Lyndy tossed the lasso over his shoulder and tugged on his waistcoat as Ned drew the wagon beside what looked like a giant metal water hose. But he hesitated to follow as Ned jumped down.

This wasn't what Lyndy had expected. He'd envisaged panning the river, spying the golden nuggets' sparkle through the crystal clear water or a dark, cold gaping hole blasted into the side of the mountain. But this. This was an expansive pit, devoid of topsoil and vegetation, cut into the hillsides where the rerouted river used to run, crisscrossed with boulders, boards to walk upon, iron water pipes, and elevated wooden troughs thick with bone-dry dirt. Giant piles of sand and gravel lay haphazardly on either side. It smelled of dust, dirt, and rusty metal.

And it was deathly silent.

Ned patted the hose apparatus and began explaining how the operation worked as if he'd been saving up his words the entire trip. With no bird song or leaf rustling, Ned's voice echoed eerily against the man-made rock ledges, spouting *hydraulic*, *sluices*, *tailings*, and a few other terms Lyndy had little use for. He just wanted to find some gold.

"Was all this here when you bought it?" Lyndy admired the hard work that must've gone into it and said so.

"Yes, the infrastructure was all here. But gold doesn't find itself. It takes a lot of hard work to find any."

"How much gold have you found so far then?"

"Not an ounce." Seeing Lyndy's surprise, he added, "Though not for a lack of trying. Are you game to try?"

"I am. I fancied bringing a bit back to England with me."

"Rather have a nugget of gold than a fossil for your souvenir from Montana, huh?" Ned laughed as he grabbed a canvas sack of tools from the back of the wagon. The metal tools clanked together as he flung the sack over his shoulder. He paused momentarily, admiring the view, then slapped Lyndy on the back. The taciturn man who'd driven them across the prairie was now a distant memory. Lyndy returned the hopeful smile spreading across Ned's face. "Well, let's see what we can find, shall we?"

Purdy Sullivan struggled, tugging and pulling, the muscles in his back straining until he finally freed his foot from his boot. He tossed it onto the floor beside the other one to lie among the crumbled paper Purdy had discarded earlier, the thud not as satisfying as he'd hoped. What had he been thinking? He'd arrived in Colter City with perfectly functioning, stylish footwear. Yet he'd let himself be mesmerized, manipulated by the sweet sound of jangling spurs, the hard crunch of thick soles on the town's wooden platform sidewalk. One day in town, and Purdy had to have a pair of boots like the cowboys. And for what? They'd set him back more than a pretty penny, and in a land where most men wore them, no one even noticed. Not even the ladies. Sure, he didn't have to worry about snake bites, but spending much of his time clomping back and forth between the hotel and the telegraph office or out at the dig site, when would he see a snake? They still smelled of fresh leather, but the elaborate stitching had already dulled with dust. And at night, it took him a hell of a time to get the damn things off.

No wonder they say cowboys die with their boots on.

Purdy propped himself up against the rails of the brass bed's headboard and tried to get comfortable, but with the cushions the hotel called pillows so thin, he could still feel the metal poking him in the back. He shifted the typewriter onto his lap, balancing it on his knees, and shifted his back again against the headboard. He stared at the blank sheet of paper he'd fed it earlier. Who was he kidding? He'd tried writing at the desk, standing up at the dresser, even placing the typewriter on the floor. Nothing worked. It wasn't that he had writer's block. Purdy didn't believe in that. A writer writes even if it's nonsense. You just put your fingers on the keys and pressed. The problem wasn't getting words on the paper, as the litter of paper on the floor could attest. The problem was he didn't have anything left to say. First came the story about his rescuing Lord Atherly. His editor back east loved that. And then his follow-up with the death at the dig—was it or wasn't it an accident?—went over almost as well. But now what? He'd attended the inquest, which was a waste of time unless he counted the argument between the two paleontologists. But who wants to read about two academics arguing over ancient sun-bleached bones? Sure, Professor Gridley had accused Dr. Moss of stealing from him, but so what? Who cares? Readers want sensation and scandal, not intellectual arguments.

Purdy yawned, luxuriously stretching his arms high and wide. It had been a long, fruitless day.

If only those visiting aristocrats would do something interesting. American readers loved gossip about the British nobility. The story about the earl proved that. Purdy knew it wasn't just the rescue that made it his most famous piece. And his most lucrative one. No, no one but the locals would care if he'd come across a scruffy miner who'd lost his way or a homesteader's wife thrown from her wagon. He needed something bigger. If only Lord and Lady Lyndhurst would give him a story. And not the love story about an American heiress and her British beau. No, Purdy needed blood or bravery or—.

A knock on his hotel room door cut Purdy's reverie short. He set aside his typewriter, cringing at the loud creak as the bed sagged beneath him, and padded across the thin carpet in his stocking feet. How far he'd fallen. The glittering opulence of the Palmer House in Chicago danced in his memory as Purdy opened the door. The faded wallpaper, the dim lighting, the boy in shirtsleeves and suspenders standing expectantly in the hall snuffed the memory out.

"You Mr. James Sullivan?"

"I am," Purdy confirmed over the deafening pounding in his ears. Anything bearing his Christian name meant trouble.

The boy, barely a wisp of stubble above his upper lip, thrust an envelope at him. "Telegram for you."

Fixated by his full proper name on the envelope, Purdy absentmindedly dug into his pocket for a coin. He slapped it into the boy's outstretched palm and waved him off, unaware if he was still there when he closed the door. Purdy grabbed his letter opener from the desk and read the telegram through the slit he'd made in the envelope. *As if that would lessen the blow.* Clutching it in his fist, Purdy dropped to the edge of the bed and glanced over his shoulder at his typewriter.

"Gosh. Wouldn't you know? I was right," Purdy said out loud as if the whole thing surprised him. But it didn't. Not really. He'd just never dreamed it would come now, after all he'd done.

Purdy groaned as he bent to retrieve his boots again. He couldn't take any chances wearing anything else where he was going tonight.

CHAPTER 17

Mama barely waited for Lyndy to halt the wagon when she leaped down. She paused only to pour herself a quick cup of coffee from the pot on the smoldering fire before joining Terence, who was already excavating the new find.

"She's certainly keen," Lyndy grumbled, a victim of too little sleep. Coming back empty-handed from the mine last night had done little to dull his ardor. How were they to know Mama would abandon her chores and urge Stella and Lyndy out the door barely after sunrise?

Remembering the night before, Stella kissed Lyndy's cheek. "As were you last night."

Placated a bit, Lyndy smirked. "Yes, but you realize we now each have a parent obsessed with ancient bone and rock?"

He had a point. No amount of kneeling bent over in the dirt under a hot sun could dampen Mama's enthusiasm. She'd hinted as much over breakfast. But who could blame her? Even from here, Stella could see the unearthed shape waiting to be fully revealed.

"Wait until we get there, and you'll see why."

As they strolled toward the quarry, they passed the research tent, its flaps fastened open. With tables upturned and fossils, equipment, tools, and papers strewn into a chaotic mess on the ground, the research tent was in shambles.

Once inside, the sheer extent of the destruction was evident. Plaster jackets protecting some fossils were flipped upside down, chunks of plaster scattered among the wreckage, its white dust floating in the sunlit air. As if neither man knew where to start, Professor Gridley and Lord Atherly stood in the middle of the tent, gaping around them.

"What happened?" Stella gasped.

"Aurelius Moss is what!" Professor Gridley exclaimed, wincing as if the words were too loud in his ears.

She squatted and began gathering things up.

"No, no, Stella dear," Lord Atherly offered her a hand, "you mustn't. Not yet. Miss Landstrom is scheduled to arrive soon, though her task will not be as expected. She was supposed to photograph the new find."

Disregarding his father's admonishment of Stella, Lyndy righted several overturned chairs. Lord Atherly gratefully collapsed into one of them. "What will you have her do now, Papa?"

"Document the destruction, that's what," the professor answered for him. "I won't let Moss get away with this too."

"Maybe Dr. Moss stole your notebook, Professor, but why do you think he's capable of this?" Stella gestured around her.

With the professor holding his forehead and saying nothing, Lord Atherly explained, "It appears Dr. Moss has recently published a paper in a highly reputable journal using data that Gridley collected."

"He stole it from me is what he did. Claimed the work to be his own," the professor said, bitterness marring his usual congenial tone. "And now, with his own camp less than five miles away, he's out to ruin me altogether."

"Didn't you post a guard?" Lyndy asked.

Lord Atherly shrugged. "What with the new safes and Terence's display of the rifle yesterday, we didn't think there'd be any need."

"However did you sleep through it?" Lyndy said.

As one, the two middle-aged men dropped their gaze to their shoes, hanging their heads like truant students found skipping school.

"We perhaps had a bit too much whiskey last night about the campfire," Lord Atherly admitted sheepishly.

"Was anything taken?" Stella asked.

"That's the thing." Gridley removed his spectacles and rubbed them with his handkerchief. "From what we can tell, absolutely nothing."

"The notebooks and the smaller valuable specimens were locked up," Lord Atherly said. "We couldn't secure the larger ones, some of which are quite valuable and yet not too large to be carried off. So why would Dr. Moss not take them?"

"Because Moss is an idiot and doesn't know a horse hoof from a mastodon tooth," Professor Gridley concluded. "That's why he has to steal from me."

"But nothing more was stolen. Could an animal have caused this?" Lyndy said. "Perhaps a hungry bear in search of sustenance?"

Stella tried not to smile. Lyndy was so eager to encounter the Montana wildlife. But Stella knew better. At least when it came to poisonous snakes and predators like bears. She'd tried to tell Lyndy how dangerous they could be, but the fact that he could end up injured or worse hadn't stopped him from hoping for a glimpse.

"It's always possible," the professor said. "It's why we keep the firearms handy. But if it was an animal hoping for a meal, why ransack the research tent and not the other tents or the wagon or kill the horses, for that matter?"

The professor was right. This did seem more like the handiwork of malicious humans than starving creatures. With the missing notebook and the conversation Stella overheard, Dr. Moss was most likely the culprit. For if not Moss, then who? Onie Drucker bent on retaliation? Some of the thrill-seeking townspeople up to no good?

Murmuring voices, her mother and Terence, as they worked in the quarry, reached her through the tent's canvas walls. Could Terence have done it? He'd threatened Mr. Drucker with a rifle, and he hadn't gotten along with Harp. But Terence was fastidious when it came to his work. Was he capable of such destruction?

So concrete were her mother and Terence in her mind's eye that Stella grabbed for the back of Lord Atherly's chair when Purdy Sullivan's head, with Letti Landstrom peering over his shoulder, popped into view. Why was she so much on edge?

"Mr. Sullivan. What are you doing here?" Professor Gridley demanded.

Purdy strolled in like he was the expedition's patron and had come to check up on the researchers' progress. Letti followed, lugging in her camera and wooden tripod, her jaw gaping at the mess.

Purdy produced his notebook and a new brown pencil, licking the sharpened point as he poised to write. "My gosh, Professor. What happened here?" He hadn't answered the question.

"Out, you!" Gridley demanded, pointing at the reporter. "Miss Landstrom was invited, but you, my friend, were not."

Lyndy, who'd been hoisting Letti's camera over the mess, set it on an open spot on the floor and hastened to stand shoulder-to-shoulder with Professor Gridley to block Purdy's advance. "You heard the professor, Mr. Sullivan."

"But Professor, Lord Lyndhurst," Purdy pleaded, flashing a disarming smile. "This is news. Don't you want the world to know about your troubles here?"

"No, Purdy, that's exactly what we don't want," Professor Gridley said. "After Harp's death, we can't afford any more bad publicity."

"But no publicity is even worse, wouldn't you say?" Purdy insisted. "Lord A, please. My readers love stories about you and your fossil-digging adventure."

"Love reading about his woes, more like," Lyndy muttered as he forced the reporter to back out of the tent.

"Lady Lyndhurst, I beg of you." Purdy put his palms together, imploring not to be evicted from the tent. "You want the world to know more about your father-in-law than he got himself lost, don't you?"

"Of course, but that's not up to me." Stella shrugged.

"Mr. Sullivan!" Lord Atherly suddenly pushed up from his chair to stand at full height, whacking his knuckle against the edge of an upturned table. "I am most obliged to you, young man, but that comment and your entreaty to my empathetic daughter-in-law is well beneath you. Now, please, do as the professor asks and leave."

"But Lord A—"

With a loud bang, a puff of smoke, and a flash of blinding light, one of Letti's camera flashes exploded behind Stella, causing everyone but the photographer to flinch. With echoes of last year's near-fatal explosion ringing in her ears, Stella grabbed Lyndy's hand. While the others tried to dissuade Purdy, Letti had managed to set up her camera and tripod. Each subsequent flash explosion interrupted the argument, bringing all conversation to a halt as everyone held their ground. A consummate professional, Letti appeared oblivious to the tension in the tent.

"If there's nothing else you need from me, Lord A," Letti said when she finished documenting the damage and dismantling her camera. "I'll go back into town with Purdy and develop these for you."

"But I'm not going back yet," Purdy argued, his hands on his hips.

"Yes, you are." Terence, who must've heard the commotion, stepped into the tent, brandishing a bristle brush. *At least it's not the rifle.* Stella relaxed her grip on Lyndy's hand. Terence waved the brush at him, his voice calm but commanding. "We've had enough of your kind of publicity. Unless you know some way to mitigate this disaster?"

Why was Terence handling the destruction so well? Stella would've expected a violent outburst. His work was in rubble on the floor, and he'd barely raised his voice. Could he have done it after all?

"All right. All right." Surrounded on three sides, Purdy held his hands up in surrender. With Stella holding one end of the gangly tripod and Letti the other, the two women followed him out, Lyndy with the camera a few steps behind.

Purdy approached as if to help with the equipment but grabbed Letti's shoulder instead, leaning in to her to whisper, "Remember our agreement," before releasing her. He ambled away, whistling.

Letti's face flushed when she caught Stella watching her. Letti hurriedly took the tripod from Stella and clumsily walked the last few yards alone. Purdy was leaning against the wagon, waiting.

Once Lyndy had gingerly laid the camera in the back and the photographer had climbed in, Purdy slung up into the wagon, snapped the reins, and the pair rumbled away.

What was that about?

"Sweet Pea," Stella's mother called. Slapping the dirt from her split skirt, she walked toward Stella. "Thought I'd take a break and give you a hand cleaning..." Mama's gaze drifted past Stella's shoulder. "Terence?"

Stella whirled around to find Terence, his face as white as a sun-bleached bone, clutching the tent's flap, but it couldn't hold his weight. He slid to the ground, threatening to pull the tent down with him. Lyndy reached him first.

"Bloody hell!" Lyndy shifted the assistant's weight to him and, with his arm wrapped beneath his shoulder, nearly dragged Terence inside, setting him as gently as Letti's camera in the ladderback chair.

"Are you all right, Terence?" Stella held out a canteen of water.

His breath was ragged and shallow. Still, he waved off Stella's offering as if it were a wet stocking. "I'm all right. I'm all right." He didn't look all right.

"Are you hurt? Do you feel sick?"

"I said I'm all right!" Color flooded his cheeks as he shot up out of the chair. "But my skull is gone!"

The pounding feet of galloping horses drummed in Stella's ears. Sheriff Becker's shout followed. "Professor Gridley?"

Setting down the fossils piled in her hands on the nearest table, she crossed over to the tent's entrance and poked her head out. She brushed aside the wisps of hair the breeze blew across her eyes. The sheriff was tying up his horse as Mr. Drucker swung down from his saddle.

"The sheriff's back."

Stella shot a glance over her shoulder at Terence. Consumed with sorting through fossils on the back table, he didn't notice. Everyone had pitched in to search and clean up the tent, with Terence directing the placement of every table, chair, plaster jacket, and piece of paper. Except Terence's fossilized skull was still missing.

Terence had refused to answer Stella's questions about the missing skull. Professor Gridley then explained how his assistant had unearthed a skull on a recent prospecting trip, potentially of a new bear ancestor. Stella initially pictured the giant head of a grizzly, which confused her. Why were they searching under piles of papers for it? Wouldn't they have spotted the large skull right away, even in this mess? But when the professor had described it further, Stella understood. The bear ancestor's skull was only two and a half inches wide.

But then, if it's so important, why wasn't it locked up in the safe?

"What does he want now?" the assistant grumbled.

"Now, now, Terence. Sheriff Becker didn't lose your skull."

"Lose my . . . ? *I* didn't *lose* anything." Terence shot daggers at the professor.

Professor Gridley had removed his spectacles, fogging them with his breath, and didn't notice. He was still cleaning them with a handkerchief when Sheriff Becker and Mr. Drucker stepped inside the tent. Terence went back to his search.

"What happened here?" Sheriff Becker glanced at the coating of plaster dust covering the ground. The chalky scent was inescapable. He pulled a smooth stone from his vest pocket and weighed it in his hand.

"Back again, Sheriff?" Lord Atherly said. "We'll make a fossil hunter out of you yet."

"I'm afraid I'm here on business." Sheriff Becker flashed Lord Atherly a strained smile that quickly disappeared. "Mr. Drucker here says he showed you proof that two of your horses belong to him, and you ran him off at the point of a gun."

"Lord Atherly didn't. I did." Terence didn't bother to look up.

"Well, Mr. Brochard, I've seen the paper and am satisfied. I'm here to see that Mr. Drucker gets his horses back."

"We paid good money to the Smiths for those horses, Sheriff. If we give them to this man, will we get our money back?"

"You'll have to take that up with the Smiths, Professor."

"We're academics, Sheriff. Money isn't in unlimited supply."

"Ask your rich lord to help you out." Mr. Drucker jabbed his thumb in Lord Atherly's direction.

"Onie," the sheriff warned. "I told you to be quiet and leave it all to me."

Stella didn't need to see Lyndy tug at his waistcoat to feel his frustration. But she was proud of him. He kept quiet. It was Lord Atherly who couldn't let it lie.

"I say, Mr. Drucker. My money isn't in unlimited supply either. This will be the third pair of horses we'll be obliged to purchase. If I'd known that would be the case, I would've been better off purchasing mules."

"Don't worry, Lord A," Mama said, brushing plaster dust from her hands. "Stella, Lyndy, and I will simply go back to the ranch and get Clem to round up a couple more horses for you."

"That is most kind of you, Mrs. Smith."

"And at no charge. You shouldn't be put out because some bad character sold Clem stolen horses. Besides, he'll be right put out to know he'd been taken like that."

"And what about me? I'm the one who—"

"Quit whining." Sheriff Becker cut off Onie Drucker's complaint. "I'd be obliged if someone got Mr. Drucker's horses now, please."

No one moved.

"Very well. We'll get them ourselves." As Sheriff Becker motioned for Onie Drucker to follow, Terence skirted the table and strode toward them, blocking their way.

"This is ridiculous, Sheriff! Just look at this!" His hand swept out to incorporate the tent's interior, causing Onie Drucker to flinch and back up. "Instead of harassing us and confiscating our horses, you should be out there tracking down who's trying to ruin us. Don't you realize careers are at stake here?"

"We even know who it was," Professor Gridley chimed in. "Dr. Aurelius Moss. And we know where to find him."

"Professor, you think Moss stole my skull?"

Sheriff Becker pushed the brim of his hat back with his finger. "I'm sorry about the tent, but unless you have proof it wasn't simply a mischievous bear, I'm too busy to deal with a dispute between feuding paleontologists."

Everyone in the tent flinched at the sheriff's ill-chosen wording.

"But that skull—" Terence began.

"Now, Mr. Drucker will fetch his horses, and we'll be on our way." To stop Terence from saying more, he added, "And if you try and stop him, I'll have a mind to arrest you, Mr. Brochard, and take your rifle, to boot."

Terence stepped aside to allow the sheriff and Onie Drucker to leave, glowering at them from under hooded eyes as if trying to burn holes into their backs. Stella gave him a wide berth as she and her mother followed them out of the tent.

Once at the corral, Onie Drucker climbed over the fence and dropped into the trampled dirt. He clicked his tongue, produced a crabapple for each horse, and slipped on the halters he'd brought with him when they approached. They obviously knew him. Sheriff Becker opened the gate. As Onie led the horses past, Stella confirmed what she'd suspected. The brand on the horses' hips was the same as on the horses Ned Smith had shown her. Had they all been stolen? Would the sheriff expect Ned to give them all up? Wouldn't that be a huge financial blow? What did Mama think of all this?

Stella stole a sideways glance at her mother but found no answers there.

As they watched Sheriff Becker and Onie Drucker lead the mares away, Mama put her arm around Stella's shoulder. Lyndy, his father, and the professor soon joined them as if the air in the tent was too stifling. Behind them, a wind kicked up as Terence stormed past, slapping his hat on his head and making his way to the quarry.

"Better put the rifle away, Papa," Lyndy suggested as Terence picked up a small shovel and began stabbing at the ground. Mama's slight nod mirrored Stella's own. Seeing the professor's surprised but pained expression, Lyndy added, "Just to be on the safe side, eh?"

CHAPTER 18

Stella closed her eyes and let the long, willowy fishing rod relax in her hand. Welcoming the darkness that enveloped her, she listened to her breathing, slowing to match the gentle rush of the water swirling past, pushing against her legs. When she opened her eyes again, she was surprised, for a split second, at the splendor of the scene around her: the rocky bottom of the crystal-clear stream, the flat grassy bank, the evergreen trees. Too skinny to provide much shade, richly pine-scented trees grew sparsely nearby but thickened into a green blanket as they climbed the sides of the pointed mountain range looming in the near distance. A small herd of elk browsed among the trees. Birds, silhouetted against the sky, soared high above. A few miles upstream from the Ninebark Ranch house and its surrounding lush valley meadow, Stella felt a world away from the expedition camp and all its woes.

Yet she wasn't alone. About eighty yards downstream and similarly outfitted in rubber waders, Lyndy stood midstream with his back to her. His presence was a comfort, as steady and reliable as a lodestone. Stella watched, mesmerized, as his fishing line swished methodically back and forth in the air. The clinging beads of water, sparkling in the sun, made the line iridescent. As Lyndy finally flung the line loose, all the tension Stella had been holding drained from her muscles, down into her waders, and into the water.

How could I have not wanted to come?

After the sheriff and Onie Drucker took the horses, Stella had returned to the Ninebark Ranch with Lyndy and her mother, hoping to pick out a couple more they could bring back to camp. Then, she'd intended to seek out Dr. Moss to see if he was the culprit. With his new dig on a neighboring ranch, he had to be somewhere nearby. But Mama had other ideas. After explaining the futility of finding Moss's dig without some sense of its location, Mama had Junior fetch fly fishing equipment from one of the outbuildings—rods, reels, waders—and then proceeded to pack two suppers, one to send with the horses back to Lord Atherly and Professor Gridley and one for Stella and Lyndy to take to the river.

But Stella didn't want to go fishing. She wanted answers. Neither her mother, Junior, nor Clem seemed surprised Stella knew how to fish. Lyndy had taught her before they were married. But they didn't know that the last time she'd done it, she'd fished a body out of the river. And yet here she was, after being escorted by Clem to a good fishing spot on his way to bring horses he could spare back to the camp. When had Stella ever been able to say no to her mother?

Stella bent to touch the water. Despite it being July, the water was freezing. That, too, brought back painful memories—of a swim of desperation in the Solent near the Isle of Wight just before the wedding. But this water was only thigh deep, and she could see her feet grounded in the river bed. Nothing about this was the same.

Almost the opposite.

It was as if she was being baptized again, the haunting memories being washed downriver. She could start again and enjoy the sport. And not just the sport, everything. She could let go of not only the memories but also her concerns about her relationship with her mother. If she and her mother weren't close, if her mother didn't love Stella as she had when Stella was a child, how could she have known what Stella needed to ease her mind? Stella could release the questions around Harp Richter's death and everything plaguing the dig that buzzed and fluttered in her brain like fireflies in a jar. At least for a while. And could this be what Stella needed to do to get pregnant? Hadn't the doctors told her to relax?

Stella's laugh bellowed up through her belly and burst from her as an overwhelming hope filled her. Lyndy glanced back, the sun catching the white of his teeth as he smiled. He'd been worried about her, worried about conceiving an heir. He'd hoped this trip would fix everything or, at least, put off their troubles for a while. And maybe he was right. She had needed to come all this way to see her mother, to see Lord Atherly transformed by his passion, to experience this beautiful, magical river and be reminded that she was capable of anything and everything would be all right.

"Everything all right, my love?" Lyndy shouted, his sonorous voice carrying across the water.

"Couldn't be better!" she called back, raising her rod to get back to the business of fishing.

Laughing, Stella plopped beside Lyndy on the horse blanket he'd thrown on the ground. His wife's shirtsleeves were soaked, hair had slipped through the restraints of the bun she'd managed without a maid's help, and she was still sporting the ridiculous rubber waders Junior had procured for her.

And she'd never looked more beautiful.

Lyndy twirled some of her silken strands around his finger before tracing the entire length of her neck. He kissed her skin.

She tasted of salty perspiration and rose water. She giggled, ticklish as she was, but leaned into him, turning her face toward his to make it easier for their lips to meet.

"Who knew falling into an icy stream while fly fishing could be so romantic?" she whispered, the featherlight touch of her lips on his. Her tone was airy but said with a hint of melancholy she couldn't hide from him.

What was she thinking? About the German homesteader's death? Papa and all the mishaps at the dig? How Clem selling Papa's stolen horses might affect Ned and her mother? Dwelling on any one of those could account for her unease. Each was unsettling on its own, but put together, they were enough to rattle him. And Stella was far more empathetic than Lyndy ever pretended to be.

Or could it be far more personal?

Lyndy knew too well how the specter of their familial duty, their need to conceive a child, hovered over them every time they were intimate. He despised it as much as he adored being this close to her. Yet all he could do was reassure her of his love and loyalty.

And to, of course, enthusiastically try and try again.

"Come here, my love." Lyndy cupped the back of her head and, holding her gently, kissed her sweet mouth.

She eagerly embraced him, pulling him closer as they rolled onto their sides on the ground. Lyndy wiggled his fingers into the bun and pulled it loose, relishing her shampoo's lingering fresh orris root scent as her hair cascaded around them. Stella tugged the braces that held up the waders from Lyndy's shoulders as he eagerly responded in kind. Getting the waders off might prove awkward, but he was more than willing to give it a go. Stella unbuttoned his shirt, slipped her hand beneath the cotton fabric, and laid her hand over his beating heart. It beat faster at her touch. Laying his hand over hers, he held it there, reminding her she had his heart, as much as if she held it in the palm of her hand. His lips had begun tracing the length of her collarbone when a not-too-distant explosion boomed, echoing in their ears and resonating in the ground where they lay.

Stella jerked away and bolted upright, nearly clipping Lyndy in the chin in her haste. "What was that?"

"Our love made the earth shake," Lyndy quipped lightheartedly.

Stella had been tense all morning and seemed to finally relax, but that bloody blasting might ruin everything. He'd have a bone to pick with Ned. Realizing the pun, Lyndy chuckled to himself. He urged her back into his embrace, unwilling to let anything spoil the moment, but she resisted, her body rigid as she braced for another explosion.

"No, Lyndy. This is serious. It couldn't have been lightning." Stella stared up into a perfectly blue sky. "It might've been a gunshot." A second blast reverberated beneath them again. Stella clutched the blanket in her fist. "That was too powerful for a gunshot. Do you think they have cannons here?"

"It's all right, my love." Lyndy grudgingly sat up and pecked the patch of bare shoulder he'd managed to free of her shirtwaist. "I imagine it's just Ned dynamiting his mine. We're not far from it here."

Stella craned her neck to force Lyndy to meet her questioning gaze. "What do you mean? You said he used water to remove the creek bed to get at the gold, not dynamite."

"I also said he'd not found any that way and would mine for ore instead if need be. Didn't realize he'd give up on the gold so soon, though." Lyndy punctuated his sentence with another kiss on her shoulder. Unlike Ned, Lyndy wasn't willing to give up so easily. He nibbled on her neck.

"Ned doesn't strike me as the type to quit either." She ignored Lyndy's attempts to divert her attention back to him. "Just imagine all he went through to build up such a successful ranch. Mama too. But why would he be using dynamite? That's really dangerous."

"We're quite safe."

"We might be, but it would shatter Mama if something happened to Ned."

"I'm certain Ned knows what he's doing. Like you said, he's a seasoned frontiersman. He wouldn't do anything reckless. Besides, your mother is quite strong and capable of more than she knows. She's much like her daughter in that regard."

Stella's smile unfurled across her mouth and lit her face like a beacon on a stormy night.

Good Lord, how he loved that smile.

"Oh, Lyndy. You do know just the right thing to say." She took his face in her hands and rewarded him with a kiss so full of promise it made his heart skip a beat or two.

Stella lifted her head from Lyndy's shoulder as their buggy rumbled along the driveway toward the ranch house. "Oh, no. What are they doing here?"

Onie Drucker stood beside the sheriff in the stable yard. With his hat pulled nearly over his eyes, he kept his head down, digging his boot heel into the ground. Becker was talking to Clem, who was holding the reins of a chestnut Quarter Horse, its coat still slick from a ride.

"I just got back from helping out with the harvest, Sheriff," Clem was saying as Lyndy halted the buggy nearby. "Give me a minute to take care of Rusty, and I'll be able to give you all the time you want."

Stella climbed off, twisting her hair back into some semblance of a bun while Lyndy flipped their horse's reins around a nearby fence post.

"What's all this about, Sheriff?" Lyndy asked before Stella had a chance.

"Seems the Smiths bought more of Onie Drucker's stolen horses." Becker pointed to Onie, who remained more interested in the ground than what was being said. After the reaction at the camp, he was probably more than willing to let the sheriff do the talking. But his anger hadn't abated; the hole in the ground he'd dug attested to that.

"I don't know what you're talking about, Sheriff." Clem patted Rusty's shoulder while acknowledging Stella and Lyndy's arrival with a friendly nod. The horse nudged him with his muzzle, and Clem gently stroked the horse's long white blaze. "I bought those horses fair and square off a homesteader eager to sell. I got a bargain, I admit. But it was a fair price. I didn't steal anything."

"Well, that may be, Clem. But that homesteader was in no position to sell you another man's horses."

"What are you saying?"

"You'll have to give them back to Mr. Drucker here."

Clem, having been preoccupied by Rusty, seemed to focus on Onie Drucker for the first time. He rubbed the stubble on his chin with his knuckles and squinted at him. As if the scrutiny was unwanted and unwarranted, Onie kept his head lowered. Only the scowl on his face was visible.

Clem's disbelieving snort reminded Stella of Tully, her Thoroughbred, when Stella arrived in the stables empty-handed. Tully did love her treats.

"It's this man's word against mine." Clem Smith was as calm as if he, and not Stella and Lyndy, had just come back from fishing. "And I'll say it again, Sheriff. I didn't steal any horses."

Sheriff Becker frowned, weighing a smooth stone in his palm, doubt creeping across his face as he glanced sideways at Onie Drucker. From what her mother had told her, Becker had known Clem for years, and from Stella's impression, Clem Smith was the type of man whose word was worth something. The sheriff had known Onie Drucker for a few hours. But the sheriff was a lawman, and the law was on the side of this stranger.

The sheriff let out a resigned sigh. "I am sorry, Clem, but

Mr. Drucker's got the papers to prove those horses belong to him. I have to insist."

"If you must, you must, but you won't get any help from me." Clem led Rusty around, turning his back on them, and walked the tired horse back to the barn.

"Where are they?" Becker called.

"In yonder barn," Clem pointed toward a distant barn without looking back.

"Come on, Onie."

The pair trudged across the work yard as Clem and Rusty disappeared into the shadowy interior of the closer barn.

"I wonder how many horses Clem bought?"

Ned had shown them off to Stella a few days ago, but they'd been grazing with a dozen others. Could it be so many? She got her answer when the sheriff and Onie Drucker entered the second barn and reappeared with three more horses.

"How did they know Clem had more of the stolen horses?" Stella wondered out loud as Onie Drucker, mounted on one, led the other two past, leaving Sheriff Becker to hike back toward the house alone.

"Good question," Lyndy agreed, his arms folded across his chest as he eyed Onie Drucker suspiciously.

"Even a woman like you could make that guess," Onie Drucker snipped. "They do run a horse ranch, after all."

Whatever he meant by "a woman like you," Lyndy was quick to take offense. His jaw tightened as his anger flared. But he squeezed his forearms in an attempt to keep it in check. "I say, you disrespect my wife with such demeaning insinuations again, and I'll unseat you from that horse whether you own it rightfully or not."

Stella suspected Lyndy didn't know any more than she did what Onie Drucker was insinuating, but the effect was that the man blanched and kicked his horse, spurring it to trot away. Stella was glad to see the back of him. But she still wanted a valid answer.

"How did you know—?" Stella began to repeat her question to the sheriff as he stepped into the saddle when Ned, on the back of a buckskin Quarter Horse gelding and covered in fine dust from head to foot, galloped into the yard and dismounted with the skill of an acrobat. Relieved to see him in one piece, Stella marveled he didn't twist an ankle or buckle a knee as he landed two feet from Sheriff Becker.

"What in all tarnation is going on here, Sheriff? I just saw a fellow taking off with those horses Clem bought the other day."

"That was Onie Drucker, Ned, and they're his horses."

Ned removed his hat and coughed as he swatted dust from it. "Clem sold them to him, did he? I didn't think—"

"No, Clem didn't sell them. I let Onie take them."

"Not without paying, you don't." With the reins still in his hands, Ned grabbed a handful of his horse's mane and lifted his foot toward the stirrup again. Sheriff Becker, guessing Ned's intent to ride after Onie Drucker, snatched hold of the bridle and loomed over him. Ned was a tall man, but Becker was bigger.

"Nothing you can do about it, Ned. They were stolen horses."

"Like the ones he took back from Lord Atherly and the professor." Stella had meant it to be clarifying, but it had the opposite effect. Ned scowled in confusion. "The ones you sold them?"

Mama had known all about it. Hadn't she told Ned?

"What's this? Did you have a hand in that, too, Hank?"

"I'm sorry, Ned, but the man had a right to them."

Ned threw his hat on the ground and swore. The skin along his hairline was pale and free of dust. "Damn it all, Hank. What are you trying to do, bankrupt me?"

"Now, now, Ned. I know it isn't fair, and losing three horses set you back some, but didn't Clem say you got them at a bargain?"

"Bargain or not, you know what horses cost. Besides, do

you know what folks will think when they hear about this? They'll think we peddle in stolen horses. The market's been bad enough as it is. If they aren't calling for our necks, you can sure bet they won't be calling to buy our horses."

"I'll be sure to let it be known you did nothing wrong, Ned. All you'll be out is the three horses. I can promise you that."

"Like hell! Can you promise Claxton doesn't pay me another call?" When the sheriff's mouth set in a hard line, Ned swiped his hat up from the ground. "Didn't think so." He stormed into the house, slamming the screen door behind him.

"I didn't want to have to do this," the sheriff muttered to the audience he had left, "any more than I wanted to take away your father's horses, Lyndy."

"We all know it's not easy being a lawman," Stella assured him. She'd learned from Inspector Brown back in the New Forest that carrying out his duty as a policeman often clashed with his personal desires. However, Sheriff Becker seemed more constrained by politics than usual. "I'm sure when Ned calms down, he'll understand you were only doing your job."

Becker tipped his hat in appreciation and took his leave. When the dust from his horse had settled, Lyndy slid his arm around hers and whispered, "You're sure, are you?"

"Not in the least," Stella admitted, "but I certainly hope so."

CHAPTER 19

Lord Atherly dabbed his lips with his napkin before tossing it beside his tin plate. He'd eaten little of their evening meal. Not that it hadn't smelled appealing. His stomach rumbled and gurgled in protest, but he ignored it, his mind preoccupied elsewhere.

How dare Moss or one of his ilk set up a rival camp nearby (though granted, *nearby* here was a relative term)? *The audacity of the man.*

"You can take it away, Murphy. I'm finished."

The Irishman they'd hired as cook frowned at the sourdough biscuit with one bite taken out, the half-eaten portion of beans, the strips of steak wallowing in gravy. He may have silently transferred his displeasure to Lord Atherly before carrying the plate away, but Lord Atherly ignored that, too.

"I say, Gridley. How far do you suppose Dr. Moss's camp is from here?"

Lord Atherly hadn't bankrolled this expedition and come all this way for some usurper to steal what he'd spent half his life searching for. When someone stole a specimen from his study in England, the shock nearly killed him. He'd never contemplated such evil. With his constitution far more hale and hearty than ever, he was more inclined to do something about it.

The professor, still sopping up the last vestiges of gravy with his biscuit, paused to consider. "About three miles downstream. Can you believe he had the gall to camp along the Cottonwood? Seems it crosses the Claxton ranch, too."

Lord Atherly slapped the table decisively, rattling the near-empty tin cups of coffee. "What say you to taking a look?"

Gridley untucked the napkin dangling from his open collar and dragged it across his mouth, wiping away any specks of gravy. "I say, let's go. Terence can meet Miss Stella, Lyndy, and Katherine when they return with the other horses. I want to see what the shyster is up to."

After a quick word with Terence insisting he continue without them, the two men hitched up the surrey with the eagerness of boys setting off on an adventure. For over an hour, they followed the creek as it snaked along the foothills, speculating whether it was Moss or his surrogate who stole the notebook and fossils and whether he killed poor Harp Richter. When Lord Atherly decided to speak in Moss's defense, Gridley reminded Lord Atherly of Dr. Hale, whose rivalry with Gridley had resulted in the *Miohippus* fossils being stolen from Lord Atherly's study last year. Moss had been one of Hale's students and, with his mentor's disgrace, had taken it on himself to perpetuate the rivalry: bribing landowners to prevent Gridley access to dig sites, criticizing him in the press, and publishing Gridley's work as his own. By the time they spotted the rival camp, Lord Atherly's jaw was clenched against the ungentlemanly oath raring to burst from his lips.

Could there be any doubt Dr. Aurelius Moss was capable of murder?

Tying the horse in a stand of cottonwoods far enough from

the creek to avoid detection, Lord Atherly and the professor scuttled toward the camp, their backs hunched over, hoping the water's babbling would drown out their approach. With a smooth granite boulder acting as cover, they lay on their bellies in the prickly grass and waited. Lord Atherly fought the urge to spit and sneeze as bits of grass tickled his face and went inside his mouth.

If Frances could see me now.

Moss's camp was far more primitive than theirs: two canvas tents, an uncovered, makeshift wooden platform table, an uneven ring of stones with a cast-iron pot slung above it, a couple of tapestry-backed folding chairs that looked more suited to a cabin parlor than an expedition camp, and an unhitched covered wagon filled with specimen crates. A marvelous palomino gelding was hobbled close by but far enough away to allow it to graze. But for the smoke that wafted up from a recent fire, the camp looked uninhabited.

"Do you think anyone's about?" Lord Atherly whispered.

As if in answer, Moss flung the flap of the farthest tent open and stepped blinking into the afternoon sunshine. He was smartly dressed, the jacket of his well-cut suit flung over his shoulder, a book clutched under his arm. How he camped out in this rugged landscape and remained unrumpled and tidy, as if his valet had just dressed him in warmly pressed attire, Lord Atherly couldn't guess. Clutched in his other hand was a thick blue and white porcelain coffee cup. Moss took a sip and tossed the remaining contents on the ground before setting the cup on the wooden table. He seemed to be alone.

Moss stood by the dying fire, reading his book. Lord Atherly couldn't see the title on the spine.

Lord Atherly momentarily dropped his gaze, suddenly self-conscious, and followed the progress of a single ant crawling along the ground. What was he thinking, instigating this out-ing? He'd never done anything like this in his life. He was the Earl of Atherly, a member of the British peerage. How could he stoop so low? Yet here he was, hiding in the grass, desperately trying not to breathe too loud and spying on this person as he did the most mundane things.

After Moss strolled to the back of his wagon, Lord Atherly used the noise of Moss's rummaging, moving crates about, as cover to raise his concerns.

"Perhaps we were mistaken, Gridley. Perhaps we should turn back."

Without taking his attention off his rival, Gridley pinched his lips tightly, causing them to disappear. The professor was far more convinced of Dr. Moss's evil nature than Lord Atherly. But after a few moments of consideration, Gridley finally nodded in resignation. Lord Atherly began to inch backward but froze when Gridley clutched his arm and pointed. Moss had found what he'd been searching for. Clutching a rifle, Moss strolled back to the fire and settled into one of the folding chairs. He retrieved a cardboard box of cartridges from the ground, crossed a leg over his knee, and started humming as he slid open a box. Moss was reloading his gun.

Lord Atherly didn't wait to see more. He scrambled backward, scraping the palms of his hands, then scuttled around like a crab. With the professor at his side, he crawled on all fours for several yards before launching, stumbling to his feet. He spirited toward the hidden surrey, his breath quick and shallow, his muscles burning in protest.

"What in the blazes . . . ?" Moss cursed.

A gunshot rang out from behind them, and they instinctively ducked their heads. A bullet whistled past, lodging in the trunk of one of the cottonwood trees. It was head high. Winded and top-heavy, Professor Gridley lost his balance and stumbled in fright, his knee smashing into a rock.

"Blast it all!" he cried out in pain.

Lord Atherly grabbed the fellow by the crook of his arm and hauled him to his feet. He shoved him toward the wagon, which Gridley used as support, and dodged around it to untie the horse. As Gridley clutched the rails to hoist himself up and onto the plank, Lord Atherly leaped nimbly beside his companion and snapped the reins. As another shot rang out, the horse tore off like the devil was closing in on them, and Gridley, not secured on the bench yet, nearly tumbled out because of the abrupt backward force. As it was, his hat flew from his head. As it soared past like a low-flying bird, Lord Atherly clutched the reins so hard his knuckles turned white. He dared to glance over his shoulder. Moss had reached the trees they'd just left.

"I'll fix you!" Silhouetted by the setting sun, Moss rested the butt of his rifle against his shoulder, the barrel aimed directly at them.

Soon, they'd be out of range. Lord Atherly surprised himself by bursting into euphoric laughter. With the wind whipping against the brim of his hat and his heart matching the horse's hoofs pounding against the hard ground, Lord Atherly had to admit it surpassed being holed up in his study examining fossilized bones.

And then the wheels hit a prairie dog mound or a boulder or a tall clump of grass, and the surrey jolted as it careened along the creek, jostling the two men, their shoulders colliding hard against one another. Lord Atherly struggled to slow the horse. Instead, one tug strap snapped and then the other. The gelding pulled free of the iron shafts, and the surrey tilted as one of the shafts jammed into the ground, abruptly halting their momentum.

Lord Atherly strained for the reins, now flapping uselessly behind the fleeing gelding. A dark mass that must be Gridley shot over his head, momentarily blotting out the purplish hues of the sky. Lord Atherly found his seat again briefly. Then flew. Airborne, his mouth gaped open like the nighthawks darting above, eating insects. The surrey crashed in a deafening mass of splintering wheels, collapsed rails, and broken planks before tumbling over the edge of the creek bank. As the ground loomed large, Lord Atherly, despite his years in the saddle, flinched and tensed his muscles. Instead of a controlled roll, he bounced and tumbled down the ravine after the broken surrey like a rag doll, slamming against exposed roots, rocks, and hard-packed earth. Collapsing at the bottom, he lay as cracked and broken as the spokes of the upside-down wheel still spinning on its axis beside him. Gridley was nowhere in sight.

"Not again," were the last words Lord Atherly whimpered, the taste of blood on his lips, before the darkening sky closed in.

"How'd you find Lord Atherly and the professor, Clem?" Mama asked as her brother-in-law dropped into the open chair at the table.

Eager to hear what Clem had to say, Stella passed him the green beans she'd just been spooning onto her plate. In contrast to the strict rules of dining followed at Morrington Hall, Stella found the lack of formality in the Smith home refreshing. Lyndy, from the look on his face, still didn't know what to make of it.

"I wouldn't know," Clem said after helping himself to the green beans and then accepting the basket of rolls Maria offered him. "They weren't in the camp when I brought the pair of horses around. Just that assistant fella was there. He didn't offer up where Lord A and Professor Gridley were, so I didn't ask."

"Oh, Clem," Mama sighed, her frustration echoing Stella's silent disbelief. "How can you not have asked?"

Stella had encountered few people who lacked curiosity. More often than not, they were curious but refused to admit it.

Her mother-in-law, Lady Atherly, for one. Lyndy, when they'd first met, had been another. Could Clem Smith be one of those rare individuals who did what needed doing and asked for no more out of life than to spend his day with his horses and a glass of whiskey now and then? Could he truly not be interested in where Lord Atherly and the professor had gone? If only Stella could be like that. She couldn't silence her mind if she wanted to.

More often than not, her need to learn, to grow, to prove herself, to know was all-consuming. Even now, in the quiet of Mama's kitchen, with supper's lingering scents and congenial small talk of the weather, roundups, and the harvest around the table, Stella's mind brimmed with questions. Where were Lord Atherly and the professor? They were keen to unearth the fossil Mama had found and had numerous specimens to catalog and box up. Where could they have gone? Was Moss guilty of sabotaging the expedition, as the professor suspected? Had they gone to confront him?

Yet something held her back from asking.

The peace she'd found fishing had been shattered. The blasting at Ned's mine and Onie Drucker had seen to that. Was she hoping if she resisted the urge to voice her questions, she'd reclaim that sense of peace? Or was it the worry about something she couldn't put her finger on that crept at the edges of her mind like a spider spinning its web? Instead, she sought answers by watching her mother, but Mama always smiled when she caught Stella staring.

What was Stella missing?

"When you're finished, mind you feed those wolf pups, Junior," his father said. Since the incursion into the kitchen, the pups had been confined to a distant barn.

"I'm done now, Pa." Junior swiftly pushed back from the table, threw down his napkin, and raced out of the room.

"Any luck at the mine, Ned?" Lyndy asked, shoveling up

another bite of cherry pie. "We heard the blasts when we were fishing. Find anything of value?"

Ned coughed as he shook his head slowly, like its weight was more than he was used to. The lines across his forehead were deeply etched with disappointment. "Not a thing. Seems it's a tired-out, worthless piece of land."

"Should've known." Clem held out his cup, and Maria obligingly poured him the last of the coffee from the pot. It barely filled the cup halfway. Ignoring the irritation plain on Ned's face, Clem swigged down the coffee before pushing back in his chair, claiming to be exhausted and heading for his bed.

"Sounds like a good idea," Ned said, though Stella suspected he'd wanted to say something else. "I'll bunk on the sleeping porch, Kate. Got an early start tomorrow and don't want to disturb you."

Mama offered him her cheek, which he duly kissed. "Much appreciated. Sleep tight!"

Stella and the others bid the brothers goodnight and moved to the front porch at Mama's suggestion. With a borrowed woolen shawl of her mother's tight around her shoulders, Stella sat in a rocking chair between Lyndy and her mother, still sipping her cup of coffee.

"You're unusually quiet, my love," Lyndy whispered.

"Everything all right, Sweet Pea?"

"I'm fine. Just tired, I think."

"I can imagine. You've had little peace since you arrived."

"The fishing trip was perfect for that. Thank you for suggesting it, Mama."

"Don't thank me. It wasn't my idea."

With a subtle tilt, her mother indicated Lyndy, who was rocking like a man who'd never been in a rocking chair before or known its purpose, jarring the chair every time he hit the side of the house.

Stella should've known. She wanted to leap up and kiss her husband but didn't dare as he continued pitching back and forth with such vigor that Junior said as he strode toward them, "I made that rocker, Lyndy, and you're fixing to break it."

Lyndy chuckled and, fiddling with the top button of his shirt, slowed his pace. They chatted about this and that for a while, the Kentucky Thoroughbreds, the earthquake, and a possible trip to the national park. Eventually, they fell into a companionable silence, watching the darkening blue sky flare with oranges, pinks, and purple as the sun set and listening to the creaking rockers, the hum of insects, and a distant hoot of an owl. Mama reached over, taking Stella's hand and intertwining their fingers, and they rocked gently in synchrony. Her mother's warmth spread from her hand to envelope Stella's whole body. She never wanted to let her mother go. But too soon, Mama announced she was heading to bed and suggested they do the same.

They rose, and Stella wrapped her arms around Lyndy, resting her cheek against his shoulder as she allowed him to guide her toward the door. It was such a luxurious feeling, this drifting off to sleep on her feet, but as Mama and Junior disappeared inside, Stella caught a flash of movement out of the corner of her eye.

It was enough to break the spell. Her muscles tensed, and her mind reawakened with questions. Was it a hungry pronghorn hoping to raid the kitchen garden or a coyote rooting out rabbits? Or a lumbering bear following the scent of easily pilfered food? She raised her head and squinted into the dark, her vision having adjusted, and recognized the creature's outline in motion. It wasn't an animal. From his build, it had to be Clem Smith as he headed toward the stable. Hadn't he gone to bed a while ago?

"Look, Lyndy." Stella spoke so only he could hear. "It's Clem."

"Poor chap. Seems the work of a ranch manager never ends." They watched as Clem disappeared into the stable.

"I wonder."

"Perhaps there's something wrong with one of the horses?"

That was Stella's first thought. But then, why hadn't he brought a lantern instead of picking his way stealthily across the work yard in the dark?

CHAPTER 20

～⁕～

The morning began cool, with a light breeze and a blue sky so vast it beckoned Stella for a ride. Stella eagerly obliged. Wearing a split skirt, she could straddle the saddle, opening up a new way to ride. Every time she gripped the horse's flanks with her thighs, her muscles had to adjust to the balance point. It was such fun she never wanted to ride in a buggy or wagon again. And practical. To keep herself and her horse safe as they galloped across the prairie, she had to focus, leaving no room for questions and concerns. And she had them in spades.

Stella had slept well, but thoughts of Clem Smith accosted her the moment she awoke. As she and Lyndy had undressed for bed, from their bedroom window Stella had seen Clem emerge from the barn and ride off. What was he doing out that late? And where had he gone? When they'd saddled up their borrowed Quarter Horses—Gin, a palomino mare, and Chester, a red dun gelding—Clem's horse, Rusty, wasn't in the stable. And no one had seen Clem this morning—he'd skipped the hearty breakfast she and Maria had prepared. So why, like Ned, was he up and gone before the sun? Or had he not returned yet?

A flutter of feathers and wings erupted from the grasses as a bird was flushed out by the approaching horses. As Gin skirted the nest, Stella fought to keep her balance. She'd let her focus slip. To refocus, she deeply inhaled, savoring the leather scent mingled with the fragrant wildflowers crushed beneath Gin's hoofs, and realigned herself with Gin's rhythmic motion beneath her. Then she looked at Lyndy. Beside her, Lyndy twirled his lasso, at ease on Chester, as if born to the saddle—which, in a way, he was. He was getting better at lassoing every day. Yet, despite the lasso and the well-creased black Stetson hat that Clem had given him, Lyndy's nails were too clean, his boots too new for him to be mistaken for a real cowboy. He lacked the carefree, sun-worn swagger that defined those hardened men who worked the ranch or walked the streets of town. But Stella wasn't going to tell him that, especially since he looked adorable playing the part.

"Race you!" she shouted, urging Gin to pick up the pace.

Caught off guard, Lyndy fumbled with his lasso and fell behind by a length. Stella was the first to pull up beside Lord Atherly's cabin on the edge of the dig camp, laughing and boasting of her win. But the silence dampened her enthusiasm. It was reminiscent of the morning they found Harp Richter's body.

"Good morning!" Stella flung her leg over the saddle and slid down. A horse whinnied in greeting from the corral. "Professor Gridley?"

"Hello?" Lyndy joined her in hitching the horses to the nearby fence post. "Papa?"

Stella's stomach clenched as she glanced around the empty camp.

"Bloody hell. Not again."

She squatted beside the fire ring—the pile of gray ashes was cold. "No one's built a fire this morning. Clem did say your father and the professor weren't here when he brought the horses." The pair of Quarter Horses watched from their new corral, tails swishing but their eyes wary.

"And you think they haven't been back since yesterday?" Stella shrugged.

Lyndy dashed to his father's cabin while Stella headed for the sleeping tent. "Papa's bed is made."

Stella peeked into the sleeping tent through a slit in the flap opening, half dreading finding the men undressed and still in their beds, half praying she would. The tent was empty. "Same here."

A horse whinnied again, but not from the corral. In eager anticipation, Stella stepped away from the tent as a horse and rider approached. "Professor?"

The man had the same stout silhouette, but that's where the similarities ended. As he drew closer, the scruffy, curly hair beneath his hat became more evident. It was a stranger.

"Can we help you?" Lyndy positioned himself between the rider and Stella. The man raised his hat in greeting.

"Just come with breakfast, I have." His strong lilt made his words difficult to understand but marked him as a recent immigrant from Ireland. He slid down, unbuckled a sack, and confidently strode toward the table. Lyndy stepped in his way.

"And you are?"

"Murphy, my friend, hired to cook for these here men of science." The Irishman shoved out his hand. "And who might you be?"

"Lord Lyndhurst." Lyndy took the man's hand before stepping aside.

"You don't happen to know where they are, do you, Mr. Murphy?" Stella didn't wait for an introduction. "No one seems to be around."

Murphy emptied the sack of eggs, potatoes, a loaf of bread, and a large can of corned beef. "Well, I don't rightly know, lass.

They're usually up and about and complaining about the lack of coffee by now."

That's what Stella was afraid of. "When was the last time you saw them?"

"Served them their supper last night. Saw them go off in their surrey while I was washing up."

"Bloody hell. Not again." Lyndy began to pace the length of the table as if anchoring himself to the last place his father had been.

"He's all right, Lyndy." Stella laid a hand on Lyndy's arm, stilling him momentarily. He removed his hat and raked his fingers through his hair. "And we'll find him. Maybe they went over to Dr. Moss's dig. We'll find out where it is and check there next."

She sounded far more confident than she felt. What if she was feeding Lyndy false hope? Lord Atherly had already had one close call. Could he have done something fatal this time? But if so, where were Professor Gridley and Terence? Could they have all come to a bad end?

Despite all the brushes she'd had with murder, Stella refused to accept it.

Heading toward the research tent, she called over her shoulder, "I'm just going to check if they left a note or some clue about their whereabouts."

"Good idea." Lyndy lengthened his stride to catch up, leaving the cook to prepare coffee and a breakfast no one would eat.

Stella flipped the canvas flap back, Lyndy grabbing hold of it to keep it that way, and reeled at the stuffy air thick with the scent of whiskey. "Someone enjoyed themselves last night."

It was dim inside. Motes of plaster dust sparkled as they floated through the thin rays of sun streaming in from behind them. From what Stella could make out, the tables, the oversized plaster jackets, and the organized rows of fossils were as they should be. Stella ducked in and walked unhurriedly between the tables. Nothing seemed out of the ordinary except the stale whiskey smell. And there. The nearest table had a dark splotch on its edge and beneath it on the ground. Had someone spilled ink? Maybe they'd find a note after all.

With her attention on the tabletops, Stella didn't notice the sack of plaster of paris protruding from underneath the nearest one. She accidentally tripped on it and stumbled as her boot caught the tangles of a haphazard pile of twisted rope. She lunged for the table to catch herself and knocked a rock hammer to the ground. The blunt wrought-iron side landed with a thud on her toe.

"Ow!" She'd often seen the paleontologists use the sharpened pick side to free fossils from the earth. She'd never thought about how hard it was.

"Are you all right?" Lyndy, finishing tying up the flaps, poked his head in.

"Fine. Just tripped on stuff someone left in the middle of the tent."

But who would do that? The men who worked this dig were fastidious about their equipment. Had someone else been wreaking havoc in the tent—again? Had Moss come back? Had one of the town tourists? Stella bent to pick up the rock hammer. A dark, dried smudge of blood streaked from the pointed metal pick tip along the length of the wooden handle.

"Ahh!"

Stella dropped the tool as if it had burned her. Landing squarely on its metal head, it bounced before settling on its side in a darkened patch of grass. How could she not have recognized the dark splotches on the ground and table? But there was no mistaking what they were. Blood had pooled on the edge and seeped into the soil. Stella covered her mouth with both hands, stifling another cry. On the other side of the table, partially hidden behind more sacks of plaster, lay a body. A man's body, his feet tangled in a length of coiled rope.

Stella rounded the table, and Lyndy was suddenly at her side, his arm wrapped around her shoulder.

"Everything all right?" The cook appeared in the tent opening, clutching kindling for the fire.

"I wouldn't come in if I were you, Mr. Murphy."

Lyndy's warning only flamed the cook's curiosity. He picked his way cautiously toward them, his focus on Stella's obvious distress. "Are you all right, my lady? I thought I heard . . . Jesus, Mary, and Joseph." Spotting the body, he dropped the branches, genuflected, and backed out the way he'd come.

Lyndy squatted beside the figure sprawled on his stomach on the bloodied ground. The dried, crusty grass crackled as he shifted the body to see the dead man's face. Stella squeezed her eyes closed so tightly they hurt and held her breath, listening for the slightest indication of Lyndy's reaction. *It can't be Lord Atherly. It just can't be.*

"Is it . . . ?"

Lyndy let out his breath in a shutter. "No." He knew who she meant.

Hesitant but curious, Stella cracked her eyes slightly as Lyndy let the body settle again. The glimpse she caught was enough to emblazon yet another macabre image on her memory—bits of grass clinging to the blood encrusting his forehead and hair, the colorful but upside-down pith helmet by his side, the flash of light when the sun reflected off the cracked pince-nez lenses pressed into the ground by his weight, Terence Brochard's pale waxy face, twisted in haughty denial, his eyes frozen in an unseeing stare.

CHAPTER 21

Fighting the morbid draw of the dead body at their feet, Stella's gaze swept the tent; the intensifying aroma of burned bacon wafted in from outside. As if she'd see something new. As if she'd find answers on the tables, among the fossils, and not in a patch of blood-soaked grass. Something nagged at her memory.

"What do you think, Stella?" Lyndy rubbed his finger across the prominent crease of his dimpled chin. "Another accident?"

By all appearances, Terence had tripped over the plaster sacks and rope, hitting his head on the rock hammer on the table. And from the stench of whiskey permeating the place, he'd been drunk. The similarities to Harp's death were unmistakable. As they'd discovered in the few days since they'd arrived in Montana, accidents weren't uncommon here. But so, too, were there many similarities to Reverend Bullmore's demise last spring. The first dead body she'd ever seen. But Reverend Bullmore's death was no accident.

And Terence didn't drink.

"I don't know. It just doesn't look right."

"Could you be wrong?" Lyndy offered gently. "You thought Harp's death was suspicious, too. And that was an accident."

He was right. By all accounts, Harp's death had been a terrible accident, and yet even that might have been predicated by others' misdeeds. Despite the official ruling, the jury was still out on that. In Stella's mind, at least.

"I may have been wrong about Harp, but you have to admit, Lyndy, there are too many things here that need explaining. Like Terence drinking?" Stella picked up a whiskey bottle she'd spotted under a table. It was empty. "You heard how much he was against it. And what were the sacks and rope doing there? Where anyone could trip on them? Yet another unwelcome visitor to the tent? Moss or one of the town tourists wouldn't move rope and plaster. Terence wouldn't have left them lying around, and I don't see your father or the professor doing it either. And where are your father and the professor?"

Stella dropped her focus back to the body, tension spreading from the base of her neck across her shoulder blades. Her head started to pound.

"Did they find the body early this morning and have gone to fetch the sheriff?" she continued, scrutinizing Terence's prone form. "Or did they not even come back last night?" Stella hesitated, hugging herself. If only she didn't have to say it. "And then there's Clem sneaking out in the middle of the night."

"You suspect Clem Smith? Have the two men even met?"

"As far as I know, they met yesterday when Clem brought the new pair of horses."

"I'll grant that Terence was as irritating as a bloodthirsty mosquito," Lyndy admitted, "but even so, one encounter with the chap would not be enough for Clem to want to kill him unless there was some history between them we don't know about or . . ."

Stella sighed. "Or it was an accident." Lyndy accepted Stella's concession with a nod of the head.

Stella squatted beside Terence again, having noticed one hand was tightly clenched. She began prying his fingers apart. Her fingertips brushed against something hard. Maybe she'd been too quick to concede after all.

"I know the western prairie is supposedly fraught with danger, Lyndy—snake bites and hypothermia and starvation, drought and bears—but do you really think this camp is so dangerous that two men accidentally died here within days of each other? And then there's this." She held up the splintered fossil fragment she'd found in Terence's grasp. And then she remembered.

The precious *Hypohippus* jaw. Stella hadn't seen it anywhere.

The couple simultaneously looked up from the body at the sound of horse hooves drumming on the ground. Someone was approaching.

"Maybe that's your father or the professor."

Without waiting to see if Lyndy followed, Stella sprung to her feet and dashed outside. Mr. Murphy was gone, cut raw potatoes left behind on the table, blackened bacon left in the pan. In his place, Purdy Sullivan, the journalist, and not Lord Atherly or the professor, trotted toward camp. With his hat jauntily tilted to one side, he was whistling. He let the notes sour on his lips and fade into silence when he spotted Stella.

"Miss Stella?" Purdy stood up in the stirrups, looking around as if expecting to see something or someone that wasn't there. "What are you doing here?"

"I was about to ask you the same thing."

Purdy slid from his saddle, his eyes restless, searching. "Lord Lyndhurst with you?" He craned his neck at the opening in the tent. When Lyndy appeared, Purdy bit his lip.

"What do you want, Purdy?"

"Quiet, isn't it?"

"Just answer the lady's question, Purdy." Lyndy's arms were so tightly crossed that when Purdy slipped by to enter the tent,

Lyndy was too slow to stop him. "I say! I wouldn't go in there if I were you."

Purdy snuck by but emerged almost immediately, his mouth gaping, his fingers shaking as he pointed over his shoulder. He swallowed so hard Stella could trace the path of his Adam's apple from feet away. "There's a dead man in there."

"We know." Lyndy grabbed the journalist's arm and escorted him back toward his horse. Purdy put up little resistance, shuffling clumsily as he stared over his shoulder at the tent.

"It looks like Terence Brochard."

"It is."

"But how, when, why?" With his hand still shaking, Purdy produced his small notepad and pencil from his waistcoat breast pocket.

"We don't know any more than you do." The journalist's pared-down stutterings had echoed Stella's thoughts. She wished she knew more. Though she doubted she'd tell him if she did.

Purdy stared at the gaping hole where the body lay, chewing on the end of his new pencil. "Have you told the sheriff and the coroner yet?"

"No." And Stella hoped Lord Atherly and the professor would arrive before they had to. "We just found him."

Purdy's gaze swung from the tent to Stella, his slack features lengthening, a sly smile slowly animating his face. He snapped his fingers, shoving his notepad and pencil back into his pocket. "Leave it with me, Miss Stella. I'll go tell them. I'll fetch Sheriff Becker and—"

"And wire your newspaper at the same time?" Lyndy quipped. Stella had been suspecting the same thing.

"And why not? My readers back east are going to love it." He rubbed his hands together, his eyes gleaming with excitement. How could anyone, even a hardened reporter, face tragedy with giddiness and ghoulish glee? "And to think, this is even better than . . ." He stopped short when he caught Stella's eye as if he was about to reveal something he didn't want her to know.

"Better than what, Purdy?"

"Ah, nothing."

"You know you never did tell us what you were doing here." Lyndy crossed his arms against his chest, waiting.

For that, Purdy didn't have an answer, and before they could interrogate him further, he flung his leg over the saddle and dug his boot heels into his horse to spur the gelding on. With his horse kicking up grass and dirt, he raced away like he was outrunning a bullet.

Stella wrapped her arms around her shoulders, trying to keep the shivering at bay. Why hadn't either of them ever learned how to build a fire? When had the morning turned chilly? She bounded up from her seat and began pacing, as Lyndy might do, waiting for him to return. As he emerged from the sleeping tent, a scarlet wool blanket draped over his arm, the wooden and metal clattering of wagon wheels announced the arrival of the sheriff's party. With him, he'd brought the coroner. Purdy drove a dogcart with Letti Landstrom on the bench beside him.

Claxton had prevented Letti from photographing Harp's body or the scene of his accident. Yet here she was. What had Purdy argued that changed the coroner's mind? From the rumblings called between the wagons, Stella soon had her answer. *Absolutely nothing.*

"You have no right to obstruct our rights," Purdy fumed across the gap as the wagons stopped. Purdy carelessly tossed the reins to the floor and jumped down. "It's called freedom of the press, Claxton."

"Seems our intrepid journalist has recovered from the shock." Lyndy draped the blanket around Stella's shoulders. She flinched. The blanket was the color of blood.

"And that is why I allowed you to accompany us, Mr. Sullivan." Elmer Claxton brushed the lapel of his jacket before alighting at his leisure. Purdy grumbled, his hands on his hips, waiting to confront him face to face. "But there is no wording in the United States Constitution that stipulates that I must allow you to hire a female photographer to take pictures of the deceased. It just isn't decent."

What wasn't decent, the request or the fact that it was a woman taking the pictures? Suspecting the latter, Stella tugged on her ear, repressing a flash of annoyance. Besides, another man was dead. Why were these two bickering like stray dogs over a meaty bone?

"But, as they say, Claxton, a picture is worth a thousand words. My readers will love it. Scenes from a murder in far-flung Montana." Purdy's eyes sparkled as if he was envisaging the headline, but Claxton shattered the dream with the sharp snap of his suspenders.

"There will be no pictures! I will be the judge of whether it is a murder or not."

Sheriff Becker, who'd been securing both wagons, strode past the feuding men. "Where can I find the body, Miss Stella?"

"He's in there." As if needing an excuse, Stella shrugged off the blanket before pointing him in the right direction.

He strode away but doubled back, scanning the camp. "Where are the others?"

"Papa and the professor aren't here, Becker. The camp was empty when we arrived."

"And when was the last time either of you saw the professor and your father, Lord Lyndhurst?"

"The last time you did, Sheriff."

Sheriff Becker nodded, considering this, and then strode toward the tent.

"Were you not listening?" Elmer Claxton raised his voice to stop Purdy and Letti from retrieving Letti's equipment from the back of their wagon. "I said you don't have my permission to take pictures."

"No law says you can keep us from setting up her camera." Purdy took the tripod from Letti's shoulder and planted it into the ground.

"I'll do it." Letti blocked Purdy's attempt to snatch the camera brusquely out next. She elbowed him aside and gingerly lifted it out herself. Letti attached the camera to the tripod and then stepped back to assure Claxton she had no intention of doing more.

"Fine." The coroner pinched his lips together in consternation. He wasn't a man used to being disobeyed. "But see that you stay here and not an inch closer to that tent, or I'll find a law that will put you both behind bars. Wait for me, Becker." This he shouted as the sheriff ducked his tall frame to clear the open flaps.

Sheriff Becker ignored him and disappeared into the shadows of the tent. Swearing under his breath, Claxton stomped toward the tent, hustling to catch up. When Stella and Lyndy fell in behind him, the coroner rounded on them, his face flush with exertion and anger.

"And that goes for you two, too. Stay out!"

"The bloody cheek." Lyndy yanked on the hem of his waistcoat as Claxton entered the tent without them. He then demanded of the journalist and photographer, "Does either one of you know how to make a damn fire?" Purdy dropped the potato half he'd picked from the pile on the table, and Letti stopped fiddling with a lens cap. Both nodded. "Thank goodness. I could kill for a cup of tea."

Stella winced at Lyndy's choice of words but couldn't agree more. After helping collect wood and kindling found behind the cabin, Stella settled in to learn. Purdy created a teepee shape with the logs as Letti stuffed twigs and small branches beneath it. Letti rummaged through her handbag and surprisingly produced a matchbox. Stella tried to catch a glimpse of Letti's gun but couldn't peek fast enough. Soon, the fire was crackling.

After Lyndy filled the kettle from the river and placed it over the flames, the water began to heat up.

"If your mother could see you fetching and carrying like a footman," Stella teased. She loved seeing him step outside his role as heir to the manor house and couldn't resist having a little fun.

"Why do you think I do it? I'm counting the days until I can see her expression when I describe the details. It's worth every ache, pain, and blow to my pride."

"I should've known." She playfully swatted his shoulder as she rose. "But don't think you're fooling me, Lord Lyndhurst. I know how much you're enjoying yourself." Lyndy laughed, having been caught out.

Though Purdy was too busy scribbling in his notebook to notice, back at her camera, Letti watched curiously from the corner of her eye. From their banter, an outsider would think Stella and Lyndy had forgotten the grisly scene the sheriff and coroner were inspecting just yards away. But this was how they'd come to cope. There had been too many deaths, too many murders, and if Stella gave in to the sadness, the senselessness, the heartbreak each one brought, she'd never smile again.

At least she'd stopped shivering.

"I'll go get the tea and cups," Stella said as Lyndy unnecessarily poked the fire, sending orange sparks in the air. One ember landed on Purdy's pant leg. The reporter didn't notice. Stella kissed Lyndy on the cheek. "Where do you think your father keeps them?"

"I noticed them on a stand by his bed."

Despite being able to keep the melancholy at bay whenever a stranger or acquaintance died, Stella still couldn't stifle the fear for her father-in-law. "Where are you, Lord Atherly?" she whispered, entering the earl's cabin.

The one-room cabin, a far departure from Lord Atherly's opulent and overly cluttered study back home, held little more than a bed, a nightstand, and his steamer trunk full of linens and clothes. And no clue as to the occupant's whereabouts. All his fossils, hand lenses, notebooks, and stationery were kept in the larger research tent. The bed was made with one of Maria's patchwork quilts folded at the foot—she'd made a similar one for Stella and Lyndy's bed. The floor was hard-packed dirt and bare except for a pair of spare boots by the door. But for the lingering sweet, musky scent of Lord Atherly's expensive shaving cream, she wouldn't have guessed he had been here in days.

The tin and a short stack of teacups were where Lyndy described they'd be, along with a stack of plain white handkerchiefs, a shaving mug, and a small photograph taken of the couple and her in-laws at Stella and Lyndy's wedding. She had never seen it before.

Oh, Lord Atherly! Touched by the sentiment, she snatched the cups and tin of tea and hurried out. If she wanted to banish her fears, she had to act. Now.

CHAPTER 22

"Lyndy, we have to go find him." Stella found him still stoking the fire. His cheeks were flushed from the heat, and the acrid smoke was making his eyes water, but he wouldn't stop.

Purdy's head shot up from his note taking. "Find who? Is someone missing?" He glanced around, scanning the camp. "Where are Lord A and the professor anyway?"

Before Stella or Lyndy could answer, Sheriff Becker and Elmer Claxton emerged from the tent. Becker was slipping the smooth stone she'd seen before into his vest pocket.

"Like I said, I will be the judge of that." Claxton was wiping his hands with a handkerchief. Was that blood on it?

"But their absence is telling, Claxton." Becker's tightly crossed arms threatened to burst his shirtsleeve seams. "There must be more to it than meets the eye."

Whose absence? Stella deliberately caught Lyndy's eye. Were they talking about Lord Atherly and Professor Gridley? Did Sheriff Becker think they had something to do with Terence's death?

"Again, I will be the judge of that, Becker."

"Don't you mean the inquest jury will be the judge?"

Purdy put his finger to his lips and waved Letti over. As the two men bickered, Purdy and Letti tiptoed behind the lawmen as stealthily as one could, carrying a bulky tripod and camera. Stella ignored the pair and homed in on what the lawmen were saying.

"You are too keen to cry murder, Becker. The man tripped and hit his head. It doesn't matter when or who wasn't here to witness it. The man drank too much and paid the price."

Stella set down the tea things she'd been holding. Should she tell them about Clem? He might not have even been involved. And besides, it would devastate her mother if her brother-in-law was accused of murder. But how did Stella clear Lord Atherly without implicating Clem?

"But what if that man doesn't drink?" Stella decided not to reveal all that she knew. "Terence was very clear he abhorred it."

"You see, Claxton, as Miss Stella says, it's too much of a coincidence that a dead man who didn't drink is found reeking of whiskey." The sheriff and coroner strode toward the fire.

"Tea?" Lyndy offered, holding up the steaming water kettle. Becker shook his head.

The coroner grimaced like Lyndy had suggested he drink from a chamber pot. Luckily, Lyndy glanced away at that moment to pick up his teacup. "That's probably why our man waited until everyone else had left camp. So, he could secretly imbibe."

"And a precious fossil is gone," Stella added. "That makes it all the more suspicious, doesn't it?"

"Like your supposed missing notebook?" The coroner rolled his eyes.

"I agree with Miss Stella, Claxton. There's a possibility of foul play here. Even more so than with Franz Richter."

"Exactly," Stella said. "There are too many coincidences to ignore."

"Like Lord A and Professor Gridley being conveniently nowhere to be found."

Distracted by Purdy and Letti tiptoeing out of the tent, Stella went to agree with the sheriff but stopped. "No, wait. That's not what I meant." But it was too late.

"You have a point, Becker," Claxton punctuated his words with the sharp snap of his suspenders, "and I'm nothing if not a fair man. Find the British lord and his paid paleontologist and see what they have to say for themselves. They'll need to testify at the inquest anyway. In the meantime, get this body to town for an autopsy. Then we'll see if it was an accident or murder."

"No, you misunderstood—" A small, muffled explosion and a blast of light cut off Stella's objection. Everyone's attention turned to the research tent in time to see smoke emanate from it.

Elmer Claxton marched to the tent in time to meet Purdy and Letti, who were stepping into the fresh air, still blinking from the brilliant flash. "I told you—no pictures."

Claxton grabbed the camera, but neither Letti nor Purdy would let go. The trio tugged and pulled at the fragile equipment like children fighting over a toy. Stella would've laughed if she wasn't stewing over the sheriff's accusation. Had she been complicit in his conclusions? How was she going to fix this? The photographer won the tussle when Letti kicked at the coroner's leg, forcing him to release his hold.

"Becker, do your job!" Claxton rubbed his shin, his face twisted with anger.

"That's all I ever try to do."

The sheriff ordered Letti to haul her equipment to her wagon alone while directing Purdy to help him get Terence's body into his buckboard. As the two men carried Terence's body past, his arms dangling and a sheet of canvas draped over his head to conceal his fatal, bloody wounds, the coroner glared over the swaying, lifeless form at the sheriff.

"That's not what I meant. You should confiscate that camera and arrest those two."

"I think we've got bigger problems, don't you?" Sheriff Becker grunted under the strain of the dead weight. "I may take orders from you when it comes to suspicious deaths, but there's no law that says I have to listen to you about anything else. Now let's go, Sullivan. I'm not as young as I used to be."

"And you've got two suspects to track down," Claxton reminded him.

"You wager they hold the answers to this man's death?" Purdy said, flinging Terence into the wagon like a sack of potatoes. Sheriff Becker shrugged.

Lyndy leaned in. "I'll wager we'll find them before he does."

"We have to." Stella had a knot form in her stomach as the wagons rattled away. "That's a bet we can't afford to lose."

"Here comes Mama." With the knot in her stomach tightening with dread, Stella paused, one foot in the stirrup.

Her mother wasn't alone. Judging by the kickup from the horses riding alongside the wagon, she'd brought the whole family, Clem included. Gin and Chester whinnied in greeting. Stella planted her foot on the ground again.

Lyndy took the reins and snapped them forcefully, the leather cracking sharply against the hitching post. "What are they doing here?"

It wasn't the question Stella wanted to ask, watching Clem slip from the saddle. Still, the edge in Lyndy's voice, which had nothing to do with her mother's arrival and everything to do with the worry he was trying to conceal about his missing father, drew her attention back to her husband.

"Who knows, but thank goodness they are. Now they can help look."

Stella bit her lip. Attempting to soothe Lyndy, she hadn't been completely honest. Of course, the more help, the better their chances of finding the missing men. And, of course, she wanted to spend as much time with her mother as possible. But from the moment she encountered the dead body, Stella's mind had swirled with doubt, worry, and confusion, with Mama and Lord Atherly at the core. Stella couldn't let a killer get away with murder. Even if Elmer Claxton ruled it an accident, even if Sheriff Becker dropped his investigation. It wasn't who Stella was. But would seeking the truth cause more harm than good? She refused to consider that Lord Atherly killed Terence, but what if Clem had done it? How did Stella protect Lord Atherly from suspicion and her mother from yet another betrayal?

And how do I face Mama knowing what I know?

Mama held up the large wicker basket on her lap. "We brought dinner! Thought we'd bring it to you, and I could show these men folk the fossils I found."

Her mother smiled so hard it hurt Stella's heart to look at her. Soon, Stella would have to tell her something that would banish the smile and the joy behind it. But Stella didn't have to utter a word. The moment Ned helped her mother alight from the wagon, she knew.

"Something's wrong, Sweet Pea. What is it?" Her gaze shifted from Stella's face to take in the camp and the quarry. "And where are the others? I thought Terence would've beat me to it." She knew how keen they were to get her fossils out of the ground. They still weren't sure what ancient animal they belonged to yet.

Stella hesitated, the words stuck in her throat. Lyndy slipped his arm around her waist and spoke them for her.

"We have terrible news." He squeezed Stella closer, their hips touching. Whether he hoped to comfort her or anchor himself, she didn't know, but Stella relaxed a little in Lyndy's closeness. "Papa and Gridley are missing. We found Terence dead in the tent, and that bloody sheriff thinks Papa and Gridley had something to do with it."

"My land! I don't believe it," Mama exclaimed.

Clem and Ned regarded them in frank disbelief. Stella couldn't look either of them in the eye, staring instead at the sewn tear running across the knuckles of Clem's well-worn buckskin gloves. Maria leaned against the wagon, fanning herself with the small tray she'd already fished out of the basket. Junior, who'd been playing random notes on his harmonica, nearly dropped it. And then everyone started to talk at once.

"How can another man in this camp be dead?" Clem asked.

"It's unthinkable," Maria exclaimed.

"Why do they reckon it's anything other than an accident?" Ned said.

"Did you say Lord A and the professor are out on the prairie alone?" Junior said. "But neither of them has the survival skills of a baby pronghorn!"

"What are we doing standing around talking for?" Mama's voice cut through the others. "We need to go find them."

"Agreed." Clem and Lyndy echoed each other.

"That's where we were heading, Mama."

"That Becker is plum crazy if he thinks Lord A and the professor had anything to do with it." Junior grabbed the reins of his horse and leaped back into the saddle. Everyone but Maria and Ned followed suit.

As Maria handed out fried chicken drumsticks for the trail, Ned paced between the horses and the fire ring. Once, he paused to peek into the tent. Mama called to her husband from her perch in the wagon.

"What is it, Ned?"

"Doggone it. It's just too much, Kate. We can't keep doing this."

"Doing what?" Stella patted her mare, tugging and chewing

on the bit. Stella was as eager as Gin to ride, to escape the questions and the discussions and do something. She couldn't find all the answers, but she could try to find Lord Atherly.

"This!" He removed his hat, a dark band of sweat ringing the inside, and gestured between the tent and the quarry. "I don't know how to say this, but I'm gonna have to shut this all down."

"Oh, no, Ned. You can't do that." Mama's words could've come from Stella's mouth.

"Do reconsider. My father has poured everything into this venture."

"I don't like it any more than you do, but when we find Lord Atherly and Professor Gridley, I will have to insist they pack it all up and hightail it out of here."

"But you invited Lord Atherly and the professor here. And doesn't Mama have a say? Don't any of us have a say? Doesn't your word mean anything?" Stella's tone was harsh, but his unilateral decision stung. He sounded like Daddy.

"Besides, Pa, we all know Lord A had nothing to do with Terence's death." Stella could've hugged her brother for coming to Lord Atherly's defense.

"But two deaths in a week? Can you blame me?" Ned shook his head like a stubborn bull. "No, I've made my mind up." He coughed into his fist, his features hardening. "Accident or no accident," he jabbed a finger toward the ground at his feet, "this dig is on my ranch, and I can't afford to ruin my reputation by being associated with it."

"But Ned—" The bitter edge to Mama's tone spoke volumes.

"He's right, Kate," Clem agreed. "He's doing what's best for the ranch."

After a grim glare at both Smith brothers, Mama snapped the reins and drove off.

Stella, a grim resolve hardening in her chest, held up Gin as the others followed, each taking different directions across the prairie. She bit a chunk out of her drumstick, the skin crackling as she chewed, watching Clem urge Rusty into a fast canter and head south.

And what if Ned was harboring a murderer? What would be best for the ranch then?

CHAPTER 23

Lyndy deliberately forced air from his lungs, his heart still beating hard against his chest like a bird fluttering and rebelling against its cage, and marveled at the man beside him by the fire. Papa was like some bloody phoenix. *Thank God!* Lyndy handed his father a small glass of whiskey, suppressing the urge to rearrange the horse blanket he'd hastily flung around his father's shoulders, and tried to ignore how Papa's hand shook as he raised the glass to his lips and downed the entire contents in one go.

"Another," Papa croaked, passing the glass back.

"Are you certain you don't want to see a doctor, Papa?"

"You've already washed my wounds. And my leg will heal in time. What more could a physician do?"

Would Lyndy ever be able to erase the image of his father, planted in the grass, his face caked in dirt and blood, a swath of his ripped trousers wrapped around his head, the other securing a wagon spoke to his leg, the splintered remains of their wagon scattered about them? It looked like a battlefield. Gridley had done his best playing nursemaid, but neither had been up for the long walk back to camp. Though in obvious pain, Papa had managed to put weight on his leg and mount Lyndy's horse with some aid. His leg, thank goodness, wasn't broken. Gridley, himself battered and bruised, had climbed up behind Ned under his own power. Papa had leaned heavily on Lyndy as they rode, gingerly picking their way back toward camp, and would've slipped off several times if Lyndy hadn't steadied him.

"Yes, but—" He tossed the blood-soaked handkerchief he'd used to wipe the gash on his father's face into the fire. It sputtered a few moments before flames engulfed it.

"If you're pouring..." Professor Gridley leaned closer, wagging the glass held out in his hand.

His cheek had swollen and was already turning color. Without his spectacles, the paleontologist's eyes appeared smaller, his face more vulnerable, less extraordinary than before. Like he'd lost a part of himself. He clutched the spare pair (they couldn't find the original pair beneath the debris) in his lap. Suffering from a terrible headache, the professor claimed they hurt him to wear. Eyeing the whiskey bottle, Gridley forced a wan smile. Lyndy emptied its contents into the two men's glasses. How was Lyndy going to tell them Ned was closing the dig?

And that their prized jaw fragment was gone?

"Are you up to telling what happened?" Ned rested his elbows on his knees across from them.

Not long after they'd all spread out to search the valley, Ned and Lyndy had crossed paths not far from the gold mine. Together, they'd ridden toward Claxton's land, planning to inquire after them at Moss's camp. They'd found the missing men less than a mile out. That was less than an hour ago. Stella and the other searchers had yet to come back.

"I haven't the foggiest idea." Papa took another sip of whiskey. "The surrey simply seemed to come unhitched."

"Which is odd." Ned studied the fire. Although the one Purdy had gotten started had all but gone out, with a bit of prodding and the addition of Papa's bloody rags and the makeshift wheel spoke stint, they'd gotten it roaring again. "That's always been a reliable vehicle on the ranch. That's why I sold it to you in the first place. And I fixed the wheels myself."

"We've been using that since we got here," Papa said. "And it's always handled fine."

"Having that ravine in the way didn't help," Gridley added.

"You two must've been going along at a good clip for the surrey to come apart like that." Ned raised an inquisitive eyebrow as if he'd asked a question. Neither Papa nor the professor contradicted him.

"Why were you going so fast?"

"I'm just grateful you found us before wolves or bears or some such did." Gridley chuckled nervously. He hadn't answered Lyndy's question.

"Not to mention poisonous snakes or black widow spiders."

Lyndy waited for Ned to chuckle next, but he never did. "You're bloody serious?"

"You bet I am." Ned threw the last of the whiskey he'd been sipping into the flames, which hissed in protest. "They were lucky. You have no idea how dangerous nights around here can be." He stood and, staring at Papa and the professor, frowned. "I am sorry. But I've got to look out for Kate and Junior and the ranch."

"You have to get back to your ranch duties." Papa squinted at Ned as he fetched his horse. "What's there to be sorry about?"

Lyndy's jaw tightened as Ned rode away, leaving Lyndy to explain.

* * *

Lyndy couldn't put it off any longer. Papa and the professor had a right to know. He had tugged on his waistcoat and opened his mouth to explain when the pounding of approaching horses diverted everyone's attention. Seeing Stella returning safely lightened his heart and eased his mind. Until Sheriff Becker came into view.

What's he doing back here?

"You found them!" Stella shouted as she slipped off her mount. "Where were they?" She hurried to Papa's side. "Lord Atherly, you're hurt." She reached out to touch the gash on his forehead, but he flinched away.

"I'm perfectly fine, my dear. Just a slight cut and a couple of bruises. That's all." He said nothing of his injured leg hidden beneath the blanket. "Not bad, I'd say, for spending the night under the stars."

"Without provisions, drifting in and out of consciousness." Gridley followed his elaboration with a mirthless chuckle.

"Professor, your face." Stella began to reach out to touch him, too, but pulled her hand back. "What happened?"

"As Lord Atherly said, we're back from the wars in one piece. And now that we are among our treasures from the earth again . . ." Gridley's gaze lingered momentarily on the quarry as if he'd forgotten where he was. "Where's Terence? It's not like him not to be out here. Did he and Katherine already get those specimens out of the ground?"

"Not exactly." Worry creased the corners of Stella's mouth and the skin between her brows. Like the news about the dig, Lyndy hadn't told them about Terence yet. Stella managed to add, "I met up with Sheriff Becker on my way back, and he has a couple of questions for you," before Sheriff Becker strode into the circle and began speaking without preamble or apology.

"Professor Gridley, Lord Atherly, I've come to question you about the murder of Terence Brochard."

Gridley sputtered and choked on the whiskey he'd just drunk.

"What?" Papa searched Lyndy's face for answers.

"It's true, Papa. Terence is dead." Before Papa could say more, Lyndy continued. "It was murder then?" This he directed at the sheriff, looming over them like the skyscrapers he and Stella had seen upon landing in New York City. He should've known to trust Stella's instincts. "And not an accident?" Lyndy rose. He wasn't of Becker's height, but close. "What changed your mind?" Becker had seemed a reasonable chap, but his face was closed and his eyes hard. Lyndy wanted to know why.

Cutting off whatever reply Becker might have given, Stella was the one who answered. "Seems the medical examiner discovered something even Mr. Claxton couldn't ignore. When we were riding back, the sheriff told me—"

Becker held up his hand to silence Stella. "If you don't mind, I should like to be the one to tell them." Sheriff Becker poked the brim of his hat with his finger, pushing it high on his forehead.

"Tell us what precisely?" Papa asked.

"The medical examiner was able to determine that the wound wasn't caused by Brochard hitting his head on the desk. Something more substantial hit him. A hammer, from the shape of it."

Professor Gridley rose from his seat, using the back of the chair to steady him. He limped toward the research tent, ignoring calls to assist him. He reemerged with the bloody weapon in his fist. In the bright sunlight, the path of the blood was clear. The hammer hadn't simply lain in the blood. It had been the cause of it. "This? Is this what killed Terence?"

"We believe so." Becker held out his hand, demanding the professor relinquish the hammer. Once in his possession, he slung it from his gun belt. "Who does it belong to?"

"It's mine, but anyone could've used it."

"Did you kill your assistant, Professor?"

"I say! Do we look like we could've harmed a flea, let alone a young man like Terence?" Lyndy was surprised but heartened by his father's passionate objection. A bit of color rose on his cheeks. "Besides, why in the Good Lord's name would Gridley want to do a thing like that?"

"Because Brochard was stealing from him." Sheriff Becker held up a small pocket notebook. "We found this on his body. I believe it belongs to you, Professor?"

Gridley took the notebook, raised it to within inches of his face, and thumbed through the pages, squinting. "It has my name on it, but I gave it to Terence to record any notes he might need to take in the field. As you can see, much of this is Terence's handwriting."

The sheriff had the decency to look abashed. "I thought this was the missing notebook from when Harp Richter died."

"No, that one was much larger, as are most of them. We store our permanent records in them and use them in the research tent, not in the field. Otherwise, we'd risk rain or mud or mishap. Hence the need for a smaller, more portable solution out in the quarry."

"If not you, then who did kill Terence?" Becker asked.

"Moss, of course," Professor Gridley blurted. "Maybe that's why he took a potshot at us."

"You went to Dr. Moss's camp, didn't you?" Stella said.

"How did you know?" Professor Gridley asked.

"Because she's a clever sort." Papa chuckled.

"What were you doing there?" Sheriff Becker said.

"In truth, we went to spy on his dig." Papa straightened his back until a twinge of pain passed across his face. "He boasted of a brilliant find, and we wanted to see for ourselves."

Papa had just admitted his curiosity got the better of him. If it hadn't resulted in him being lost and injured, Lyndy would've thought *Good for him!*

"And we thought to confront him about the data he stole from me," the professor admitted.

"Did you confront him?" Stella asked. "Is that when he shot at you?"

"No, we never did. But that didn't stop the reckless bastard from shooting at us. He almost got us, too, when the horse broke free and the wagon broke apart."

"The horse broke free?" Sheriff Becker rubbed the stubble on his chin. "That's odd." That's what Ned had said. "Seems I need to follow up on this. I'm going to ride out there and take a look. Not far from Moss's camp on the Claxton place, right?"

"Just follow the creek a few miles," Gridley explained. "And you'll find it."

"What are you thinking, Sheriff?" Stella asked.

"I'm thinking it can't be a coincidence that Professor Gridley and Lord A were kept from camp just at the same time someone was murdering Terence."

"You believe someone tampered with the surrey on purpose?" The color had drained from Papa's face again.

"I do. I'll have to see it to confirm my suspicions, but it sounds like someone tampered with the neck yoke."

"I would normally agree with you, Sheriff," Stella said. "I don't like coincidences either."

"But?"

"If someone sabotaged the surrey to make sure Professor Gridley and Lord Atherly weren't in the camp, how did they know they'd leave camp in the first place?"

"That's a good point. As far as anyone knew, we'd planned to stay put," the professor said.

"And what's more—" Lyndy began.

Stella finished his sentence. "If it was intentional, whoever did this might not have simply wanted to keep you from camp."

"Whatever do you mean, my dear?" Papa objected.

"Whoever did this to you..." Stella slipped her arm into Lyndy's and gazed into his face—acceptance, resilience, and determination outshining the fear he expected to find—before turning to the others. "Might've wanted to do you harm."

CHAPTER 24

~~~

Stella picked up another newspaper and read the headline—
PRESIDENT SAYS HE WILL CURB TRUSTS—before crinkling it
into a wad and stuffing it into the crate. Didn't Clem call him
the cowboy in the White House? Now, there was a man who
didn't give up. *So why are we?*

Stella carefully set the fossil specimen Lord Atherly handed
her among the newspaper. With Mama and the others still out
searching and the sheriff gone to examine the wreckage and to
submit the rock hammer into evidence for the upcoming inquest, Stella had finally told Lord Atherly and the professor
about the missing *Hypohippus* jaw. Lord Atherly might have
pooh-poohed the revelation that someone could be out to do
him harm, but at the news of his missing fossil, he'd gone as
white as the sugar he stirred into his tea, staggered to his feet,
and announced it was time to pack up and go home.

"You're really calling it quits?" As if Ned had given them
much of a choice.

"I'm afraid we are, my dear," Lord Atherly handed Stella another specimen to pack up, flinching when its weight caused

him pain. His hands were still shaking. "After everything that's happened, I do believe it's for the best."

"But don't you wonder who did all this? Who stole your prized fossil? Who sabotaged the dig and the surrey, killed Harp and Terence, and forced you and the professor out?"

"Of course I do." He sighed, his shoulders bent like a man twice his age. A few days ago, Lord Atherly was thriving, taking hardship in stride. But now, he was exhausted and in pain, and when Lyndy told them what Ned had decided, the fight had visibly drained out of him. It was painful to see. He patted Stella's cheek. "Besides, you are far better at all that than I."

Better at what? Was he asking her to keep looking for answers?

"Well, thank heaven!" Mama clapped her hands in prayer as she strode into the tent. "It warms my heart to see you two men alive and well. Though it seems..." She paused after a brief sweep of the activity in progress. "What's going on here?"

"We're packing up, Katherine." Professor Gridley and Lyndy hoisted the largest fossil into a crate.

"So, you heard what Ned said."

"We did. And he's right." With the specimen settling with a soft thud, the professor dismissed Mama's concern with a wave of his freed hand, a bluish-purple bruise darkening on the back. "It's water over the dam."

"But what about my fossil? Aren't you even going to try to finish getting it out?" Who couldn't admire Mama, her hands on her hips, admonishing paleontologists about a fossil left behind? It also put an idea in Stella's mind.

"Could that be what this is all about? Could Dr. Moss or whoever is stealing things and killing people want to scare you off so they can retrieve whatever Mama and Terence found?"

"I can't see how." Lord Atherly gently touched the new bandage on his head. "We already know it's not a *Hypohippus* vertebrate. What else would be worth killing for?"

Stella cringed. *How could anything be worth killing for?* But she held her tongue. It had to be a figure of speech. Didn't it?

"You tell us." Lyndy had come to stand beside Stella and her mother.

Lord Atherly and Professor Gridley looked at one another. Lord Atherly shrugged. He'd spent years obsessing about horse fossils. He couldn't imagine anything more valuable. The professor, on the other hand, took a broader view.

"Something unknown? Something that could catapult the discoverer into the highest echelons of academia?"

"Terence was ambitious, wasn't he, Professor?"

"Indeed, Miss Stella. I think a little bit too much so. But if you think he killed Harp over that specimen, you have to remember your mother hadn't unearthed it yet. Besides, like Lord Atherly said, Terence would be more likely to want to claim both the *Hypohippus* find and the unknown bear ancestor for himself. And we know he didn't steal those."

He had a point. But what else made sense?

"But what if he bragged about the *Hypohippus* fossil to someone else? And they killed him to get to it first?"

"Like Moss?" Professor Gridley spat his rival's name like a curse.

"Maybe."

"But whoever did all this, and why, doesn't change our fate." Upon unfolding a chair, Lord Atherly dropped into it. "We're no longer welcome on Ninebark Ranch."

Mama frowned. "Now, hold on there. My husband may have to look after the ranch, but I look after the people, and I say you are welcome to stay at the house as my guests as long as it takes. You fellas have been put through the wringer, and I'm not about to let you leave until you're fully recuperated."

"Does that invitation include me?" Stella's tone was teasing, but she had to ask. Her life was now hitched to Lyndy and his family. If Lord Atherly left, she couldn't see how she'd be able not to.

"Well, of course it does, Sweet Pea. Breaks my heart to think you'd assume otherwise. But all of this is based on one condition."

Stella tensed. That wasn't what she was expecting. Hadn't Daddy always put conditions on everything he ever did for her? But Mama wasn't like that. So, what did she mean?

Lyndy plopped the fossil he held carelessly into the nearest crate, heedless of his father and the professor's objections. "And what would that be?"

He'd asked so Stella wouldn't have to, knowing what troubled thoughts suddenly swirled through her mind. She reached for his hand and gave it an appreciative squeeze.

"It seems to me there is unfinished business here. My one condition is that you men pack up and leave us ladies to the important work." Mama winked at Stella, and she could've melted with relief. How could Stella ever have doubted her?

Anticipation fanned Stella's curiosity. "Important work?"

"Yes. I'll retrieve whatever ancient animal bone is out there, and you'll search this camp from top to bottom. One way or another, Sweet Pea, you and I will dig up some answers."

Stella threw her arms around her mother, kissed Lyndy on the cheek, and then got to work.

As frustrating as it was for Lyndy to admit, it was time to admit defeat. *And telegraph Mother.*

After Stella's best efforts came to naught at the dig, Papa and he had decided that Mother must be informed to anticipate their early return. With Papa in no shape to ride anywhere but to a soft bed at the ranch house, that left Lyndy to head into town. Stella, as he had expected, stayed behind with Katherine.

A stream of water, still standing after the storm, curved like a snake down the middle of the main street. Thankfully, the camp had dried quickly, the prairie absorbing the rain like a dry sponge. Here, horse hoofs and wagon wheels had churned up the rain-sodden gravel, forcing Lyndy to guide his horse through large swaths of mud. He located the telegraph office easily enough, the aromas from the dining room next door reminding him he'd had nothing but a chicken drumstick since breakfast. His stomach rumbled in response. He hopped off the saddle, splattering mud onto his boots and trousers, tied Chester's reins to a post, and went in.

The telegraph operator, already attending to a grizzled, rotund fellow wearing chaps, didn't acknowledge Lyndy's presence and forced him to wait. Clumps of mud dropped from his boot heels as Lyndy stomped about the tiny room. At home, in Rosehurst, if he'd entered an establishment, whether it be a haberdasher's or a newsstand, he'd have been waited upon immediately whether the clerk was aiding someone else or not. He was Viscount Lyndhurst, after all, and rank, as they say, had its privileges. But not here. It was something he still wasn't used to. Yes, his being a lord was a novelty, emboldening the lowest of cowhands or shop girls to approach and ask him all sorts of personal questions, forgetting to couple their interrogations with the respect he was accorded. Since arriving in Montana, he'd eaten at the table with servants, worked like a footman, and danced with shopkeepers' wives. But would he ever acclimate to such disrespectful treatment as this clerk was guilty of? He doubted it.

After several interminable minutes, pacing and clearing his throat as the clerk and his customer finished conducting their business (if debating the identity of a supposed petrified man the customer had seen was to be called business), Lyndy had gotten no further than an acknowledging bob of the clerk's head. Lyndy had opened the door to leave when the jingle of the bell seemed to alert the clerk to who Lyndy was.

"Yeah, aren't you one of them fellas that's out at that fossil dig on the Smiths' place?" It was a spectacularly vague statement, yet Lyndy could confirm he was. However, it still didn't get him any further in sending a telegram. Instead, he earned the rough customer's suspicious squint as the clerk leaned closer to say, "Did I tell you, Cyrus, that I actually saw that there man that was found killed out there this morning?"

That news traveled fast! Lyndy abandoned all pretense of waiting patiently, if he'd shown any, and wheeled around. "I say. Where did you see him?"

The grizzly chap's lip curled, presumably expressing a dislike of Lyndy imposing on their conversation, but stepped aside a few paces to allow Lyndy to approach the desk. The clerk seemed more than happy to enlarge his audience.

"At the Colter Hotel. I was there delivering a telegram. I passed the fella in the hall. I remember because he had something like a ledger tucked under his arm. He entered a room a few doors from where I was knocking and came out again before I'd been paid. And when he did," the clerk paused for effect, "he wasn't carrying that ledger no more."

Could it have been the missing notebook? The one stolen the night Harp died? But why would Terence have brought it here? And more importantly, why would he have left it? *Unless he was the thief.*

The grizzled man stroked his unkempt beard and nodded as if he, too, had been there, but he was quick to shoot Lyndy another disapproving scowl when Lyndy had the audacity to inquire further.

"How do you know it was him?"

"Because somebody greeted him by the name Brochard. Can't be too many folks called that around here."

"Hey, don't you want to send a telegram?" the clerk called as Lyndy abandoned the conversation and strode toward the door.

"Not unless you happened to hear more whilst you had your

ear to the door." The man's sputtered denials rivaling his companion's deep belly laugh reached Lyndy as he stepped out into the street.

The Colter Hotel was less than a block away, and Lyndy was soon pacing the marble-floored lobby from spittoon to the plush, cushioned borne settee and back, having again been forced to wait. However, Mr. Duval, the hotel manager, a small, dapper man with an eager face and no chin to speak of, reappeared momentarily, the delay more in Lyndy's mind than in reality, and showed him the diffidence he was used to. But when Lyndy asked who Terence might have met at the hotel, he proved as unhelpful as the telegram clerk.

"I am truly sorry, sir"—the manager fidgeted with a silver pinkie ring—"but I don't know this Terence Brochard. I simply recognized his name from those mentioned in the papers. Yours included, Lord Lyndhurst. Mr. Brochard certainly wasn't a guest of this establishment. He is the museum man who got killed last night, though, right?"

How did the news travel so fast? Was this Purdy Sullivan's doing?

"Perhaps you'd allow me to look in your register and see if I recognize any of the names?"

Duval slapped his palm to the register, expecting Lyndy to take it by force. "Now, that just wouldn't be right, my lord."

Lyndy sighed. How would Stella tease the information from this man's grasp? It was no use. Whatever charm or tactic that she employed was beyond his reach. He had relied on the unspoken rule that those of lesser standing did as he asked. Or he'd get Stella to find out. Neither was going to work for him here. Lyndy glanced about the lobby, occupied by two men perusing the town's daily paper in separate corners, before leaning conspiratorially against the desk. He could see his reflection in the highly polished surface. And approved of the cowboy looking up at him.

"Perhaps if I mentioned a name, you could tell me if they are or were staying here sometime in the past few days?"

The manager fidgeted with his ring again. "Perhaps."

"All you must do is move your head if I mention a name. Shall we proceed?"

Duval nodded slowly as if he was trying out their agreed-upon response.

Lyndy began with a name he knew wasn't in the registry to test the man's honesty and willingness. "William Searlwyn." The manager glanced at the book, then shook his head. "Amos Gridley." Again, a negative shake. "Franz Richter." At this, Duval looked up.

"I knew Harp, poor fella. What does he have to do with this?"

"Nothing, I suspect, but I must be thorough."

Lyndy then mentioned everyone at the dig site and began to expand his circle. He listed everyone at the Ninebark Ranch and got nothing more than a sardonic smile from the manager.

"Elmer Claxton?"

"Now, you are just being ridiculous, sir. No offense, but Mr. Claxton is the largest landowner in the county, with both a home in town and a ranch. Why on earth would he need a room here?"

Lyndy conceded the point but again admitted he was just being thorough.

"Well, why not ask if President Roosevelt has ever stayed here? As with every other name you've mentioned, I would have to express my regrets. Alas, our president favors the Dakotas and has never been to Colter City. But it would've been a better guess than Elmer Claxton."

"Very well then. It seems you are unable to help me."

Lyndy tugged at his waistcoat jacket and turned on his heel. As he passed, a man swatted too vigorously at a pesky fly and, losing his grip on his broadsheet, sent it soaring into the air. It fluttered and landed like an open book on the nearby plant stand.

Lyndy snatched the paper from the fern's abundant fronds, tossed it back to its owner, and returned to the desk.

Swallowing his pride, his curiosity too strong, he cleared his throat. "What about Dr. Aurelius Moss?"

Duval pinched his lips in disapproval, a remarkably good impression of Lyndy's mother, but his gaze slid to the register. Seems Lyndy wasn't the only curious one. Immediately, he secured a place on the page with his finger.

"Well, I'll be. It seems Dr. Moss is indeed a guest of ours," the manager said, all confidentiality and discreet nodding forgotten. "He's staying in Room 14."

I was right! Despite establishing his own dig, Moss didn't strike Lyndy as the kind of man who'd voluntarily sleep on the ground.

Lyndy fished a silver dollar from his waistcoat pocket and clasped it into the manager's palm. "You were most helpful. Thank you."

CHAPTER 25

Stella propped her elbow on the table and rested her chin in her hand. She couldn't take much more of this. Hushed tones, sad faces, and long stretches of silence had permeated the ranch house since Lord Atherly's and Professor Gridley's wagon rolled into the drive last night, signaling the end of their expedition. The somber mood now dragged into breakfast. With Lord Atherly refusing to get out of bed, the others finished their meal without two words between them. Stella had tried to draw Mama, then Lyndy, and even Maria, who was already at work shucking peas for dinner, from their thoughts, receiving monosyllable replies for her efforts. Absentmindedly stirring the sugar in her lukewarm coffee, Stella gave up, allowing the unanswered questions of the day before to fill the gap where lively conversation had existed in the days past.

Had Terence stolen the notebook and given it to Dr. Moss? Lyndy's trip into town had been a revelation. But did it get them any closer to discovering who killed Terence and why? If Terence was the one stealing for Moss, why would Moss kill him? To silence him? To avoid giving him whatever was promised? It didn't make sense. With Terence dead, Moss would never be able to publish the data without Gridley's suspicions of theft and murder being broadcast to the entire world of paleontology. His career, which he seemed intent on advancing at any cost, would be over. But if not Moss, then who? And how did Harp and Terence's deaths relate to sabotaging the camp and the surrey? Had Moss done that, too?

"Would you pass the cream and sugar, my love?" Lyndy asked in an undertone. He took his tea black but couldn't stomach drinking coffee that way.

As she obliged, Ned coughed, then scraped his chair back and stood, the harsh sound against the floor jarring Stella upright.

"Are you men ready?" Ned picked up his cup and slurped his last sip of coffee as Clem, Junior, and Lyndy followed him to their feet.

"Where are you going?" Mama asked.

Stella hadn't known of any plans either, but why wouldn't her mother? Stella had noticed Ned slept on the summer porch for the second time last night. He didn't have another early morning. Could it have anything to do with Ned demanding Mama leave the camp with her fossil still in the ground yesterday?

Haven't they made their peace yet?

Stella couldn't imagine letting an argument with Lyndy last overnight. But then again, he'd learned not to demand she do anything.

"We're moving a herd of Quarter Horses out of the foothills, and I figured Lyndy would want to use his new skills. Don't ya, son?"

"Quite! You're coming too, aren't you, my love?"

Being in the saddle all day, why wouldn't she? She couldn't get up from the table fast enough. "Of course, I want to go."

"Whoa, there, little lady," Ned said. "Wrangling is no task for a woman."

"Why not?" Stella pinned Ned with her stare.

"Wrangling can be risky."

"Riding astride a good steady horse in my split skirt, it's not any riskier for me than it is for Lyndy."

"I'd say." Once, Lyndy would've been the one to object, always trying to keep Stella safe. But no longer, thank goodness. He'd learned how capable Stella was. "My wife can more than handle herself in the saddle."

"That's very true." Professor Gridley's affirmation came as a surprise. Stella didn't even think he'd been listening. "From what Lord Atherly has told me, she was the first woman ever to compete in the New Forest's Point-to-Point Race on Boxing Day last year."

Stella held her breath, waiting for him to elaborate. That day hadn't ended well. But he didn't. Instead, he rubbed his elbow, as if hoping to assuage the pain before nibbling on a slice of bacon. Maybe Lord Atherly hadn't told him the whole story.

"Wrangling is also hard work." Ned hadn't given up.

"And dirty," Junior chimed in, but with a cheery note that did nothing to dissuade his sister.

"Lyndy's never done it, yet he was invited to help."

"She has a point, gentlemen." A lopsided grin spread across Lyndy's face. He was enjoying himself.

"Kate, will you talk some sense into your girl?"

Mama shrugged. "She's a grown, married woman, Ned. If Stella wants to ride out on the ranch, who am I to stop her? That would be up to her husband to do. Right?" Ned shot her an angry glance.

They were still feuding then.

"Thank you, Mama."

"That's settled then." Lyndy offered his arm, and Stella took it.

"I said no." Ned snatched his hat from the rack by the door. "She's only gonna get hurt. I can't risk another accident on the Ninebark."

"Of all the bullheaded . . ." Mama started to object.

Lyndy, who'd already slapped his hat on, raised it as if in salute. "Then I will respectfully decline to join you as well. After all that has happened, I was rather looking forward to spending the day with my wife."

Was that the sole reason Ned didn't want her to go? Because of the accidents? But not everything in the past few days had been accidents. Or had it something to do with her mother? Stella's focus fell on Clem as he grabbed his brother's arm and pulled him aside. Although he tried to whisper, his words were audible to the room.

"Are you forgetting that you let those two seasonal cowboys go, even with all the haying that needs doing? We need every hand we can get."

"Fine." Ned clenched his teeth and pointed a finger at her. "You do everything exactly as you're told, little lady, or I'll send you packing, you hear?"

Stella, bursting with excitement and vindication, nodded, letting her triumph push thoughts of Terence, the dig, and even Clem's unexplained late-night departure to the back of her mind.

"Thank you, Ned." Mama rested her hand on her husband's arm. "She'll be more of a help than you realize."

Ned grunted as he shoved the screen door open, letting it slam behind him. Stella squeezed Lyndy's arm, her smile so wide it almost hurt. She was going on a roundup.

"I always knew"—Lyndy chuckled under his breath as Clem and Junior proceeded him and Stella outside—"that I wasn't the only one who longed to be a cowboy."

Captivated by the majestic peaks looming large here on the furthest edge of the ranch, Lyndy alternated his attention between the scenery and the barbed-wire fence Clem was leading them through. It had been the third gate they'd passed. What it must've been like—wrangling herds of horses and cattle in the days of open range. Lyndy couldn't imagine. As it was, despite the herd they were looking for numbering in the dozens, not a single horse was in sight. And then a tinkling of a bell on the wind and Clem, Ned, and the cowboys that had augmented their group broke into a fast canter. They'd found the herd. Lyndy did all he could to keep up.

The old chestnut mare, wearing a bell around her neck, grazed among the evergreens along a northern slope. She wasn't alone, and once urged by Clem and Rusty to move, she led the others to follow. Quickly, the younger, stronger members, with much squealing and bluster, began to race one another down the hill and toward the distant open gate. With solid, steady horses beneath them, Lyndy and the others kept the herd together and moving in the right direction. Stella, her hair stuffed into a man's hat and a scarf covering half her face, maneuvered her horse, dodging this way and that with the skill that made him proud. If not for her split skirt, an outside observer wouldn't have been able to tell her apart from the men. With the crisp, pine-scented wind in his face, his wife whooping with joy as she chased a stray, Chester's hooves pounding the ground beneath him, Lyndy couldn't resist, at one point, rising in the stirrups and letting off a boisterous holler of his own. With the herd successfully in the next pasture and gathering near a shallow segment of the Cottonwood to drink, Clem approached.

"You've done well, both of you. Gotta couple of strays that wandered off before we got them through. Care to help me wrangle them?"

Stella slipped the cloth from her face, a line of grime outlining where it had been. "Absolutely." Lyndy similarly agreed.

"Junior, guard the gate. We'll be back shortly." Junior waved in acknowledgment as Clem continued to explain. "Luckily for us, the grass is coated with dew. They should be easy to track." Away from the heavily trampled area, he soon picked up their trail, which led over a series of small hills.

"There they are." Following where Stella pointed, Lyndy sighted the missing horses and a few more besides. "Didn't you say there were only two?" Without waiting for Clem's answer, Stella trotted toward them.

"Miss Stella, stay back!" Clem warned.

Stella made a quick pass by the closest horse before rejoining them. "I recognize those horses."

How could that be? Lyndy got his answer when one of the more curious strays drew closer. The brand on the filly's haunch was the same as that found on the stolen horses.

"These are the ones Sheriff Becker confiscated the other day," Stella said. "They belong to Onie Drucker. So, what are they doing here?"

"Bloody hell, Clem." Lyndy found it hard to accept. "Did you steal them back?"

Clem took off his hat and, despite the cool air, wiped perspiration from his forehead with the sizeable gray kerchief tied around his neck before answering. "You can't steal what is rightfully yours."

"What does that mean?"

"It's like this, Miss Stella. The man calling himself Onie Drucker, the one who claimed these horses were stolen from him, is the same man I bought these horses off in the first place. He claimed he was a homesteader looking to offload them quick. So they came cheap. I'd told him I was a horse rancher, and I'm guessing he assumed I'd sell them again at a higher price. Seeing as how we were over two hundred miles from here, he never dreamed he'd see me or the horses again. You can imagine my surprise, and his as well, when we came face to face. Not a very bright one, that Drucker."

"But he claimed they were stolen."

"Seems this wasn't the first time he'd pulled something like this, selling his own branded horses cheap to unsuspecting ranchers in hopes they'd trade or sell them. He's done it all over the state. It's just a matter of time before he comes across other horses he can 'reclaim' so he could sell them all over again. And he would've gotten away with it this time, too, if I hadn't seen him. He didn't factor in me recognizing him."

"And you know all this, how?" Lyndy asked.

"Because you confronted Onie Drucker the night Terence was killed, didn't you, Clem?" Stella's voice quivered with hope.

"But how—?"

"I saw you leave the ranch that night. I was hoping you hadn't gone to the dig and killed Terence."

"My God. That's what you've been thinking? How'd you even look me in the eye?"

"It hasn't been easy," Lyndy answered for her.

"Well, you're right about my finding Onie out. I took along a couple of cowboys and went into town. Wasn't hard to find the man spending money he doesn't have in a saloon." Clem smirked fondly at the sewn tear on his gloved hand. "We, uh, *persuaded* him to give back the horses in exchange for me not telling the sheriff."

"And those cowboys will testify they were with you, and you never went to the dig site?" Stella asked.

"We didn't have time to do anything else. We fetched the horses where Drucker had stabled them and loosened them out here. Ben and Jack were with me the whole time."

"What about Ben and Jack?" Ned and Whiskey had crested the hill and were trotting toward them. "And what's taking so long? The herd's getting restless, and we need to move on." His tight expression slackened in alarm as he spotted Onie Drucker's horses. "Clem, are those—? Please, tell me my eyes are deceiving me."

"Ned, I can explain."

"You have got to be joking!" Ned's face flushed as his horse, sensing the tension, pranced nervously beneath him. "What the heck were you thinking?"

"Hear him out, Ned," Lyndy said.

When Clem finished, Stella, who'd opened her mouth several times, itching to interrupt, said, "And you knew nothing about this?"

Ned shook his head, almost dejectedly, as if he didn't want to believe what he'd heard. As if the truth wasn't enough. "No, I thought the horses and the money we paid for them were gone for good. I wish you'd confided in me, Clem."

Where was the relief Lyndy had expected? Did Ned think Becker would still find out? Or was he disappointed his brother hadn't confided in him?

"I didn't want to get you involved. For now, we'll leave these here. But let's get a move on with the strays." Whether Clem truly wanted to move the horses or change the subject, Lyndy couldn't tell.

The four horse riders encircled the two strays in silence, he and Stella exchanging questioning glances whenever they could. Lyndy knew what his wife was thinking. The same question batted around in his head. Clem hadn't killed Terence, and Ned had gotten his horses back. Why, then, was there a pall over the ride as they guided the strays back toward the rest of the herd?

CHAPTER 26

～≥～

Lyndy pushed open the door and was met with near darkness despite the afternoon sunshine streaming in from behind. The air was thick with the fetid stench of old spilled whiskey, unwashed bodies, and smoke. If only he'd worn a kerchief like Clem's and Stella's around his neck. He allowed his vision to adjust to the gloom before scanning the large room for his quarry. The vaulted ceiling was covered in tin squares, the floors with dirt and grime from the street. Dilapidated heads of deer, pronghorn antelope, and elk stared glassy-eyed from all four walls. Round tables were scattered about. Most were empty. Several men standing shoulder to shoulder at the long wooden bar, the only surface approximating clean, momentarily glanced up to take the measure of the newcomer. Finding nothing interesting about Lyndy's arrival, they returned to their drinks. The man behind the bar dried a glass with a towel. Above his head, a sign in faded hand-painted yellow letters read WE TREAT YOU LIKE ROYALTY. Lyndy chuckled at the irony.

The Palace wasn't like any pub he'd ever been in.

A woman with bare shoulders and a plunging neckline sat at an empty table near the door, holding her head. The momentary sunlight flashed off the sequins sewn into her bright peacock blue dress, revealing a better glimpse of her face. Tired eyes, crinkles about her turned-down lips, she wasn't as young as Lyndy first supposed. Meeting his gaze, she rose languidly and took steps to approach him. When Lyndy waved her off, she shrugged and slumped back into her chair.

Thank goodness I finally convinced Stella to stay outside.

It had been her idea to confront Onie Drucker about Terence Brochard's murder. Terence had threatened Onie on more than one occasion. She'd reasoned that Onie might have returned to the camp that night to get the upper hand. On the trip back toward the ranch house, they agreed to detour into town. With Clem supplying the name of the saloon where he'd found Drucker the night before, the Palace was the first place they'd checked.

Drucker occupied a table toward the back, stooped over the near-empty bottle of rye and glass in front of him. His hat was pushed back, revealing dirt embedded in the creases of his forehead, and his arm was in a sling. Lyndy pulled out the chair opposite and sat.

"Hey," Drucker protested, his words slurred. "Did you ask if you could join me? Leave me alone."

"I assure you I won't remain in your company longer than I must."

Drucker finally looked up, squinting through tiny slits of his eyes. "You talk funny, mister. Do I even know you?"

"My father finances the fossil excavation on the Ninebark Ranch."

"Yeah, so?"

"And you swindled him out of some horses, claiming they'd been stolen."

"Who told you they weren't stolen?"

"The man you originally sold them to."

Drucker licked his lips, cast a glimpse over his shoulder, and poured the last of the rye into his glass, spilling some of its contents onto the table. Although Lyndy had carefully avoided even touching the dirty table's edge, Drucker ran his finger across its sticky surface, lapping up the liquid and sucking the liquid off his finger.

"I gave them back, didn't I? So, what do you want? Ain't gonna tell the law on me, are ya?"

"That depends."

Drucker threw back the contents of his glass and slammed it back onto the table.

"Watch it, fella!" The man behind the bar warned. "You break that glass, you pay for it."

Drucker dismissed the threat with a slopping wave, bringing his free elbow to rest on the table, his finger pointing straight at Lyndy.

"Depends on what, mister?"

"On how you answer my questions."

"What questions?"

"Where were you two nights ago?"

Drucker chortled. "That's an easy one." He pointed the finger perpendicular to the table. "Right here."

"When was the last time you were at the dig camp?"

Drucker tipped back in his chair, a self-satisfied grin spreading across his face. "When I got my horses back."

"And you haven't been back since?"

"Why would I? I got what I wanted."

"What's your connection to Dr. Aurelius Moss?" Stella speculated that Drucker could have been working for Moss.

"Oraylous, who?"

If he was lying, Drucker was a better actor than Johnston Forbes-Robertson. Lyndy moved on.

"How did you hurt yourself?" Lyndy jutted his chin to indicate the sling. "Get into a row with Terence out at the dig, perhaps?"

Drucker scrunched his nose up. He landed the front legs of his chair with a hard thud. "You're barking at a knot, mister. I don't even know who *Terence* is."

"The man who ran you off at the point of a shotgun," Lyndy reminded him.

"Oh, him." Drucker's lip curled. "Bastard."

"I'll ask you again. How did you hurt yourself?"

"I didn't hurt myself," he corrected with an exaggerated slur. "If you must know, this regular curly wolf wearing a gun thought I'd cheated him. He and his compadres broke my arm. Why do you want to know so much?"

"Because Terence, that bastard who ran you off, is dead."

Drucker's eyes grew into saucers. "I don't know nothing about any of that!" He shoved back from the table, trying to gain his feet, but stumbled. Toppling forward, he smacked his injured arm on the edge. Howling in pain, he slid sideways and crumpled to the floor.

Rising, Lyndy ignored the sudden silence, the stares boring into him from the bar and across the room, and leaned over the drunken fool. As he offered Drucker a hand up, he lowered his voice. "Now tell me how you truly hurt your arm."

"I told you. That wrangler from the Ninebark, the one I sold the horses to. He and a couple of cowboys found me here and snapped my arm clear in two."

"It's true," the man behind the bar offered. "Clem Smith and his boys caught up with him last night. Smith claimed they'd played faro with him in Billings and caught him cheating. Seems the feller got away before they could settle the score. He's been drinking here for two days, so he didn't put up much of a fight."

Clem's was a clever lie, but otherwise, he had been true to his word. The barman's tale proved neither he nor Drucker could have killed Terence. *Thank goodness.* Lyndy didn't suspecting the wrangler.

Lyndy helped Drucker settle back into his chair and ordered another bottle. Drucker eagerly accepted the peace offering and poured himself a drink.

"I answered your questions. You gonna tell Sheriff Becker about them horses?"

"No." Drucker might be a thief, but he was no killer. "As long as I don't hear that you've swindled other innocent people." Drucker had no way of knowing that Lyndy would never learn of such dealings, but he didn't have to know that.

"Here's to you then, mister." Drucker raised his glass to Lyndy and drank it in one gulp. Lyndy got up, disgusted. He enjoyed his whiskey, but even in his wildest days, long before he'd met Stella, he was never one to imbibe to excess. Early on, he'd been forced to acknowledge he couldn't hold his temper while drunk. Even stone sober, it was often a challenge.

And could potentially land me in prison. Lyndy had no intention of repeating that mistake.

With his hand shaking, Drucker filled his glass to the rim and raised it again. "And here's another to your pretty wife." Whiskey dribbled from the corner of the man's mouth as he gulped it.

With his resolution still echoing in his head, Lyndy clenched his fists at his sides and warned the bounder, "Leave my wife out of this" before turning abruptly on his heel and storming from the saloon so he wouldn't do something he'd regret—*like break Drucker's uninjured arm.*

As another buggy drove by, hooves clip-clopping on the hard-packed street, its driver slowing his horses to gawk like the last two, Stella fidgeted with her wedding ring, trying to ignore it. Hadn't they ever seen a woman loitering outside a saloon before? And then it dawned on her.

Maybe she should wait for Lyndy somewhere else.

Scanning the street, she weighed her options: venturing into the Sing Toy Wang restaurant—she'd never had Chinese food before—or stopping at the café advertising huckleberry pie. Her mouth watered at the prospect of either. Or she could browse the dresses she'd seen in a dressmaker's shop window the night of the dance. Mama could certainly use a few new ones. It wasn't until her gaze lit on a sign that read LANDSTROM PHOTOGRAPHY that Stella pushed away from the pillar she'd been leaning on. Craning her neck one last time, hoping to see inside, Stella strolled away from the Palace Saloon toward Letti Landstrom's studio. Lettie had taken several pictures at the dig site. One of them might provide clues about Terence's murder.

Stella shaded her eyes from the sun and peered through the studio's large front window. The shop was simply furnished, with a few wooden benches along the walls adorned with framed samples of Letti's work, a white wicker chair bracketed by a pair of plant stands, and a painted backdrop that looked more akin to a lush English country garden than the rugged mountain meadows of Montana. Letti's camera was secured to its tripod several feet away. Disappointed Letti wasn't in, Stella began to step away. But as her gaze drifted, she spotted a shelf she hadn't noticed before directly below the window sill. On it sat a myriad of curiosities—a chunk of iron ore, a bright blue thin-necked bottle, a pile of pine cones, a small stuffed squirrel, the carapace of a snapping turtle, a squirrel skull, and a rock embedded with clusters of small fossilized shells. Stella had seen the shell-encrusted rock before it disappeared. Could this be the same one?

Stella knocked. Receiving no answer, she tried the door. It was unlocked. Stella picked up the rock, inspecting it in the bright sunlight. She was right. These were the missing brachiopods. Then she picked up the delicate skull. Something told her this wasn't from a regular squirrel. She licked her thumb as she'd been taught at the dig and placed it against it. It stuck!

Letti had stolen Terence's missing bear ancestor. But why?

"Hello? Letti?" No answer. Stella set aside the fragile skull.

Clutching the rock in her fist, Stella approached an adjacent room and peeked through the crack in the door. The room was barely bigger than a closet and smelled of sharp, vinegary chemicals. Letti wasn't here either, but a string of photographs hanging from a clothesline drew Stella forward. Settling the rock among the empty trays, the various bottles and brushes, the roller, graduated glass, and the stack of dry plates set about the table beneath them, Stella studied the drying pictures. Most were portraits of farm families, cowboys, and newlyweds. Some were taken of storefronts Stella had passed on her way here. It was the last few that interested Stella most. These were of the research tent. Stella carefully unclipped the ones taken of Terence. She'd expected the scene to look less macabre in black and white. It didn't. But the photographs didn't reveal anything new either.

Stella put them back and took down the one snapped after Harp died and another from when the tent was ransacked and compared the two. There was a striking difference. The first showed no misplacement, nothing out of the ordinary. The tent was as orderly as Terence insisted upon. Stella now knew why. It was Terence who'd stolen the notebook that night, and he knew right where to look. He did not need to upend a thing. But the second showed the tent as disturbed as Stella remembered. But seeing that moment captured in time didn't help her discover the rhyme or reason behind it. It was as if the trespasser's sole purpose was to be destructive. And yet, the stolen fossils had been sitting on Letti's ledge. Could she have overturned the tent? But why, when she could swipe the fossils while she photographed inside the tent and have no one the wiser? Could it have been an animal? Again why? What food they had was stored in a trunk in the cabin. And no ravenous critter had tried to assault Lord Atherly yet. Could Moss, hoping to steal data again, have become so enraged by Gridley locking the notebooks up in his new safes that he damaged the tent out of spite? Or could a band of mischievous tourists have enjoyed a drunken escapade at the paleontologists' expense? Stella was gripping at straws.

Frustrated, Stella picked up the rock and gripped it in her fist until the fossils left little shell-shaped indents in the skin of her palm. She put it down and examined the photographs again. There had to be something here. Studying the first one, she found nothing new. She held up the second photograph, reinspecting every inch of it. And found nothing new. Wait. What was that? Half-covered by papers flung loose on the ground was a pencil with visible chew marks. What was Purdy Sullivan's pencil doing there? Had he lost it? And if so, when?

Footsteps alerted Stella she was no longer alone. Absorbed in thought, she hadn't heard the front door. And they were coming closer, not with the natural pace of Letti going about her business but with the deliberate hesitation of a wildcat stalking its prey. But who else could it be? At the click of the door latch behind her, Stella tossed the photographs into one of the empty trays and snatched up the rock. Light flared without warning. Momentarily blinded, Stella flinched but raised the rock like a weapon.

"I wouldn't do that if I were you."

Stella wheeled around, prepared to strike, but froze midswing. It was Letti Landstrom standing before her. But in her hand, she held her derringer. And she was aiming it point blank at Stella's face.

"Miss Stella! You gave me an awful fright."

"I could say the same of you, Letti." With her heart still in her throat, Stella lowered the rock in her fist. "You're the one pointing a gun at me, after all."

"Oh, this?" Letti laughed nervously as she held up the small pistol, the barrel pointing toward the ceiling, and inspected it as if she'd never seen the intricate carving on the silver plating before. "I keep it for protection. A woman can't be too careful."

She paused, and the moment drew out long enough for Stella to imagine what Letti needed to be protected from. Would she say? She didn't. Stella was relieved. Some things didn't need to be said.

"If I'd known it was you, I'd never have pulled it out. But I'd left in a rush and realized I hadn't locked the studio's door. When I noticed motion in my darkroom, I feared the worst. I once had a drifter break in and sleep the night here. It took a lot of convincing and this gun to get him to leave. By the way, what are you doing here?"

"As you said, the door was unlocked. I just wanted to look at the pictures you'd taken of the research tent. I was hoping to shed some light on Terence Brochard's murder."

"Find anything?"

"I'm not sure." Stella hadn't lied. She didn't know if Purdy's pencil meant anything. But something kept her from telling Letti about it.

"Well, if you need a closer look, we can bring them out into the light. Maybe you'll see something you missed. I have a magnifying glass you can use, too."

Letti pulled the pertinent photographs from the empty tray and leaned past her to slide open a drawer Stella hadn't noticed under the table. The magnifying glass lay on a cardboard box labeled ROEBUCK DRY PLATES. Letti still hadn't lowered her pistol.

Stella took Letti up on her offer, gratefully stepping out into the main room where she could see people passing in the street, but she found nothing more in the pictures than she had before. Stella handed back the stack of photographs and the magnifying glass. All except the one with Purdy's pencil.

"Thank you. Do you mind if I hang on to this one?"

"If it will help." Letti set the others on the nearest bench. "Wish I could help more." She ambled over to admire one of her photographs, a large family dressed in their Sunday best proudly standing in front of their humble cabin. There must've been seven children, including a babe in arms.

And I can't even have one. Stung by a sudden desperation, Stella had to look away.

Oblivious to Stella's internal conflict, Letti stepped closer and then, as if finding the still scene wanting, shrugged as she stepped away.

"Most of my work is taking family photographs, or businesses hire me to take pictures of their stores to use in advertisements or to hang on their walls. It pays the bills, but it can get boring. Long trips out to lonely homesteads. I've done that three days running. Even had to spend the night at one."

"Was that the night Terence Brochard died?" Stella jumped at the opportunity to find out Letti's whereabouts.

"How'd you guess?" Letti shrugged brightly, continuing with her previous train of thought. "Photographing the dig wasn't the usual. I had so much fun out there. Too bad it's been plagued with calamities. Your father-in-law and Professor Gridley are such a pleasure to be around. They don't deserve that."

Letti's compliments recalled the warm welcome the photographer gave Lord Atherly that first time at the dig. Like they'd known each other for years, not a matter of days. "I don't have to remind you Lord Atherly is married."

Letti laughed, dismissing Stella's concern with a wave of her hand. Unfortunately, it still held her gun. "I don't have any designs on Lord A if that's what you mean. He's like the kindhearted father I never had."

Letti's face abruptly fell, memories, maybe of the kind of father she did have, surfacing. Stella could empathize. Her father was a horrible man, and Lord Atherly was nothing but kind. Still, Stella couldn't let her empathy stop her from pressing Letti for answers. But first things first. Stella retrieved Letti's handbag from where she'd dropped it to the floor and held it out.

"Would you mind putting the pistol away?"

Letti blushed. "Gosh, Miss Stella, you got me thinking of things, and I guess I forgot I was still holding it."

Or she still didn't feel safe. Either way, Stella breathed a sigh of relief when Letti slipped the gun into the handbag and set it with the photographs and magnifying glass on the bench. She tweaked her nose.

"You're lucky, you know. To have Lord A as a father-in-law. He's such a gentleman." Letti's hand clenched where the gun used to be. Again, bad memories flitted across her face.

"And what about Franz Richter or Terence Brochard? Were they gentlemen?"

"The men that died? Neither uttered more than a few words to me." Was that an answer? Stella wasn't sure. Stella studied Letti's expression and found no telltale sign of ill feelings.

"What about Dr. Moss?"

"Who?"

"And Mr. Sullivan?"

Letti shrugged. "Purdy? He's nice enough."

"You and he always seemed to arrive at the dig together. Do you work together quite a bit?"

"No, he just wanted photographs to send back to his newspaper. He was insistent, desperate even, though he couldn't pay much. But I was happy to oblige."

"And that's all that's going on between you?"

Letti's laugh was mirthless. "Purdy Sullivan has his eye on someone, Miss Stella. She's just not me." She glanced at the simple silver watch brooch she wore, then at her camera. "I've got Mr. and Mrs. Dietz arriving any minute. Did you need anything else?"

"Where were you the night Harp died?"

"You don't suspect me, do you?" Letti started to walk Stella toward the door. She didn't answer the question.

"Then why did you take this and the fossilized skull?" Stella raised the rock she still held.

"Believe me, I had no idea what a fuss it would cause." Letti opened the door.

Stella stood her ground. "You admit to stealing them?"

"I took them as souvenirs." She pointed to her curio shelf. "I collect unusual things to photograph, and they had so many. I didn't think they'd miss one rock and a tiny skull. I just loved those shells. But when Lord A got so upset, I didn't have the heart to admit I took them. He's been so nice to me."

Lord Atherly's distress had nothing to do with these particular fossils, but Stella didn't tell Letti that.

"But why not bring them back?"

"How?"

Stella could think of a few ways, including slipping them back onto a table without anyone the wiser. Wasn't that how she'd taken them?

After Stella bid her goodbye and stepped into the street, Letti crossed one foot over her threshold while still clinging to the door jamb.

"You won't tell Lord A I took his fossils, will you?" The woman who threatened Stella with a gun, who independently ran her business, regarded Stella with the pleading eyes of a puppy.

"No, Letti. Lord Atherly will be overjoyed just to have them back. Your secret's safe with me."

CHAPTER 27

Stella put her ear to the door, carefully avoiding the chipped, ragged edge, and knocked again. The hollow sound echoed in the empty, unadorned hallway. Hearing no motion, she finally stepped aside.

"I don't think he's in there."

Lyndy tried the door as if Stella hadn't already and, finding it locked as Stella had, pounded the side of his fist against it, rattling the loosely tacked-on brass-plated number four. They knew it wouldn't bring Purdy to the door faster, but it helped vent his frustration.

Stella put a hand on his arm. "Let's just go talk to the sheriff."

After reuniting with Lyndy across the street from the saloon, Stella had swapped information with him—she about Letti taking the fossils and finding Purdy's pencil in the photo, he about Onie Drucker's drinking binge and corroboration of Clem's story. They'd agreed that they should talk to Purdy. But with Purdy not in his hotel room, the next best option was to see if Sheriff Becker had any news.

A short walk from Purdy's cheap hotel brought them to the

county jail. After the musty odors of old carpet and stale cigars, the fresh air mingled with honest barnyard scents came as a relief. The large, square, unembellished red brick building stood behind the county courthouse, its purpose advertised by the iron bars on its windows. The sheriff stood at a corkboard plastered with wanted posters advertising rewards from twenty-five to a thousand dollars for everything from missing persons to embezzlers. Despite its faded ink, one offering four thousand dollars for the capture of Robert Leroy Parker, aka Butch Cassidy, stood out. The clean-shaven, square-faced man, who looked more like a farmer than a murderer, glared back at her.

Sheriff Becker paused pinning a new one for a bail jumper among them as they entered. "Don't tell me someone else has died?"

"No," Stella replied, "we just thought you might have news. Did you find the surrey or talk to Dr. Moss?"

The sheriff finished his task and sat on the corner of his desk, crossing a booted foot over his knee. "I had a look at the surrey, and it was plain someone took a saw to it, cutting it partway, knowing full well it would snap eventually. But who or for what purpose, I don't know yet. Unfortunately, with Lord A and the professor relatively unharmed by the incident, I have to focus my time on the Brochard case."

"And Moss?" Lyndy asked.

"He denies everything, of course."

"Even shooting at my father?"

"Even that."

"What about the Brochard case? Have you learned anything more there?"

Sheriff Becker folded his arms across his chest with slow deliberation. "Now, that's none of your concern, Miss Stella. Murder is no topic for a lady such as yourself."

Stella dismissed the rebuke. It was ridiculous. She and Lyndy had found the assistant's body. *And many more besides.* "It's officially a murder now?"

For a moment, Becker studied his well-worn, creased leather boot, picking at dirt embedded along the outward seam. "No, you're right. Claxton is still convinced the second death was an accident, too."

"It's almost as if he's being mulish on purpose," Lyndy quipped.

Could Lyndy be right? Was Claxton trying to convince an inquest jury that Terence's death was an accident, too? All so he could benefit from the Crow land sales?

"But haven't you learned more from the medical examiner's report?" Stella asked. "Didn't that confirm that the hammer killed him? Doesn't Mr. Claxton have to consider that?"

"Legally, he does, but Claxton . . ." Becker left any accusation left unsaid. "Was there anything you wanted to tell me?"

"Actually, there is. But it's more something we want to show you." Stella produced the photograph Letti had given her.

Becker held it up to the light, squinting. "What is it I'm looking at?"

"Letti Landstrom took this photograph after the research tent at the dig site had been ransacked and the fossils had been stolen."

"Okay. And?"

"Well, first of all, Letti admits to taking all but one of those fossils while shooting these photographs. She wanted some souvenirs and didn't think they'd be missed."

"And?" The sheriff's voice was growing more impatient. "I see lots of rock and fossils in this photograph."

"This is the important one." Stella pointed out the *Hypohippus* jaw fossil. "It went missing after Terence was killed."

"Are you saying you suspect the woman photographer of murder?"

"No, as I said, it was still there the last time Letti was in the tent. And she couldn't have returned for it because she was taking a family's photograph far out of town. She spent the night at their homestead. I'm sure you could check if you'd like."

"Not unless I have a good reason. But if she didn't kill him, why even bring her up?"

"Because that one fossil is still missing."

"And perhaps the killer absconded with it?" Lyndy added.

"It may also be why Terence was killed."

"Over an ancient bone?" Becker tossed the photograph onto the desk among more wanted posters. Stella readied her response, but Becker continued, "But then again, these fossil hunters have been known to do drastic stuff. Look at how those others—Cope, Powell, and Marsh, wasn't it?—went at each other in the newspapers. Imagine what they'd do if they were fighting over the same patch of ground."

"That's exactly why we think Dr. Moss might have something to do with it. He's the only one who would know the fossil's value. Outside of Professor Gridley's excavation team, that is."

"You think Dr. Moss came into the camp to steal the fossil, and Terence caught him in the act and tried to stop him?"

"Either that or Purdy Sullivan did."

"What does that dandy have to do with it?"

"That's what we'd like to know." Stella stabbed her finger on the photograph. "That pencil belongs to Purdy Sullivan. It wasn't in the photograph taken after Harp Richter died, and from what I remember, Purdy wasn't allowed in the research tent after that."

"Until, of course, he slipped in after Terence died," Lyndy said.

Sheriff Becker picked up the photograph to study it again. "So, what is it doing there?"

"That's what we want to know."

After checking at the hotel again and confirming with the desk clerk that Purdy had returned but left again, the trio had walked up and down Main Street—Stella poking her head into drugstores, haberdasheries, and blacksmiths while the men checked out the saloons and billiard parlors. They found Purdy Sullivan dining in one of a string of Chinese businesses. Though he tried to be discreet, Lyndy craned his neck at every sign plastered with Chinese characters and peered into every shop window, whether displaying drying ducks or laundry. He couldn't look more like a tourist. Stella would've laughed to see him so blatantly curious if their mission were any less serious.

Considering the modest frame exterior, the interior of Wu's was surprisingly grand, with intricate mahogany fretwork, low-dangling chandeliers, and a bright wall-to-wall red carpet. The exotic smells of ginger and garlic and who knew what else made Stella's mouth water. The proprietor welcomed the sheriff by his given name and began showing them to a table.

"Thanks all the same, Ming, but we're not here to eat." His friendly refusal implied Mr. Wu's assumption wasn't usually off the mark. Sheriff Becker was a regular customer here. "We just need to have a word with one of your customers." As he spoke, he stared at Purdy Sullivan, who stopped mid-bite, thick strands of brown noodle dangling from his fork.

"If you're here on business, Sheriff, please take it outside."

"Of course." Sheriff Becker motioned for Purdy to join them. Purdy slurped up the noodles, wiped his mouth with a napkin, and pushed back from the table. He was in no rush.

"What's this all about, Sheriff?" Purdy eyed Stella and Lyndy as he joined them.

The sheriff didn't answer until they were all back on the street. Even then, he led them away from passersby to an alley where sacks of rice had been piled on top of wooden crates filled with Stella knew not what. Only Chinese characters were stamped on the sides.

"Show him the photograph, Miss Stella."

Having rolled it up and stuffed it in her waistband, where it half stuck out, Stella produced it like the sword from the stone.

She handed it to Lyndy to hold taut while she pointed. "That's your pencil, isn't it?"

Purdy bit his lip. "So that's where that went."

"You admit it's yours then?" Lyndy let go, and the photo's edges rolled in on themselves.

"Of course. It's my lucky pencil, but I lost it."

"Could you have lost it when you killed Terence Brochard?" Sheriff Becker was goading him. The photograph had been taken before Terence was killed. But that didn't mean Purdy hadn't come back.

Purdy buckled as if he'd taken a blow to the stomach. "What? How do you arrive at that? I lost a pencil, for goodness' sake, not a weapon."

Stella could've instructed him on how even the most innocuous, mundane items could be used to kill, but instead, she asked, "Then why was your pencil in the research tent?"

"I don't know. I must've dropped it there before Terence was killed, or it wouldn't be in that photograph."

Becker shot a disgruntled glance at Stella as if her failed logic had gotten them to this point.

"But you were never allowed in the research tent," she said. "If you went in sometime between Harp's death and when the tent was ransacked, who's to say you didn't come back?"

"Who's to say you didn't kill Terence Brochard?" Sheriff Becker was insistent.

"Whoa," Purdy held up his hands, palms out. "I didn't kill anybody. I wasn't anywhere near there. And there's someone else who can swear to it."

"And who would this someone be?" the sheriff asked.

"A lady who I will not name."

"How convenient. Then it's as if you have no alibi at all."

"And you still haven't explained how your pencil got in the research tent," Stella pressed, trying to catch his eye. He refused to meet it. He must be hiding something. "Maybe you killed Terence after all."

"Why? Why would I kill him?"

"Because he caught you stealing a valuable fossil for Moss." With the photograph rolled tightly like a tube in his fist, Lyndy smacked it against his palm and took a step forward. "Perhaps Terence caught you? And you were forced to silence him?"

"Now, now. You've got this all wrong." When Sheriff Becker joined Lyndy, Purdy retreated against the crates, knocking one to the ground. A tabby tomcat darted out from under them with a malicious hiss and dashed toward the street. "I didn't steal anything. I didn't kill anybody."

"Then why were you in the tent?" Stella stood on her toes to see Purdy between the two other men's shoulders.

Beads of sweat streaked from under the band of Purdy's hat. His breathing grew fast and shallow. He licked his lips, his eyes darting over the men's shoulders to the alley's end and the street behind. A wagon loaded with metal milk jugs rattled by.

"Answer the lady." When Purdy wasn't forthcoming, Lyndy loomed closer to the cowering man, blocking any path of escape. "Why were you in the tent?"

"Because I need to keep my job!"

Sheriff Becker tapped Lyndy on the shoulder, urging him to ease off. "Care to explain, Mr. Sullivan?"

"My editor was sending me telegrams, making threats. He was cutting me off and demanding I take the next train back if I didn't come up with something big quick. But I didn't want to leave. Not yet. So, all I needed to do was . . ." He licked his lips again.

"Was to do what, Mr. Sullivan? Or should we continue this conversation at the county jail?"

"To do . . . something drastic?" He shrugged, flashing them a feeble smile. "So, I ransacked the tent."

"What? Why?" Stella squeezed past Lyndy and shouldered a startled sheriff aside to face the reporter close up. She could smell the ginger on his ragged breath.

"Because I needed to make something happen. And what

better way than to capitalize on the cursed fossil dig? First, Lord A goes missing, then Harp Richter falls to his death, and then the tent is ravaged by unknown forces. Audiences back east love that kind of stuff."

"And you were going to blame it on innocents?" Whether he intended to incriminate people or animals, Stella was appalled by the thought. Purdy refused to say, but his reddened cheeks answered for him.

"And then fancy it when Gridley wouldn't allow you into the tent," Lyndy said. "You couldn't write a story about something you supposedly knew nothing about."

Stella caught Lyndy's train of thought. "So, you did something bigger, more sensational." How far would he go for his story? Would he kill Terence? Would he . . . "That's why you sabotaged the surrey, isn't it?"

"I'd like to think it was newsworthy, yes," Purdy said.

"Are you saying you're the cause behind my father's and the professor's wagon accident?" Lyndy's hands curled into fists, crumpling the photograph. Stella pried it out of his grasp.

"Yes, I admit it. I found a handsaw in the tent and . . . well, you know the rest." Purdy put his hands up in mock contrition. "But to be fair, I spotted you driving the surrey in town. I thought it was yours, not Lord A's. That poor fellow's been through enough. I never would've done it if I'd known he'd be in it."

"But you have no problem with me and my husband spilling into a ravine?" Stella couldn't believe what she was hearing.

"I couldn't guarantee when the horse would break away, but I had high hopes. LORD AND LADY TAKE A VIOLENT TUMBLE." Purdy spelled out his headline in the air in front of him. "It would've made the front page."

"Especially if either of them had died," Sheriff Becker growled.

"I'm not denying sensational deaths, especially of important folks, sell papers. Look at all the articles about Harry Kendall

Thaw, Evelyn Nesbit's murderous husband. I have to compete with that. But I never intended for either of you to get too hurt. Surely you understand that, Miss Stella? Lord Lyndhurst?"

Purdy pushed off the crates, sending another tumbling to the ground. He winced at the sound of porcelain breaking.

Lyndy flexed his fingers, his muscles wound up like a spring, but without Stella insisting, he stepped back and shoved his hands into his trouser pockets. "No, I fail to understand your cavalier attitude toward creating havoc and chaos."

Unfortunately, Stella did understand. Purdy wasn't that different from her father. Each envisioned a goal they wanted and did what it took to obtain it—regardless of whom they hurt. "It's just good business, right, Purdy?"

"Exactly. The more newsworthy the article, the happier my editor is, the longer I get to stay in Montana."

"And what's so special about Montana?" An image of her mother joyfully uncovering her fossil find flashed into Stella's mind. "Or should I say who in Montana is so special?"

"Now, now, Miss Stella. I told you I wasn't going to say." He wagged a knowing finger at her.

So, it was a woman, then. The one who could supposedly give him an alibi. But why won't he reveal her name?

"Two deaths at the fossil dig weren't enough to keep your editor happy then, eh?" Lyndy slipped his arm protectively around Stella's waist as she stepped back.

"It most certainly was," Purdy was warming to his audience, his earlier fright seemingly forgotten. He removed his hat and placed it over his heart. His hair was slicked back with sweat. "To be honest, if I'd known Terence was going to be murdered, I wouldn't have had to stage those other accidents."

"Or did you murder Mr. Brochard because those staged accidents weren't enough?" Sheriff Becker had watched silently as Purdy regained his composure. Purdy fumbled his hat, catching it by the brim to keep it from falling.

"What? No. I told you. I didn't kill anyone."

"Likely story." The sheriff scoffed, his scowl signaling he was unaware of his pun. "James Sullivan, I'm arresting you for the murder of Terence Brochard."

He pulled a pair of handcuffs hanging off his gun belt and clapped them around Purdy's wrists. Out of the corner of her eye, Stella caught Lyndy flinch, no doubt reliving his encounter with the cold metal shackles. Despite Purdy's squirming, Sheriff Becker managed to lift his hat to Stella.

"Much obliged for your help apprehending the killer, Miss Stella."

Purdy tried to drag his feet, but he was no match for the sheriff. "But you've made a mistake."

Whether he was accusing her or Sheriff Becker, Stella couldn't tell. But watching the sheriff push the reporter into the wider street, shouting his denial, brought her no relief, no satisfaction. Purdy had admitted to some heinous things, but did Purdy murder Terence? She wasn't so sure.

Could they have gotten it wrong?

CHAPTER 28

"Where did you find them?" Papa winced as he tried to rise too swiftly from his chair, only to plop back down again. Despite the mild breeze, he dabbed his brow of perspiration.

"Take care, Papa." Lyndy rested one hand on his father's shoulder while placing the shell-encrusted rock and skull Letti had taken into his outstretched, open palms. When they arrived at the ranch, Stella had handed the fossils off to Lyndy to return while she went into the house to tell her mother what they'd learned. Lyndy had found Papa and the professor drinking tea on the porch watching Junior and Clem clean Rusty's hoofs in the stable yard.

"Someone from town pinched them." Stella had insisted Lyndy help keep her promise. He didn't mention Letti's name.

"One of the tourists from town, eh?" Lyndy didn't correct him. "They seemed a congenial bunch, and all along, one of them was scheming to steal from us."

"Perhaps you've got it wrong, Papa. Perhaps they didn't mean any harm and just wanted a souvenir. Didn't fancy you'd miss a couple when you had so many?"

"Miss a couple? Did you hear that, Gridley?" Papa broke into a fit of laughter, leaning conspiratorially toward the professor.

Did Papa actually nudge the paleontologist with his elbow? It heartened Lyndy to see his father being lighthearted again. He'd begun to despair when he'd found Papa hadn't bothered to dress.

"How little people understand." Papa held the skull to the light, admiring it like a finely cut diamond. "One fossil can make all the difference."

"Nor does the size equate to a specimen's import," the professor added. "Take this for example. With Terence having found this," he pointed to the skull resting in Papa's palm, "we may yet describe a new species. This may look small to you, but to Terence, it may have been the key to a new world and a very bright future."

"Any word of the *Hypohippus* jaw?"

"It's still missing, I'm afraid."

With his earlier mirth vanished, Papa handed the rock and skull to Gridley as if he'd lost all interest.

To curtail Papa's backslide into negativity, Lyndy pressed on with what they'd learned. "But the big news is—"

"Look here, Ned," Gridley interrupted. "Some of our missing specimens have been recovered."

"Glad to hear it, Professor."

Lyndy turned to see Ned approach. With his broad shoulders slightly stooped and a day's gray stubble on his chin, Ned looked older, more tired than he had this morning. "Long day?"

"Not any more so than usual, son. Appreciate your help this morning. Almost ready for supper, Junior?"

Junior pointed to the hoof Clem was cleaning. "Almost, Pa."

"Where did you and Miss Stella get off to?" Clem paused from his task to exchange the hoof pick for the brush Junior held.

"Had an errand in town." Lyndy didn't elaborate on how he'd checked his story by confronting Onie Drucker.

Junior pointed the hoof pick at Lyndy. "You were about to tell us some more big news. Weren't you, Lyndy?"

"Indeed." Lyndy paused to guarantee he had everyone's attention. "You should all know that Purdy Sullivan has been arrested for Terence Brochard's murder."

"I say! That is wonderful news!" Papa exclaimed. Professor Gridley agreed heartily.

"Didn't see that coming." Ned tucked his thumbs under his suspenders. "But what a relief."

"Who's Purdy Sullivan?" was Junior's question.

Clem let the horse's hoof drop and smacked him affectionately on the rump. "That reporter? What convinced the sheriff he did it?"

"What difference does it make?" Ned said. "They caught the killer. We can sleep soundly in our beds again."

"I didn't know you were worried, Pa."

"Not really." Ned forced a smile to reassure the boy. Evidently, Junior hadn't noticed where his pa had been sleeping lately.

"But aren't you curious why he did it, Ned?" Clem pressed.

Ned shrugged. "I'm curious what's for supper."

"Or how he was caught?"

"I can speak to that." Lyndy had been savoring the relieved smiles his news brought, but now he credited Stella with scrutinizing Letti's photographs and discovering the missing pencil.

"But he wasn't allowed in that tent," the professor objected. "At least not before Terence's death."

"Precisely. So, along with Sheriff Becker, we tracked down and confronted the man. He admitted to ransacking the tent and sabotaging the wagon. All for the sake of a sensational story he could write about."

"That scoundrel was responsible for our being pitched into a ravine?"

"He was, Papa."

"But that doesn't make him a killer," Clem said.

"He could've killed us." Papa nodded vigorously at Gridley's assertion.

Clem untied Rusty's reins. "Did he confess?"

"No, but he did refuse to get himself an alibi. The sheriff reasoned it was because he didn't have one. And if Purdy was willing to endanger any one of us by sabotaging the wagon, then it wasn't a stretch that he'd killed Terence for a story, too."

"I don't know. Seems like a stretch to me." Clem's doubts echoed those Stella had voiced on the ride back to the ranch. Lyndy had reluctantly agreed.

"What difference does it make?" Ned said. "The man is behind bars. We can get on with our lives."

"I wish Lord Atherly and I could."

"Why can't you, Professor?" Junior had produced his harmonica from a pocket but paused with the instrument inches from his face to ask.

Gridley adjusted his spectacles. "Well, to us, Junior, getting on with it extends to our fossil expedition. It was what we'd planned to do all summer. But to protect the reputation of the ranch he's worked so hard for, your father wishes us to leave."

"And rightly so." Papa sat up in his chair. "We wouldn't want to cause any more harm to you or your dear mother."

"Well, Pa? The sheriff got the killer. Couldn't Lord A and the professor go back to their dig?"

Ned frowned. "I don't know."

"Please, Pa?"

"Katie sure would like to finally get her fossils out of the ground," Clem said.

"I know she would. But can we keep it quiet, just between us? No sheriff, no tourists, no photographers?"

"And no meddling, usurping hack who dares call himself a paleontologist?" Gridley held up his hand. "You have my word."

Ned sighed, a weak smile flitting on his lips. He knew when he'd been beaten. "Then can't see why not."

Junior threw his hat into the air. Papa and the professor shook Ned's hand in gratitude. All around him, the other men were celebrating the end of an ordeal. Then why couldn't Lyndy shake the feeling it was only the beginning?

From the easy banter, laughter, and enthusiasm pervading the camp, an outsider might've supposed they were celebrating a holiday. Stella knew better. After days of death, stress, and worry, everyone was eager to put all the ugliness behind them. It didn't matter that Lord Atherly and the professor were still recovering from their injuries. Happily preoccupied, the pair seemed to forget their pains. It didn't matter that the inquest was set for tomorrow, and the same two were compelled to attend. This time, a man had been arrested. How could Claxton and his jury find it was anything but murder?

Or at least that's what the others thought.

After a hearty breakfast, everyone except Ned and Clem, who still had a ranch to run, packed up the wagons and rode back to camp. With all hands helping (wouldn't Lady Atherly shudder to see her son and husband working like footmen unloading a carriage?), the crates, the boxes, the trunks that had been removed found their way back to the tents that hadn't been dismantled yet. Within a couple of hours of arriving, it was as if they'd never left.

"Now for the fun part!" Lord Atherly bounced on his toes as Professor Gridley handed out the dustpans and tools.

Mama took hers eagerly. "I've been thinking about this all night. Haven't slept a wink."

Mama dropped to her knees and began to work the soil around her fossil find. As if she'd been a trained professional, she instructed Maria at her side on how to help. Stella made up the trio. At first, the three women chatted about the yield of Mama's lush garden, Maria's visit to Yellowstone National

Park, how Clem might incorporate the Kentucky Thoroughbreds into the herd, and the undeniably irritated content of the telegrams they'd begun receiving from Lady Atherly. But it didn't last. The conversation soon lapsed as Mama concentrated on her task, offering monosyllable responses. Stella, Maria, and Mama spent the next hour in silence, the sun warm on their backs, the ground hard under their knees, brushing away soil to find only more soil beneath. But what did that matter? Stella was doing it elbow to elbow with the one woman whose company she craved. Stella loved spending time with her mother, and something told her time was running out.

As a pointed projection from the primary fossil emerged beneath their brushes, the professor shouldered his way between Stella and Maria.

"Lord Atherly, come here. Come take a look!"

Professor Gridley's joyful call brought Lord Atherly, Lyndy, and Junior to his side. Lyndy put a hand on Stella's shoulder. Bending over Maria, Lord Atherly blocked out the sun. He stepped hastily to the side to let light on the specimen again.

"Is that what I think it is?"

The professor nodded, glee shining from every pore on his face. He pointed. "See the horn projection?"

"What is it? What have I found?"

"You, madame, I believe, have uncovered a member of the rhinoceros family."

"Really?" Mama beamed at the professor. Catching Stella smiling at her, she winked. Stella's smile widened.

"Rhinoceros?" Junior scratched his head. "I thought those are only found in Africa?"

"Living ones are. But recent expeditions have discovered several possible species originating in North America long ago."

"Too bad they're all gone. I would've liked to see a rhinoceros." Junior stared at the nearly completely exposed fossilized bone. "How come they died?"

As the professor happily expounded on the current scientific debate of that question, Stella, in sudden need of support, sat back on her heels and leaned against Lyndy's legs. He squeezed her shoulder affectionately as he, like the others, listened with rapt attention as the professor described how Mama's find fit into it.

Junior's word choice had sparked the embers of questions burning at the back of Stella's mind.

Why did Terence die? So that Purdy Sullivan could write about it? Stella internally shuddered at the senselessness of it. But did Purdy even do it? All the evidence against him was the pencil in the photograph. *And his willingness to do anything, no matter how careless or destructive, for a story.* But what of his alibi? Would he finally name his companion if his neck was in a noose?

And if not Purdy, who else could it be?

As if the image she'd conjured in her mind came to life, Dr. Aurelius Moss tore into the camp, pulling his horse up abruptly at the quarry's edge. The soil and dust the horse kicked up billowed around them, getting in their mouths and causing everyone to cough.

"What do you think you're doing here?" Professor Gridley shouted, drawing everyone but Mama to their feet.

Lyndy had told Stella of the professor's promise to Ned. And his unease over the arrangement. And he'd been right to be concerned. It was a promise the professor couldn't keep. Curious tourists from town might stumble in, and here was Dr. Moss just hours after they'd returned. If Dr. Moss breathed one word about their return to the dig, Ned might change his mind.

Dr. Moss slid from the saddle, brandishing a large notebook. He hurled it into the dirt, and it landed with a soft thud on the professor's feet. "You're a crook, Amos."

"That's rich coming from you, Aurelius."

"I say!" Lord Atherly brushed the dust off his chest. "What's the meaning of this, coming onto our site throwing accusations," and indicating the notebook, "and valuable information about?"

Stella retrieved the notebook and began flipping through its pages. Drawings, diagrams, and notes scribbled along the margins accompanied the copious writing. It was the one taken the night of Harp's death. "You did have the stolen notebook!"

Dr. Moss ignored Stella's accusation, snatching the notebook from her grasp as he stormed past. "I should've shot you when I had the chance, Amos." He leveled it like a knife inches from the professor's face. "You falsified the data, didn't you? When did you stoop so low?"

Undaunted by the threat, Professor Gridley removed his glasses and began wiping them vigorously with a cloth. "When you stooped to stealing it."

"I . . . Well . . ." Dr. Moss blustered, his face red with fury. Of course, Dr. Moss couldn't deny it. He'd brought the evidence with him. "I certainly wouldn't have bothered if I'd known how worthless it was."

"It's worthless because I suspected you. When you published on *Clupea* in Wyoming, I thought perhaps it was a coincidence that you managed to find and identify the extinct herring species independently. But I wasn't sure. My find last year seemed groundbreaking. To test my hypothesis, I kept two sets of notebooks. One with the real data, which I kept hidden in a trunk under my cot, and a falsified set that I'd swap out daily. For months, I've assumed I was wrong that you or one of your cronies were spying on me. But then I got a copy of the *American Journal of Science,* and there it was—a paper that included my data with your name on it. I didn't know how you were doing it, stealing my research, but when the falsified notebook went missing the night Harp died, I knew you had to be behind it."

"You meant to humiliate me?"

"Humiliate you and expose you for the fraud I've always suspected you were."

"But you didn't come into camp that night, did you, Dr. Moss?" Stella asked. Given all the professor's injuries and eviction from the excavation, she and Lyndy had agreed to put off telling Professor Gridley what they'd learned from the clerk at the telegraph office. But if there was ever a time to get answers, it was now.

"Why would I?"

"Moss is right," Lyndy said. "Why would he when he could get Terence to do it for him?"

"Terence?" Professor Gridley blanched, dropping his glasses into the dirt. "Terence was the spy?"

"Amos? How could you not have known?" Dr. Moss magnanimously picked up the glasses and handed them back. Professor Gridley's whole arm was shaking as he grabbed them. "That man was as ambitious and hungry as a prairie fire. And he certainly wasn't getting any closer to the museum directorship he coveted by being your drudge."

"Basically, he wanted the professor's job," Mama said.

Moss shrugged.

"But Terence was at the doctor's that night," Professor Gridley argued. "He couldn't have been in the camp when Harp died."

"Supposedly he snuck back," Moss explained. "Claimed he knew of Harp's secret habit of taking more than a swallow while everyone else was gone."

"Terence killed Harp?" Junior pushed his way among the adults. "I thought it was an accident."

"It was, boy," Moss said. "It was. Terence admitted he might've left the corral gate open and used the horses bolting from the warning shot Harp set off to cover his escape. From what Terence told me, Harp was staggering and shouting in pursuit of the horses as Terence slipped away."

His story fit what they already knew. But could they trust him?

"Says you," Professor Gridley grumbled.

"And what are you insinuating?"

"That you're a liar. You steal research and publish it as your own. Why should we believe a word you say?"

"And none of this is to say you didn't kill Terence." Lyndy nudged Junior back toward Stella's mother, who put a protective arm around his shoulders. "Perhaps he'd decided to confess to the professor about the theft or was even blackmailing you?" Stella had considered the same possibility.

"Or it could've been you who killed Harp and are now blaming Terence, who conveniently can't defend himself," Lord Atherly said, getting into the spirit of throwing accusations around.

"Now that's absurd." Dr. Moss flung his hands in the air in frustration. "I didn't even know this Harp fellow. And besides, why would I want Terence dead? He was useful to me. I got Amos's hard-won research to claim as my own, and all I had to do was give Terence co-authorship. It was his research, too, after all."

"But you were sole author on the last paper I read," Gridley said.

"Terence was to be co-author on the one describing the *Hypohippus*. We didn't want to announce to the world what we were doing. He was still working for you, after all. He planned to leave your excavation in a few days and join mine. It's only a couple of miles away. Who wouldn't believe us?"

It was diabolical how well they'd planned it. Except they hadn't expected Professor Gridley to be equally devious. *Or for Harp to die the same night.*

"He still could've turned on you, deciding he wanted sole claim to the work. And when he did, you struck him." Stella wasn't willing to give up on the idea of Dr. Moss killing Terence. For if not him, who?

"She's right, Aurelius," Gridley added. "You still haven't explained that possibility away."

"Oh, but I can. You see, I couldn't have killed Terence because I stayed over in Helena that night."

"What were you doing in Helena?" Stella asked. "Can Sheriff Becker find witnesses who will back you up?"

"Fortunately, or unfortunately, depending upon how you look at it, five men will be more than eager for the world to know where I was that night."

"And who are these men?"

"The panel holding a discipline hearing against me. I held a position at the state university until recently, and it seems someone has accused me of intellectual dishonesty."

"If only that were a jailable offense," Gridley said.

Moss shrugged. "Either way, they had no proof. And neither do you."

"You're quite despicable, Moss." Lyndy spat the words at the rogue paleontologist with a vehemence he reserved for grooms who abused horses, men who harassed women, and Stella's father.

Stella couldn't agree more.

With a bob of his head and wink, Moss clicked his tongue. "That may be true. But I'm no killer."

CHAPTER 29

Stella's back shivered as Lyndy's lips caressed her skin. Fastening the buttons on her dress, he kissed her after each one, steadily making his way toward her neck.

Since leaving their lady's maid and valet behind in Kentucky, they'd fallen into the habit of helping the other dress or undress when necessary. Working around the house or ranch or helping out at the dig, Stella more often than not found herself in a simple linen shirtwaist and split skirt, which was easy for her to don by herself. But just in case, her lady's maid, Ethel, had packed a few dresses, like the one she'd worn to the dance and this one, a cream-colored muslin and lace lawn dress perfect for an afternoon spent at the Claxtons'. Lyndy was particularly enthusiastic and helpful with the undressing part.

Though he seemed to be thoroughly enjoying himself now, too.

"Are you sure you want to go?"

The coroner's wife had invited Stella, Lyndy, and Stella's mother to tea. Of course, with questions still zipping around her mind like fireflies trapped in a jar, Stella couldn't refuse. Yes, it had taken some time to clean up after a long morning at the dig camp, especially with Lyndy "helping" her in the bath. And yes, she'd have to endure the scrutiny of the coroner, who seemed so bent on keeping the sheriff from doing his job.

But where else could Stella learn why? And who knew what else she might glean about the coroner and his unsuspecting wife?

On the other hand, Lyndy could've easily stayed behind at the dig. Or tagged along with Ned, who'd visited the mine again, or even helped Clem here with the horses. Stella envied his choices. The Smith brothers hadn't extended an invitation to her to do anything. And she was too sensitive to Mama's feelings to force herself on them. But with all his choices, Lyndy volunteered to accompany her and her mother to the Claxtons'.

"Katherine did say that Mrs. Claxton grew up on an estate in the Midlands, and I'm gasping for a proper cup of tea," was his reply.

Was he admitting he was missing home?

"Mama also hinted that Mrs. Claxton is a gossip and might talk your ear off." Which Stella was counting on.

"The price I'm willing to pay." Lyndy chuckled as he finished with her buttons and nuzzled into her neck, his breath hot against her skin.

Or maybe he was as curious about the Claxtons as she was?

"Get a move on, you two," Mama called down the hall. "The wagon is ready!"

No fancy dinner bells or stoic, polite footmen to prod them into action here. In a small way, Mama's house reminded Stella of the McEwens at Glenloch Hill in Scotland. They had servants, but the formalities were kept to a minimum compared to Morrington Hall. Here, in Montana, there were no formalities at all.

Like it had been during her childhood.

A pang of nostalgia, a fondness for a memory that wouldn't bear scrutiny, caused Stella to pause, to face Lyndy and kiss him quick but hard, leaving him breathless as she pulled away and hurried from the room.

"We don't want to be late," Mama insisted, sitting on the driver's side of the wagon, the reins in her hands. With Lyndy's help, Stella joined Mama on the front bench, Lyndy climbing into the back.

But why the rush? It was unlike Mama. Unlike the lifestyle Stella had witnessed, where the rising and setting of the sun dictated more what and when something got done than any arbitrary strike of the clock. She hesitated to ask but couldn't help herself.

"Elizabeth and her husband are the closest thing we have to royalty around here." Mama laughed with a tingle of nervous truth. "He might even be Montana's governor someday. And although she's always been kind, Elizabeth's never invited me over before. Ned asked that we make a good impression. So, we don't want to be late."

"But I thought Mr. Claxton and Ned were friends?"

Mama laughed. "Whatever gave you that idea?"

"Why is Mrs. Claxton inviting you now then, do you suppose?" Lyndy leaned forward to ensure his words carried over the rumble of the wheels.

"Because you and my Sweet Pea here are the closest thing to royalty Elmer and Elizabeth Claxton are ever going to encounter around here." This time Mama's laugh was full-bellied and sincere.

Eased by seeing her mother relax, Stella settled in for the ride. But the grassy cart trail they'd been following turned into a hard-packed gravel drive far quicker than she had anticipated. Within minutes of leaving Mama's, another white-washed ranch house appeared. Considering how wealthy Mr. Claxton was rumored to be, it was surprisingly not as large as the one Ned had built.

"I didn't realize you lived so close to the Claxtons, Mama. I got the impression they lived in town."

"Elmer lives in town. Elizabeth prefers the ranch." Mama shrugged with mock innocence. "If you catch my meaning. She hosts her teas here." Perhaps Stella would learn more about the coroner than she bargained for. "Elizabeth does stay in town, on rare occasions, but always uses her garden as an excuse to return. Your mother would love it, Lyndy."

"And it would be the only thing."

Mama chuckled. "Yes, I just can't picture Lady Atherly out here. But then again, I thought the same of Elizabeth Claxton." They passed an orchard of apple trees, and Mama pointed. "When I first came out here, the Jonases owned this ranch, along with that mine Ned is tinkering around with. Mrs. Jonas established the garden, which produced so many vegetables she'd sell them to us. But about six months back, they packed up and went to California. And now Elmer owns the ranch, though he sold the mine to Ned after a spell. I miss Mrs. Jonas's watermelon. We just can't seem to get it to grow."

"Do you know why the Jonases left, Mama?"

"No, but from what I've heard, they took a financial hit and couldn't pay their mortgage."

"Did Claxton hold the mortgage on it?"

"On that and about half the properties in the county."

That wasn't the first time Stella had come across that information. "Does he own a mortgage on the Ninebark?"

Mama shrugged. "Ned and Clem don't tell me about the business side of things, so I wouldn't know about that."

"Well, for all your sakes, Katherine, I hope not." Lyndy sat back as Mama pulled up on the reins and parked the wagon by the Claxtons' front door, scattering a cluster of clucking chickens.

Stella hoped not, too. But finally, here was something Stella could do for her mother. Determined and happy, Stella let Lyndy help her from the wagon, rewarding him with a kiss.

Ned had been thankful for the horses they'd brought. And not too proud to accept them. If he did have a mortgage, perhaps he'd let her and Lyndy pay it off. But Ned and Clem probably wouldn't want to discuss it with her either. So how to broach the subject? She could bring it up with Lyndy first after supper. She'd argue it was for her mother and brother's sake. With Mama not getting a penny of Daddy's fortune, it was the least Stella could do.

"Please, Lord Lyndhurst, help yourself." Mrs. Claxton held up the etched silver teapot. "More tea?"

Lyndy obliged, placing the last buttermilk scone onto his plate before handing her his cup and saucer. "I thank you."

Mrs. Claxton smiled prettily at him, carefully showing him not a hint of teeth. She'd had a maid greet them at the door and escort them into her parlor, a modestly sized room that paled compared to Morrington's drawing room but attempted to capture the spirit with its uncomfortable but fashionable settees, hand-painted wallpaper, and framed paintings of all sorts and sizes covering nearly every inch of the walls. A three-tiered tray filled with cakes, scones, and finger sandwiches that would've easily found a place at any afternoon tea back home awaited them. After greetings were dispensed with, and vague excuses for Mr. Claxton's unexpected absence made, she'd launched into a conversation of polite pleasantries in her high-timbered tone—Hadn't the weather been lovely? Had they enjoyed the dance? Had they had an opportunity to meet the mayor's wife? Except for the addition of small cups filled with smoky, saucy beans laced with bits of steak shavings, the occasion was reminiscent of any such visit Lyndy had ever had to endure. Only when the lady's wolf pup, an energetic bundle of gray fur, was allowed to pounce into the room, did he have the sense he was anywhere but England.

The quality of bergamot in the tea was especially sublime. *But as of yet, the gossip isn't forthcoming.*

"I heard you visited that old gold mine, Lord Lyndhurst?" Mrs. Claxton stroked her pet's back while the creature tried to stretch around and nibble on her fingers.

Internally bristling that this stranger knew his movements, Lyndy hesitated, contemplating the steam rising from his cup. Wasn't that one of the benefits of these wild, wide-open spaces? A bit of privacy? Yet, to be polite, he confirmed that he had.

"It does sound romantic, doesn't it? A gold mine. Like something out of a dime novel. I wanted a nugget to display in my curio cabinet when Elmer first acquired it and the ranch, but it seems it hasn't produced gold for ages. Poor sucker who bought the old place. Elmer says it's completely worthless."

How could Mrs. Claxton not know Ned Smith was the "poor sucker" she'd referred to? More to the point, how could her husband sell his neighbor a mine he knew to be worthless?

"Even for iron ore?"

"You'd have to ask my husband, my lord. What do I know of these things?" Her laugh was light and yet grated on Lyndy's ear. "I was just disappointed not to get my nugget. More tea?"

"Thank you, but no."

Lyndy had only admitted a part of why he'd joined Stella, although she might've guessed. He'd hoped they'd learn more about Elmer Claxton. And yet, with the conversation finally turning that way, suddenly, he couldn't wait to leave. Embarrassed for Ned, disgusted by Claxton, and irritated by the coroner's willfully ignorant wife, Lyndy would have made their excuses and insisted they go if Stella hadn't suggested Mrs. Claxton hand the wolf pup to Lyndy. Lyndy loved his horses and dog, Mack, and had steadily become more acquainted with Junior's exuberant pups. They were jolly good fun. The moment the soft, fluffy, wiggling pup started to wrestle and play in his arms, Lyndy was smitten.

Absorbed with warding off the pup's scratches and teeth, he barely registered when, in response to something Stella asked, Mrs. Claxton said, "It was all done through the post as far as I could tell."

"May I ask why?"

"I have no idea why my husband granted Dr. Moss permission to set up his camp. Though if he'd known what a handsome man he'd turn out to be, I doubt he would have." Mrs. Claxton's giggle was short-lived as she realized the other two women were not laughing.

"He probably wants to profit from it as much as Ned did." Stella's mother's tone deepened and darkened when she added, "That is, before Harp and the professor's assistant got killed."

"No, no, Katherine," their hostess corrected. "As Dr. Moss explained to my husband over dinner the other night, there is no profit in it. 'Only glory,' or so Dr. Moss said. The museum the doctor works for expects everything he might find, but if and when a fossil is displayed or described in a scientific journal, my husband will be given credit for providing the location. I assumed it was the same for Ned."

"I must have misunderstood." Katherine shifted in her seat. "As I told my daughter and Lord Lyndhurst, Ned doesn't explain business matters to me."

"But won't it be exciting? My humble little ranch, and the Ninebark, of course," she hastened to include, "mentioned in world-class museums and journals read by people all over the country?"

"It certainly will be." Katherine set her teacup on her lap. "And maybe it will go a ways to undo the taint these murders have had on the ranch's reputation."

"I hope so, Mama." Stella set her teacup and plate with the unfinished lemon drizzle on the table before her.

"Elmer explained that those were both accidents, Katherine. No one can blame Ned or the Ninebark for that."

It was kindly spoken, but Stella was frowning when she rose and drifted over to the aforementioned curio cabinet. It was a three-dimensional scrapbook of their hostess's travels—cloisonné vases from the Orient, displays of matching necklaces, bracelets, and brooches decorated with Italian scenery, miniature bronze replicas of the Reims Cathedral and Eiffel Tower in France.

On her way back, Stella paused by Mrs. Claxton's writing desk beside the cabinet, lingering over an array of writing implements. Among all the expensive engraved, silver-plated ones, his wife chose a simple graphite pencil. What she wanted with it, Lyndy could only guess.

"Do you have any idea why your husband would ignore the evidence of the medical examiner and declare, before the inquest, that those deaths were accidents, Mrs. Claxton?" Stella settled beside her mother, tapping the pencil in her palm until the wolf pup tried to lunge for it. Then she clutched it tightly in her fist.

"Weren't they?" The coroner's wife glanced at the pencil before meeting Stella's gaze.

"One was declared such and might have been. But the other was something worse. At least according to Sheriff Becker."

"Ah, that explains it then." Mrs. Claxton chuckled as if describing the antics of toddlers in the nursery who wouldn't share their blocks. "Those two have been locking horns like a couple of big-horned sheep ever since Hank Becker was elected sheriff. I wouldn't put it past Elmer to oppose him out of spite."

"But doesn't Mr. Claxton also have to follow the law?" Stella asked. She said nothing of her suspicions that the coroner was manipulating his verdicts to avoid spooking newcomers from buying up Crow land—if Mrs. Claxton was even aware of her husband's abuse of power.

"Dear Lady Lyndhurst," Mrs. Claxton chided Stella. "Surely, you've been here long enough to know my husband is the law."

"And here I was assuming Sheriff Becker was the lawman." Lyndy sucked on the edge of his thumb after the wolf pup succeeded in piercing it with his sharp needle-like teeth.

"For things like street brawls, bank robbery, and eviction notices, of course. But when it comes to determining matters about death, Elmer decides."

"As he decides when he calls in a bank loan?"

"Whatever do you mean, Lady Lyndhurst?"

Stella didn't answer, and Lyndy wasn't even sure what she meant. Instead, she deliberately set the pencil on the table opposite Mrs. Claxton. Then she smoothed her skirt as he'd seen his mother do before making a biting comment. He'd never seen Stella like this before. Lyndy braced for what his wife had to say next.

"Have you heard, Mrs. Claxton, that despite your husband's declaration to you that Terence Brochard's death was an accident, Sheriff Becker arrested someone for his murder?"

"Oh?" With a guilty smirk on her lips, the woman leaned in as if she couldn't hear otherwise. "And who was it?"

"Purdy Sullivan."

"Ow!" Distracted by the wolf pup's teeth scraping the back of his hand, Lyndy only heard the clatter when the fine, thin porcelain met with the edge of the table. Mrs. Claxton had dropped her cup and saucer onto the floor. With a sudden burst, the pup sprung from Lyndy's grasp and began licking the milky, sweet liquid remnants from the cracked dishes and carpet. When Lyndy looked up, Mrs. Claxton was as white as the milk in the creamer, all the blood drained from her face.

Stella locked eyes with Mrs. Claxton, waiting for the coroner's wife's reaction. She immediately shied away from Stella's gaze.

"Is that so? Who would've guessed." Mrs. Claxton scooped up the wolf pup and rose. Lyndy bounded to his feet. "It was so kind of you, Lord and Lady Lyndhurst, to visit my humble home." She tugged the bell pull and asked the responding maid to escort them out. The visit was abruptly over.

"Our pleasure, Elizabeth." Mama petted the pup in Mrs. Claxton's arms. "Your home is lovely."

Mrs. Claxton flashed a feeble smile. Stella echoed her mother's sentiment and followed Mama and the maid on Lyndy's arm.

Behind her, Mrs. Claxton sighed in relief. But Stella couldn't leave. Not yet. Whispering to Lyndy to meet her outside, she doubled back to find Mrs. Claxton studying the pencil in her hand, the pup curling up in her lap. Both she and the pup started at Stella's return.

"Is there something I can do for you, my lady?" Mrs. Claxton slipped the pencil beneath a discarded napkin on the table as if it were of no consequence. That little act confirmed what Stella suspected. It was Purdy's pencil.

"Yes. You can tell me whether you're going to give Purdy an alibi or not."

Stella had seen them together at the dance and, at the time, thought little of it. But now, knowing that Mr. Claxton spent most of his days and nights in town, it wasn't a stretch to assume Mrs. Claxton was the "unnamed lady" that Purdy refused to incriminate.

"I don't know what you mean." Mrs. Claxton reassured the sleepy pup with a few long strokes along its back.

"Of course you do. That pencil belongs to him. He was here. Maybe even the night Terence was killed. How else would it be among your things?" Stella lifted the napkin. "Unless you happen to chew on your pencils too?" Mrs. Claxton's face blushed a bright crimson, but her words failed her. "If you don't admit he was with you, he might hang for a crime he didn't commit."

Stella had never been comfortable with the idea of Purdy as the killer. He was a scoundrel, creating havoc and instigating dangerous conditions in hopes of capitalizing on his dastardly deeds. He was a sneak thief, a cheat, a liar, but a cold-blooded killer? Stella hadn't thought so. He'd done everything in the shadows. Not once had he had to face the immediate consequences of his actions. Could he have done it? Wielding the rock hammer in his hand, bashing Terence with it, and looking the assistant in the eye as life faded away? It seemed too out of character. Purdy Sullivan seemed too much of a coward. But

Stella had been wrong before and had to accept Sheriff Becker knew something she didn't.

Until she'd spied the chewed pencil on Mrs. Claxton's writing desk.

"You're right. I have been 'entertaining' Mr. Sullivan, and he was with me on the night the man fell into Cottonwood Creek and when the professor's assistant died in the tent. He was quite ghoulishly ecstatic. He couldn't quite believe his luck."

"Seems that luck has run out."

Mrs. Claxton stared at the pup in her lap as she continued to pet it. "What are you going to do now?"

"Nothing. But you need to tell Sheriff Becker that Purdy was with you that night."

Her head jerked up. "I couldn't possibly do that."

"For goodness' sake, why not?"

"My husband can never know."

"But he wouldn't have to. Not necessarily. You'd be telling the sheriff."

"But don't you see? The sheriff is my husband's political rival. It would put me in a very compromising position to tell him such an intimate, damning detail."

"As if swinging from a noose isn't a compromising position?"

Stella was losing her patience and purposely painted a harsh reality for this seemingly genteel woman. Stella's mind raced back to when Lyndy was in such a position and how she'd do anything, anything, to see him cleared of the murder he didn't commit. So why was this woman even hesitating for a moment? All it would take was one word, and her paramour would be free.

"I am fond of dear Purdy." A faraway look and a flit of a knowing smile brightened her face. "I wouldn't want him to face the gallows, especially if he didn't do it."

"Then you'll tell Sheriff Becker?"

"If needs be. Though as discreetly as possible."

Mama poked her head into the room. "Lyndy said you'd be right out." Lyndy, standing behind her with a look of surrender on his face, shrugged. "Is there something wrong, Sweet Pea?"

"No, Mama." Stella stared meaningfully at the coroner's wife. "Everything's fine."

But in reality, they were back to where they started, with an unknown killer and no suspects.

CHAPTER 30

Stella was the first out of the wagon. While Lyndy practiced his lasso from the back and her mother chatted about how odd Mrs. Claxton seemed at the end of their visit, Stella had taken the few minutes it took to ride back to mull over what she'd learned about Terence's murder. It didn't help. She'd been uneasy about Purdy's arrest, but at least the semblance of safety had emboldened Lord Atherly and the professor to return to the dig, and Mama and Ned were on good terms again. But with Purdy's solid alibi, Stella couldn't piece together who killed the professor's assistant. When Mama slowed the horses near the house, Stella was less at ease than when she'd left. But nothing a ride couldn't cure.

She was about to ask Lyndy if he wanted to saddle up when Junior rushed out of the nearest barn, sending a hen squawking in protest. He looked as if he'd been impatiently watching for their return.

"Hey, Lyndy!" he called. "Uncle Clem is going to brand the new calves. Want to come?"

The invitation wasn't extended to Stella, but unlike wrangling the horses out on the prairie, Stella had no inclination to invite herself. To Lyndy's silent inquiry, she said, "Go ahead."

Mama shook her head and chuckled as Junior eagerly led Lyndy toward the dairy barn. "Not my idea of entertainment." When Stella continued to stare silently after them, Mama wrapped her arm around Stella's shoulders. "You all right, Sweet Pea? You haven't uttered two words since we left the Claxton ranch."

"I'm fine."

"Oh, good. I thought something Elizabeth said might've upset you. She certainly was odd there at the end." Unlike Lyndy, who would've known Stella was bluffing, her mother took her at her word. Although she could innately sense Stella's melancholy, her mother didn't know her well enough to know more. It made Stella even sadder. "Maybe you're just tired. I sure am plumb worn out. I swear eating cake and chitchatting is more exhausting than cooking and cleaning."

As her mother headed toward the house, Stella hesitated. She wasn't ready to go inside. Not yet. Maybe she could go for a ride alone? Then she noticed the fly-fishing equipment was still in the buggy they'd taken fishing.

Her mother turned to see what kept Stella and followed her daughter's gaze. "The men must be really busy not to have put that away by now."

"I'll do it. Where does it go?"

With her mother's instructions in her head, Stella strolled past the row of bunkhouses to a smaller barn, the rods clutched in her hand, the heavy rubber waders draped over her forearm. She found a few empty pegs among the tack on the near side of the barn wall and gratefully relieved herself of the burden. She breathed deeply, filling her lungs with the mingling smells of straw, soil, leather, and rotting wood. These were the scents of her childhood, the happy memories of escaping her father and finding solace in the shadowy spaces beneath stable rafters.

Soothed, she took another deep breath before stepping outside again.

But instead of heading straight back to the house, she poked her head into the various buildings along the way. She lingered in the horse barns, greeting the few stabled inside, and upon finding a tractor housed in a shed, she climbed into its high, metal seat. When she came upon a small open-sided wooden structure barely bigger than an outhouse, she hesitated briefly at the cold draft wafting up the dark stairwell. Uneven stone stairs, blasted out of the granite, led to the root cellar a dozen feet underground. Stella shivered at the sudden temperature change. Shelves filled with canned goods and glass jars lined the walls, with space left beneath for trunks and baskets overflowing with potatoes, carrots, turnips, and beets. In the farthest corner, she came across an old, rusty strongbox, the kind that banks used to store gold and valuables on overland stagecoaches. Stella moved a basket of rutabaga from on top to the ground and lifted the metal lid. What romantic notion had she gotten in her head, thanks to Lyndy, that made her sigh audibly in disappointment upon seeing only a dirty, crumpled cotton shirt inside? No gold bars or burlap sack filled with coins. She was dropping the lid back on when it hit her. Those dark spots on the shirt weren't rust from the box.

They were blood.

Stella seized the shirt and was startled to touch something hard among the folds. Before she could untangle it, something dropped with a clank to the bottom of the box. It was the missing *Hypohippus* fossil jaw, with a shard broken off. Reeling at the implication, Stella tossed the shirt back in, slammed the lid shut, and stepped back as if putting distance between the evidence and herself would erase its meaning.

Why did she have to be so nosy? Why couldn't she have left well enough alone? She'd never been so close to her mother. And now? She'd been fretting from the moment she suspected a killer lived at the ranch. Would her mother ever forgive her? Terence deserved justice, yet the cost seemed too high.

And why did Stella have to pay the price?

Stella squirmed at the hidden shirt wrapped tightly around her waist like a cinch. She was wearing the shirt of a killer. But she had to be positive she'd got it right and didn't want anyone else to see. She found Maria in the kitchen frying up fish and onions. The smell turned Stella's nervous stomach almost queasy.

"What are you doing, Miss Stella?" When Stella lifted her dress to retrieve the soiled shirt and revealed her petticoat, Maria waved the spatula at her, flinging droplets of melted butter around.

"I have to show you something." Stella produced the bloody shirt and swiftly let her skirt drop.

Maria set the spatula down and lifted the heavy cast-iron pot with both hands. "Mrs. Smith warned you were a little unconventional, Miss Stella, but what is that?" The pot landed on the back burner with a dull thud. "Do you want me to wash it? I'm not sure I can get those blood stains out, though. I've had lots of practice—these men are always cutting themselves—but that's been setting for days."

Stella had already confirmed it didn't belong to Junior; despite her brother's broadening shoulders, he still wasn't as large as a grown man. It could belong to a cowboy or a ranch hand who, for reasons unknown, had killed Terence. But Stella didn't think so.

"No, but because you do all the washing, I figured you could tell me whose shirt this is."

Stella could have asked her mother as easily. Mama would know. But Stella didn't want to involve her. Not yet. Not until Stella had learned for sure, one way or another, whom it belonged to. If she could, Stella wanted to shield her mother from learning the Ninebark Ranch harbored a murderer. Maria, on the other hand, didn't have a personal stake in the answer.

"Does it belong to Clem?" Stella held it out for Maria to take.

Looking skeptically at Stella, Maria wiped her hands on her apron and took the shirt. The housekeeper held it before her, stretching it out at the shoulders. "No, Miss Stella. This isn't Mr. Clem's."

She so wanted to be wrong!

Stella had come to Montana to deepen the bond with her mother, not destroy it. To make her life easier, not harder. To show her love, not reveal a murderous hate. But how could Stella not reveal this killer? Like Mama leaving the fossil in the ground, Stella couldn't imagine it.

"Do you know whom it does belong to?" Stella also couldn't imagine the damage Maria's next few damning words, words Stella suspected but never wanted to hear, would do.

"Of course. It belongs to Mr. Ned."

CHAPTER 31

~~~

A creaking floorboard and stifled cough caused Stella to turn. Ned stood in the doorway, the grime of the mine etched into the lines on his face, his hand frozen in the act of brushing back his forelock. Shock flashed across his face when he noticed the shirt Maria held. Had he overheard them? He knew she'd found the missing fossil jaw fragment. But did he suspect Stella had unraveled the whole sordid truth?

For a split second, their eyes met. Then Ned wheeled around and dashed down the hall for the door.

"Mr. Ned?" Maria called.

Stella launched after him, but he had longer legs and a head start. Stella slowed only long enough to grab the leather handbag she'd left among the hats on the rack, and yet by the time she had reached the porch, Ned was disappearing into the nearest horse barn. A black barnyard cat, something dangling from its jaws, slunk around the corner after him.

Running at full speed, Stella shouted when she spotted Lyndy leisurely crossing the stable yard. "Lyndy! Stop him!" But it was too late.

Ned and Whiskey burst through the barn doors and raced past. Dust from Ned's mount was already kicking up on the open prairie when Stella and Lyndy reached the stables.

"What is it, Stella? What's going on?"

"It's Ned. He stole your father's treasured fossil. And I think he killed Terence."

"Bloody hell!"

To the stable hand's surprise, Stella grabbed two halters, throwing one at Lyndy. She approached Gin, cooing and patting the mare as she slipped the rope over the horse's neck and the halter over Gin's nose while Lyndy did the same for Chester.

"Don't you want me to saddle them for you?" the stable hand asked.

"There's no time." Stella waved him over for assistance. He bent next to the horse, his fingers interlocked like a stirrup. With her leather handbag wrapped around her wrist, Stella grabbed the halter rope, hiked up her skirts, and stepped into his hands. The poor man's face reddened in embarrassment as she threw her exposed leg over the horse's back. Lyndy was already heading out the door when Stella urged Gin to follow.

With Whiskey tired from the long trek from the mine, Ned hadn't gotten too far. Gin and Chester were rested and eager to run, and with the steady rhythm of thundering hoofbeats filling Stella's ears, they cut the distance between them and Ned to a few lengths. But Stella wasn't used to riding bareback, let alone in a lawn dress. While keeping Ned in their sights and avoiding any prairie dog holes or protruding boulders, Stella had to keep from falling off. Despite Gin's smooth coat, Stella's thighs chafed with every stride. She tightened her stomach and squeezed her thighs until they burned. The wind whistled past, grabbed and pulled strands of Stella's hair from its bun, adding to her struggle to stay on Gin's back.

Lyndy reached Ned first and, unbeknown to her, had snatched a stretch of rope from the wall before he'd left. Now, like a man who'd roped cattle for a living, he twirled the tied rope and flung it after Ned.

And missed. Stella's heart sank as the rope fell short, but she urged Gin on, determined not to let Ned get away.

"Stop, Ned! You can't run forever!" Stella shouted to no avail.

Lyndy regrouped and tried a second time. The rope caught Ned around the shoulders, enough to unseat him when Lyndy tugged sharply on it. Ned tumbled to the ground but, like any good horseman, tucked and rolled as he fell, tightening and tugging back on the rope as he did. The sudden tension caused Lyndy to slip sideways and nearly fall. He released his grip, flinging the rope from his hands to the ground. Ned bounded to his feet, yanked the loosened noose over his head, and sprinted away before Lyndy could dismount and gather the lasso up again. As Lyndy dropped to his feet, Stella rode past.

"Stop, Ned!"

With the galloping horse bearing down on him, Ned's desperation kept him running. Stella dug into the handbag dangling from her wrist and pulled her gun out. The very weapon that Uncle Jed stole, the one supposedly once used by Jesse James, the one that someone else had pulled on her.

Now, she aimed it at her mother's husband.

"Stop, or I'll shoot."

Whether he took her threat seriously or his adrenaline had run out, Ned halted, doubling over from the effort, his hands on his thighs, panting for breath. Stella's heart pounded as she reined Gin to a halt. Slipping to the ground, she kept the gun steady as she cautiously approached him. She had no idea how close she needed to be to pose a threat—it was a little gun, after all—but she wasn't going to give him a chance to overpower her. Yet the fight seemed drained out of him as he held up a capitulating hand. His face, still streaked with mine grime and now dust, was a mask of defeat and something else.

Could it be relief?

While she kept Ned preoccupied, Lyndy had gotten his rope. Hanging his head, Ned offered no resistance when Lyndy tied his hands, grabbed his horse's reins, and led him back toward the house.

Stella patted Gin, more for her comfort than the horse's. She could barely get the words out but had to hear him say it. "You did more than steal a fossil, didn't you, Ned? You killed Terence."

"God forgive me. I did."

Unwilling to risk Ned escaping, they'd led the horses and walked back. Lyndy had tried to persuade Stella to ride, as she was still wearing the dressy strapped sandals she'd donned for Mrs. Claxton's tea. However, Stella opted to walk with the men rather than risk Ned doing something they'd all regret while Lyndy turned his back to help her mount.

Now, her feet were blistered, and her head ached from the strain of anticipation. *How am I going to tell Mama?* As they arrived, her mother stepped out on the porch. Wiping her hands on the apron tied around her waist, she let the screen door slam behind her. Despite the long road back, Stella hadn't been prepared for the hurt and confusion on her mother's face.

"Stella? Where'd you get that gun? And why are you pointing it at my husband?"

Stella hadn't wanted it, and still didn't, but because of its connection to Jesse James, Lyndy wouldn't let her throw it away. He'd brought it to Montana, thinking Mama could give it to Junior when he came of age. But after talking to Letti, and with a killer on the loose, Stella had slipped it in her handbag for protection. Why she was pointing it at Ned was more difficult to explain.

Stella didn't attempt to explain either. Instead, she kept the gun trained on Ned's back and kept quiet, her tongue too heavy to speak.

"Well, if Stella won't tell me, will you, Ned?" Ned shied from Mama's questioning gaze.

Her mother's voice grew more desperate and louder as she took the stairs and approached them. "Will someone please tell me what is going on?"

Seeing Lyndy about to take on the burden, Stella discovered she couldn't let him do it. *She's my mother*. Such devastating news should come from her. "Ned killed Terence."

"What are you talking about?"

"Maria!" Lyndy called as the curious housekeeper poked her head through the crack in the screen door. "Have someone fetch the sheriff, will you?" Maria's head instantly disappeared. The screen door banged closed again.

"What? No!" Mama covered her face in her hands.

When her mother slipped to her knees in the drive, Lyndy motioned for the gun. Stella lowered it, shoved it into Lyndy's hand, and ran to her mother. Stella dropped into the dirt beside her, resting her hand on her mother's knee.

"I'm so, so, sorry, Mama. I didn't want it to be true."

Her mother grasped her arm like a rope dangling over a cliff but addressed her husband, still staring at the dust on his boots. "Did you do it? Tell me Stella is wrong, Ned. Tell her she's wrong."

"She's not wrong."

Mama buried her face in Stella's shoulder as Stella wrapped her in a firm embrace, unable to fathom the depth of Ned's betrayal. How would she feel if Lyndy had just admitted to killing a man? She couldn't imagine.

"How did you know?" Her mother's hoarse whisper was muffled by tears and the linen fabric of Stella's dress.

"I didn't, for sure, until he fled at the sight of his bloody shirt. But I suspected at the tea when Mrs. Claxton put you straight about the profitability of the dig. I realized that if you had such an expectation to gain financially from it, then Ned must have, too."

Mama raised her head, her cheeks wet with tears. "But what difference did that make?"

"Ever since we arrived, I've learned of one financial setback or disappointment after another for Ned. The drop in sales of horses, the failed investment in the gold mine, and the loss of the horses Onie Drucker claimed were stolen. Even while the harvest season approached, Ned cut back on the number of cowboys he employed. When I remembered Mr. Claxton was here the morning Harp was found, I wondered why. The two men weren't friends. But if he held the mortgage on the Ninebark, as he does on half the county, I could think of plenty of reasons why he might want to speak to Ned. And none of them were good."

"Is this true, Ned?"

"We haven't been making a profit for years now."

"But you never said."

"A man doesn't discuss his failures with his wife."

"But Clem knows?"

"Clem didn't know the half of it."

"Is that why you were adamant about closing the dig? To keep anyone from learning the truth about our financial situation?"

"I couldn't risk losing a single sale because of the scandal."

"Fancy what this news will do, eh?" Stella couldn't blame Lyndy for his cutting remark. She was thinking something along the same vein.

"But losing money doesn't make you a killer." Mama wiped the corners of her eyes with the heel of her hand. She struggled to push herself off the ground, even using Stella for support. She stepped on her apron and nearly tripped. "Why did you kill Terence, Ned? Why?"

Ned hung his head and kicked a pebble in the dirt. He coughed into his fist, unable to meet her gaze. "I didn't mean to."

"But you did!" Mama charged at him, her fists raised. Stella leaped to her feet, grabbing her mother's apron strings to stop her. But she missed, and when Mama reached her husband, she began pounding his chest. When Lyndy tried to step in, Ned waved him off. The big man grabbed and held Mama's fists as easily as if she were a child. She leaned against him, sobbing. "Why, Ned? Why?"

"I was trying to save the ranch, Kate. I was doing it for you and Junior."

"You were hoping to stave off Mr. Claxton by selling fossils from the dig, weren't you?" Ned answered Stella with a nod. "With Clem gone to confront Onie Drucker and Lord Atherly and Papa supposedly nowhere around, you found you had the perfect opportunity to visit the dig that night."

"Is that why you slept on the summer porch?" Mama asked. "So you could slip out without me knowing?"

"I didn't need to bother you with it."

"And you stole Lord A's fossil?"

Ned spoke with more than a hint of the defiant steel Stella had come to associate with him. "Kate. A man can't steal what's rightfully his, now can he? And everyone was making such a fuss about it. Even you and your rhino. How was I to know it wasn't worth the dirt they dug it out of?"

"But Terence interrupted and confronted you," Stella continued.

"He didn't confront me. He sneered at me in a way that made my blood boil."

"He was reeling from having the tent ransacked and having his fossilized bear skull stolen."

"And possibly worried you'd seen him trying to steal data sheets again," Lyndy added a guess.

"He wasn't reeling. He laughed at me." Ned's lip curled slightly in disgust. "When I expected money, payment for letting the dig use my land, he claimed the only one getting paid was him. Something about a job at some museum. The sole benefit I was going to get was bragging rights. What good were they going to do me? But when I decided to try my luck in selling some of the rocks, he railed at me and accused me of stealing. But like I said, a man isn't a thief for taking what is rightfully his. That's why, even now, I couldn't get rid of that cursed jawbone. You would have to find it, Miss Stella."

"Is that when you killed him? Because he accused you of stealing?" Stella couldn't grasp how it could be that senseless, that Ned could be so callous.

"No. That's when he attacked me. When I went to take Lord A's fossil, the man snatched it first and stabbed me with it." Ned jutted his chin toward his upper arm at the exact location where Stella found blood on the hidden shirt. "It snapped while we fought over it."

"Then he tried to kill you. You were acting in self-defense. You were justified." Mama was grasping at straws.

"It was a deep scratch, is all, Kate," Ned admitted, looking into his wife's eyes. "But it was deep enough to wound my pride, to push me to my limit. What with Claxton threatening to take the ranch, after everything we've put into it, after *he* sold me a worthless mine, I couldn't take another blow. Especially from some smug upstart. I snapped. I grabbed the first thing my fingers wrapped around and smashed him with it."

"The rock hammer."

Stella started at the unexpected deep voice. Sheriff Becker reined in his horse and dismounted. Distracted by Ned's admission, she hadn't heard him arrive. The cowboy Maria had sent rode up alongside.

"Your man here found me less than half a mile away. I was already on my way here to deliver you this." Becker flipped open his saddlebag and pulled out a manila envelope. "I hate to do it, but it's an eviction notice. Claxton demanded I deliver it today."

"Hank, Ned killed the professor's young assistant." Mama

spoke as if she were talking about a family who'd just moved to town. She had to be in shock.

"Yes, I overheard his confession as I rode in. I'm awfully sorry." He handed the eviction notice to her and replaced the rope Lyndy held with handcuffs. "Ned, you're under arrest."

They all stood staring in silence as Sheriff Becker led Ned away. After glancing somberly over his shoulder once, the sheriff pulled his stone from his pocket and pitched it into the dirt. Having had a hand in this, Stella braced herself for the guilt she'd feel when Ned looked back, remorse and regret etched into his features, begging his wife for forgiveness. But he never looked back.

CHAPTER 32

Stella noticed her mother's gaze wandering around the parlor, taking in the scene before her. Clem, his legs sprawled out before him, absently rubbed the whiskers on his chin. Lyndy stared at the steam rising from the coffee Maria had made. He'd yet to take a sip. In the corner, Professor Gridley and Lord Atherly feigned interest in the chessboard between them. How many times had the professor's hand hovered over the pieces, only to be withdrawn again? All the while, the somber tune Junior played on his harmonica drifted in through the front door from his perch on the porch's top step. Feeling the weight of her mother's troubled look, Stella offered a sympathetic smile when their eyes finally met.

"I can't believe it's happened again." Mama surveyed the room methodically as if trying to memorize every inch. "Forced to leave a home I love."

Then her focus fell on the two-horned rhinoceros fossil resting on the tea table. Lord Atherly and the professor had brought it when they returned from the dig for supper. No one had been in the mood to eat.

Noticing the object of Mama's interest, Lord Atherly lamented, "I wish I could say I don't have an inkling of what you're feeling, Katherine."

With the sale of the ranch or its reverting to Mr. Claxton, the expedition's future was as doubtful as Mama's. Hoping to capitalize on the news that Dr. Moss had left the state on the earliest train ahead of the state university's verdict out of Helena, Lord Atherly and Professor Gridley had been excitedly discussing expanding onto Moss's site when they'd learned of Ned and the eviction notice. Seeing Lord Atherly's face fall in disappointment hurt almost as much as watching her mother struggle. Her father-in-law had been through so much during his time in Montana. All he'd wanted to do was search for his fossils.

But between them, Ned and Mr. Claxton had ruined everything. For Lord Atherly, for the professor, for Clem, Junior, and Mama.

"I'm so sorry." Stella had long tired of repeating it, but what more could she say?

"If there's anything we can do." Lyndy offered as he had countless times before. Mama shook her head again.

"We can sell off as many horses as it takes, Katie." Clem had taken the news of his brother's crime and the eviction notice like he did everything else—with quiet strength. He'd shaken his head, cursed under his breath, and then asked what needed to be done. When Mama insisted there was nothing to be done but sell the ranch, he'd taken time to consider the options. Now, he was presenting them in a pragmatic tone. "We can—"

"I'm gonna stop you right there, Clem. There's no use. I don't want to sell any more than you do. This is where my life is. This is where my boy grew up. But this here tells us what we have to do." Mama had been clutching the eviction notice in her fist since Sheriff Becker handed it over. "My husband, your brother, has given us no choice. We either pay the mortgage by selling, or we'll be thrown out on our ear by this time tomorrow. Besides, who's going to buy horses from a murderer's family?"

"If that's your thinking, Katie, who's going to buy a murderer's ranch?"

"You're right." Mama slumped back against her chair. "What are we gonna do?"

Stella wished she had the answer. If only there were something they could do.

And then she remembered. Clutching Lyndy's hand as hard as Mama did the eviction notice, Stella bolted upright. How obtuse could she be? Hadn't she already planned to bring it up tonight? Chalking her muddled thinking up to the double blow of Ned's crime and Claxton's callousness, Stella shrugged it off. Everything was clear. She knew what she had to do.

Without taking her attention off her mother, Stella rose, pulling Lyndy up with her. Startled, he set down his cup with a clatter.

"Excuse us for a minute." Stella dragged Lyndy into the hall.

"What is it, my love?"

Stella considered making her case—the relief she'd feel being a force for good instead of shouldering the burden of being the one whose discovery sent Ned to prison, the fears it would alleviate of losing her mother a second time, how it would solve not only Mama's problems but his father's too. But Lyndy would already know all that. And he would understand how important this was. She'd considered seeking his permission because he controlled her inheritance, but she knew she only had to ask.

"I want to pay the mortgage off on the ranch so Mama can be secure. We can use the sale of the Kentucky—"

Lyndy didn't flinch. "Of course. What do you think I meant when I offered to help?"

Stella threw her arms around him. "I do love you." From the look on his face, her kiss surprised him.

"As I do you, my love. I only wish Ned had come to one of us with his financial troubles in the first place."

Without waiting another moment, Stella dashed back into the parlor and knelt before her mother, taking her hand in her own.

"Mama. Lyndy and I have agreed on how to help, and we won't be taking no for an answer."

"What is that, Sweet Pea?" As she patted Stella's cheek, Mama's tone recalled distant memories of when Stella was small. Sounding indulgent but not listening.

"You're going to let us pay off the ranch. Not just the debts but the whole thing. And put the title in your name."

"What? But how?"

"We'll use the money we'll get from selling off the Kentucky house." Stella reveled at the poetic justice of using her father's estate to save the ranch. *Daddy, who kicked Mama out, will be the one to secure her future.*

"I'd be willing to stay on if you'll have me," Clem said. "And Junior can take his father's place." The slight flinch at referencing his absent brother was all that showed the pain it had caused. "He's old enough now."

"I am." Junior stood tall in the doorway, the harmonica sticking out of his breast pocket. "What Pa did was wrong, but he was doing it to save this ranch. Let me help do what he couldn't."

Mama shook her head, looking skeptically from Clem to her son to Stella. "Really? Do you think we could do it? Do you think Mr. Claxton will let us?"

It was Lord Atherly who'd risen from his chess game to answer. "Mr. Claxton is a businessman, Katherine. If my son offers him cash in hand, he won't evict you solely on principle. Besides, it would be bad for his election chances if news got out that you had the money to pay off your mortgage, and he wouldn't allow you."

"And what about Ned? What about the shame of the murder? Will anyone ever buy anything from us again?"

"It might be difficult in the beginning," Lyndy said, "but the scandal doesn't hold the same weight here as it might in England. People will forget."

"And with our discoveries, the Ninebark Ranch's name will soon be more renowned for unique fossil specimens than recent deaths." Professor Gridley, rubbing his hands excitedly, sounded more like Purdy Sullivan than an esteemed academic. Then he captured Lord Atherly's queen.

Mama reached out and took both of Stella's hands in her own. "Do you think so?" All heads affirmed her desire. "Oh, Sweet Pea! How can I ever thank you?"

"There's no need. I'm just so happy to be able to help." Stella's heart swelled to bursting.

"No, my darling girl." She cupped Stella's cheek again. "I do need to thank you. I left you, and you not only welcomed me back with open arms but saved me from financial ruin. I'll never be able to repay you."

Stella fought the tears of relief and love welling in the brim of her eyes. All she had ever wanted was to feel her mother's love again, to feel that bond she'd so truly missed. This was more than she could ever have hoped for. "Don't worry, Mama. You already have."

"What a treasure you are, Stella, my dear. Who else could've meshed her two vastly different families into one?" Lord Atherly smiled at Mama and then put his hand on Junior's shoulder.

"And does that include Mother, Papa?" Lyndy chuckled.

"Pshaw. Your mother's not here, my boy."

"Thank goodness."

When Lyndy wrapped his arms around Stella's middle, snug-gling into her, and rested his chin on her shoulder, Mama winked, the first hint of her old self twinkling in her eye.

"And may that family grow in numbers soon."

"Mama!" Stella gasped with embarrassment. Stella hadn't thought about the state of her womb in days. And of all the times to bring it up.

"Hear! Hear!" Lyndy whispered, his breath tickling her ear.

ACKNOWLEDGMENTS

I had planned to write some version of Stella and Lyndy's adventure in Montana from the outset of the series. However, only after I began the research in earnest did I realize how much of a personal adventure it would prove to be. Luckily, I had many experts who enlightened me along the way.

I would like to thank Kallie Moore, Collections Manager, UM Paleontology Collection at the University of Montana, Department of Geosciences, who answered my questions and led me to Earl Douglass and the extremely useful PBDB (Paleobiology Database); the extremely informative and helpful crew of the Montana Dinosaur Center who led the expedition that allowed me to get hands-on experience digging for fossils; the National Park Service staff at the Grant-Kohrs Ranch National Historic Site including Park Ranger Jaeger Held and Interpretive Park Guides Olivia Hathaway and Miriam Glatfelter, and Erica Berger, Interpretive Guide at the Museum of the Rockies 1890s Living History Farm, who all helped educate me about Montana in the early part of the twentieth century. If I got any of the facts or details wrong, that's on me.

I would also like to thank my team at Kensington: my editor, John Scognamiglio, my publicist, Larissa Ackerman, production editor, Robin Cook, copy editor, Carolyn Pouncy, for all their help in getting this book into your hands. And I'd be remiss not to mention the cover artist, Andrew Davidson. I think he's outdone himself this time.

Finally, I want to express my heartfelt thanks to my family, without whom this book wouldn't have been possible. Cheers all!

AUTHOR'S NOTE

Although this is a work of fiction, I draw from historical facts, people, and places for inspiration and to create stories that feel authentic to their time and place. In this book, I scattered in mentions of more than my usual list of real-life characters including notorious criminals, Butch Cassidy and Jesse James, an infamous murderer, Harry Kendall Thaw, and his victim, Stanford White, well-known actors Johnston Forbes-Robertson and Evelyn Nesbit, explorers, John Colter and John Wesley Powell, politicians Governor Joseph Toole and President Theodore Roosevelt, and a whole host of acclaimed paleontologists: Edward Drinker Cope, Earl Douglass, Othniel Charles Marsh, and Charles Doolittle Walcott.

Historical figure Evelyn Cameron, though not mentioned by name, was the inspiration behind not only the Letti Landstrom character but I incorporated many aspects of her life into several of the female characters. A native Brit, she was a pioneering female photographer, horse ranger, and diarist who is credited with popularizing the split skirt in Montana, and whose diary and photographs are instrumental in documenting ranch life in late nineteenth and early twentieth century Montana.

The Grant-Kohrs Ranch National Historic Site near Deerlodge, MT was the inspiration for the Ninebark Ranch. Once the center of a ten-million-acre cattle empire, it is now a part of the National Park Service. During the years that Conrad Kohrs and his half-brother, John Bielenberg, ran the ranch, "Johney" made significant advances in horse breeding. Breeding Thoroughbreds to hardy native mares, John Bielenberg developed what is considered the forerunner of today's Quarter Horses.

Although the fossil dig site is fictionalized, I used the comprehensive Paleobiology Database (PBDB) to determine which fossils had been discovered when and where. According to the PBDB, *Hypohippus* wasn't discovered in Montana until 1961, very near where Earl Douglass documented the first occurrences of *Miohippus* in 1902. Many fossil hunters may expect to find dinosaurs in Professor Gridley's excavation site. However, to be as authentic as possible, I used Earl Douglass's sites in west central Montana as my general setting of Cottonwood Creek and the Ninebark Ranch. Dinosaur fossils are found further to the east. For those who might be interested, Earl Douglass's biography, *Speak to the Earth and It Will Teach You: The Life and Times of Earl Douglass, 1862-1931*, by G. E. Douglass, a compilation of his diaries, is an invaluable resource and fascinating read.

Along with diaries, period newspapers often reveal some of the best historical details. Events such as the ceding and sale of land once owned by the Crow (or Apsáalooke), the sell-off of mines stripped of their gold, the San Francisco earthquake and fire, the very public murder of Stanford White by Harry Thaw, and the references to Theodore Roosevelt as a cowboy in the White House were found among the broadsheet pages of the day.